got this book off of the comm...

Prais

LAWRENCE

irresistible playboy-detective,

ARCHY McNALLY, and the bestselling series

November 2006

"Vincent Lardo continues [the] McNally sleuth series in superb style . . . His twisted plots and humorous characters are entertaining and provide a fun, quick read."

—*The Tennessean*

"[Lardo] admirably reproduces the same frothy tone Sanders brought to Archy's misadventures . . . virtually indistinguishable from the seven Sanders churned out."

—*Fort Worth Star-Telegram*

"You're only saddened when it ends."

—*The Palm Beach Post*

"Archy McNally is a raffish combination of Dashiell Hammett's Nick Charles and P. G. Wodehouse's Bertie Wooster." —*The New York Times Book Review*

"You never know what that scamp Archy will get himself into." —*San Antonio Express-News*

"McNally is the Nick Charles of the '90s."

—*Ocala (FL) Star-Banner*

"As crisp as a gin and tonic." —*St. Petersburg Times*

"An enduring character." —*The Indianapolis Star*

"McNally is a charmer." —*The Orlando Sentinel*

Turn the page for more rave reviews . . .

McNALLY'S CHANCE
An Archy McNally novel by Vincent Lardo

A romance author's missing husband embroils Archy in a page-turner of the first order . . .

"What more could you ask of a Palm Beach mystery?"
—*The Palm Beach Post*

McNALLY'S FOLLY
An Archy McNally novel by Vincent Lardo

In a play filled with murderers, Archy must separate the actors from the genuine article . . .

"A frothy caper . . . involving an eclectic cast of richniks . . . If you've liked previous McNallys, you'll enjoy this one."
—*Fort Worth Star-Telegram*

McNALLY'S DILEMMA
An Archy McNally novel by Vincent Lardo

A Palm Beach crime passionnel *puts Archy in a compromising position . . .*

"The detection is as insouciant as the detective himself . . . to be effortlessly enjoyed." —*The Boston Globe*

McNALLY'S GAMBLE
Archy basks in the sun and sin of Palm Beach—where the rich count their schemes before they're hatched . . .

"Lawrence Sanders has honed a voice for Archy McNally that is wonderfully infectious. You can't help falling for him!"
—*The Washington Times*

McNALLY'S PUZZLE
All the pieces fit in McNally's latest case—money, sex, and murder . . .

"Sanders's novel is easy reading, partly because of the amusing one-liners that McNally delivers throughout the chase."
—The Associated Press

McNALLY'S TRIAL

Archy—and his new sidekick, Binky—investigate the deathstyles of the rich and famous . . .

"Passion, greed, murder, and wit—they are Sanders's stock in trade, and McNally is his most delightful character."

—*Chicago Tribune*

McNALLY'S CAPER

Archy is lured into a Palm Beach mansion as mysterious as the House of Usher—but twice as twisted . . .

"Sibling rivalries and passions . . . " —*The Orlando Sentinel*

McNALLY'S RISK

The freewheeling McNally is seduced by the very temptress he's been hired to investigate . . .

"Loads of fun." —*The San Diego Union-Tribune*

McNALLY'S LUCK

McNally returns—and the case of a kidnapped cat leads to ransom and homicide . . .

"Entertaining . . . sophisticated wit . . . This is a fun book."

—*South Bend Tribune*

McNALLY'S SECRET

The rollicking bestseller that introduced Lawrence Sanders's most wickedly charming sleuth, Archy McNally . . .

"Witty, charming . . . fine entertainment." —*Cosmopolitan*

THE McNALLY NOVELS

Lawrence Sanders McNally's Alibi
An Archy McNally novel by Vincent Lardo

Lawrence Sanders McNally's Chance
An Archy McNally novel by Vincent Lardo

Lawrence Sanders McNally's Folly
An Archy McNally novel by Vincent Lardo

Lawrence Sanders McNally's Dilemma
An Archy McNally novel by Vincent Lardo

McNally's Gamble • *McNally's Puzzle* • *McNally's Trial*
McNally's Caper • *McNally's Risk* • *McNally's Luck* • *McNally's Secret*

Guilty Pleasures
The Seventh Commandment
Sullivan's Sting
Capital Crimes
Timothy's Game
The Timothy Files
Caper
The Eighth Commandment
The Fourth Deadly Sin
The Passion of Molly T.
The Seduction of Peter S.
The Case of Lucy Bending
The Third Deadly Sin
The Tenth Commandment
The Sixth Commandment
The Tangent Factor
The Second Deadly Sin
The Marlow Chronicles
The Tangent Objective
The Tomorrow File
The First Deadly Sin
Love Songs
The Pleasures of Helen
The Anderson Tapes
Private Pleasures
Stolen Blessings
The Loves of Harry Dancer
The Dream Lover

Lawrence
SANDERS

McNally's Alibi

An
Archy McNally Novel
by Vincent Lardo

BERKLEY BOOKS, NEW YORK

This is a work of fiction. Names, characters, places, and incidents either are the product of the author's imagination or are used fictitiously, and any resemblance to actual persons, living or dead, business establishments, events, or locales is entirely coincidental.

The publisher and the estate of Lawrence Sanders have chosen Vincent Lardo to create this novel based on Lawrence Sanders's beloved character Andy McNally and his fictional world.

MCNALLY'S ALIBI

A Berkley Book / published by arrangement with
the author

PRINTING HISTORY
G. P. Putnam's Sons hardcover edition / July 2002
Berkley mass-market edition / August 2003

For information address: The Berkley Publishing Group,
a division of Penguin Group (USA) Inc.,
375 Hudson Street, New York, New York 10014.

ISBN: 0-425-19119-2

BERKLEY®
Berkley Books are published by The Berkley Publishing Group,
a division of Penguin Group (USA) Inc.,
375 Hudson Street, New York, New York 10014.
BERKLEY and the "B" design
are trademarks belonging to Penguin Group (USA) Inc.

PRINTED IN THE UNITED STATES OF AMERICA

10 9 8 7 6 5 4 3 2 1

McNally's Alibi

1

• My potential client was a Ms. Claudia Lester. Sensing she'd prefer to meet in a grander setting, I scheduled the meeting for our conference room, as the size of my office precludes room for visitors' seating other than in my lap. Not a propitious arrangement for a first meeting, as the conference room is part of the firm's executive suite. What is also unfortunate is that the suite comprises the CEO's office, the executive loo and, last but far from least, the domain of our formidable executive secretary, Mrs. Trelawney, with whom I have a love/hate relationship. I love to sass her and hate it when she gets the better of me.

Raising her head of gray polyester, she scrutinized me from top to bottom and judged my attire—cord jacket over a pink button-down shirt, navy blue flares and penny loafers—as "Not bad."

"You utter a litotes, Mrs. Trelawney."

"A who?"

"Litotes, dear lady. Citing the vernacular, you use a negative to express a positive. You didn't say, 'You look good.' You said, 'You don't look bad.' An ambiguous compliment, to say the least."

"Perhaps, Archy, it appeared ambiguous because it wasn't meant to be a compliment—and you're late. You booked the conference room for eleven and it is now . . ."

"Just eleven, I believe."

She gazed askance at her lapel watch (yes, she really wears one) and answered, "Five past, according to Eastern Standard Time. Ms. Lester has been here since five to eleven."

"Did you offer her coffee?"

"Of course. But she refused."

"What does she look like?" I inquired.

Thinking a moment, Mrs. Trelawney answered, "Not bad for a woman her age."

"And what age might that be?"

"Somewhere between forty and death."

With that I opened the door and entered the conference room, thereby taking the first step in a case I would record in my journal as . . . No, I don't want to give away too much too soon. That's as bad as giving away too little too late. I will strike a happy medium and tell it like it happened.

Enter Archy. "Sorry I'm late, Ms. Lester. I would blame it on the traffic, but there wasn't any to speak of."

"Then let's blame it on me for being early. How do you do, Mr. McNally."

Claudia Lester was a blue-eyed blonde with a great tan, red lips and a smile as big as the rock she wore on the middle finger of her left hand. I was not yet ready to swear to the authenticity of either. Being of a kinder disposition than our CEO's girl Friday, I would place her age at anywhere between forty and fifty, with a face that had had a little work, as they say, and a figure that didn't need any. She wore a tailored suit in charcoal gray, a print blouse I would attribute to Hermès and black-and-white spectators that were a pleasing addendum to a great pair of gams.

I have long been of the opinion that women dress for the occasion in the same manner theatrical designers dress a star to complement the scene. A date with a potential lover: something girly, frilly and revealing. A date with a female acquaintance: pantsuit. Business meeting: Claudia Lester was textbook perfect.

"Can I offer you a cup of coffee, Ms. Lester?" I asked as I took the chair at the head of the polished mahogany table. Ms. Lester was seated at my immediate left.

"Your secretary already asked, thank you, but I've had my morning intake and shun elevenses."

As she obviously wanted to get down to business ASAP, I did not bother to correct her misapprehension regarding the relationship between Ms. Trelawney and me. Believing that I employed a secretary who wore a lapel watch could only enhance my reputation, at least in the working world. Eager to learn just what Ms. Lester's business might be, I opened the interview with my standard question: "May I know who recommended you to McNally and Son, Ms. Lester?"

This is usually met with a blush and a hush or a "I'd rather not say, as it was given in . . . er . . . confidence." Not Ms. Lester. "Deci Fortesque," she replied. She spoke the name in the manner of a teacher calling on an inattentive student. "Do you know him?"

I didn't know him, but I certainly knew of him. In a town rife with rich eccentrics, Decimus Fortesque was, if not the richest, surely the most eccentric of the lot. Decimus was a self-proclaimed "renowned collector," though to the best of my knowledge his most acclaimed collection was a series of ex-wives. Eight, give or take a few. For all I knew, Ms. Lester was a former Mrs. Fortesque. Decimus had boasted, at various times, of owning a fleet of Rolls Royces, a splinter from the original cross and a life preserver from Noah's Ark.

Fortesque is an old English name, but I do not believe Decimus's branch of the family arrived on the *Mayflower.* More likely they were sent over as part of the Industrial Revolution. Moneywise, this had it all over the seafarers who docked on Plymouth Rock. Where the Fortesque money came from is, like all old money in this country, unimportant; what mattered was that there was a lot of it. Where the name Decimus came from is another mystery. I doubt he was the tenth child, because the rich believe in zero population growth, giving each succeeding generation a larger slice of the pie.

I had never been employed by the man, but word of mouth in Palm Beach is the most accepted form of advertising. I can tell you without false modesty that the name Archy McNally has been known to be recommended over many a damask tablecloth, both in and out of confidence. Playing it safe, I said, "I have heard of Mr. Fortesque."

She smiled that big, red smile and nodded to say she understood my caution. I got the pleasant feeling that Ms. Lester understood many things, especially how to please a man. I don't mean to imply that she was a professional in the worst sense of that often misused word, but one trained as a hostess—in the best possible sense of that often misused word. I could see her making weary businessmen comfy on cross-country flights, cruise ships, pricey restaurants and the V.I.P. lounge of those places that feature V.I.P. lounges.

"I am a friend of the former Mrs. Fortesque. Number three, I believe, if that doesn't date me," she said.

I came back with the trite, "Who's counting?" and got a shrug for my trouble.

"Vera, the former Mrs. Fortesque, and I worked together in the days when Pan Am circled the globe. We always managed to pull those New York–to–Sydney thirty-hour shifts."

Score one for Archy.

"Now," she went on, "I find myself in a rather awkward position, if that's the correct word."

"It's as good as any, Ms. Lester, and it's the word most often used to describe the position of those who seek my help."

I got the smile and, "I like your honesty, Mr. McNally."

"And I appreciate honesty in those I represent. Anything less, and I will refuse your patronage."

"Fair enough." She opened her purse—black, shoulder strap, fine leather, I believe it was Tod's—and extracted a pack of Marlboro 100s with a filter tip. "Do you mind, Mr. McNally?"

"Not at all." I went to a sideboard that contained the standard conference-room supplies and returned with an ashtray.

"Would you care for one?" she offered as I again took my place at the table.

I had enjoyed an English Oval, the only brand I smoke, on my ride from home to office. I would indulge myself again after lunch, dinner and a final one before bed. At the end of the month I would eliminate one, my choice of which one, and eliminate one on each succeeding month until I was cured of the habit. This routine was the latest in a series of withdrawal attempts and one sworn to by ex-smokers—as were all the others.

"No, thank you. I'm withdrawing," I said.

She lit the cigarette with a match, not a Dunhill, which I considered a smart move, as too many *labels* gives the impression that one is hell-bent on impressing, and immediately turned the white filter red. The opening line of one of my favorite ballads, as rendered by Chris Conner, played itself in my head: *"A cigarette that bears your lipstick traces . . ."* And owing to Ms. Lester's former career, the next line followed quite naturally: *"An airline ticket to romantic places . . ."*

"Cold turkey?" she wondered aloud.

"No. Gradual," I answered.

"What stage are you at?"

"One after each meal and bedtime," I told her.

Inhaling deeply and directing the exhale toward the ceiling, she said, "Ah, yes, that was my favorite. And it did work. I was smoke-free for almost six months, and then along came Matthew."

"Is Matthew a heavy smoker?"

"No, Mr. McNally. Matthew is a bastard."

So we had finally reached the business end of our meeting, and his name was Matthew. The job description of a PI, especially a discreet one, is very similar to that of a psychiatrist. First we listen attentively to the client's complaint, then we go to work on finding a cure. We prescribe aspirin, a good, stiff drink, long sea voyages and, on occasion, relocating to Brazil. The human condition being what it is, their afflictions are monotonously similar, only the names are different.

"Matthew began life as Levi, a tax collector who followed Jesus," I said. "He wrote one of the gospels." It never hurts to let 'em know how clever you are.

"This Matthew is an extortionist who wants to write a

book based on my diary," Claudia told me. Her story unfolded amid clouds of smoke.

Claudia Lester had kept a diary from the day she lost her virginity to the captain of her high school basketball team to the day she found contentment as a middle-aged inhabitant of New York's Sutton Place, and all the stops along the way. She subsisted on an income derived from the estate of her late husband, who had popped the question as they soared thirty thousand feet over the Pacific.

"A very detailed diary, Mr. McNally." Puff. Puff. "And why not?" she challenged before I had a chance to ask why.

It seems Claudia Lester enjoyed penning her memoirs as she lived them, and judging from her unabashed account of her prose I would guess that her escapades read like a modern-day *Memoirs of a Woman of Pleasure*—known to the masses by the name of its heroine, Fanny Hill.

"I was attractive and ambitious. I was even offered a screen test by a producer whose name is legend in the industry, but turned him down on the grounds that acting was too much like work. The role in this costume epic went to a French gal who competed with the Sphinx for attention, and lost."

Having spent more time in the Museum of Modern Art's cinema in New York than in any lecture hall in New Haven, I immediately knew the name of the producer, the actress and the film. If Ms. Lester was as cryptic in concealing names in her diary as in this telling, woe be unto the men in her life.

She had been intimate with Hollywood producers, politicos and Fortune 500 Chairmen of the Board, one of whom she married. "He was a grandfather at the time," she admitted. "Our marriage was brief, but intense, if you know what I mean."

So intense she probably loved the old geezer to death, thereby securing a position for herself as a Sutton Place matron who lunched.

Lest I think her needle had got stuck in a groove, she said, "It wasn't all about sex, Mr. McNally. In my time I was also privy to business deals that were not quite kosher, dirty political campaigns, the sleeping arrangements aboard a Greek shipping magnate's yacht and the beard for a five-star general who was getting it on with his aide-de-camp."

Well! When it came to the prurient arts, Ms. Lester was a black belt. I had asked for honesty, and for that was not to be spared verse nor chapter of her life as a jet-setter. As any analyst licensed to probe would do, I questioned the lady's motive in keeping an account of such goings-on. Blackmail came to mind, and were that the case I would soon learn that the intent had had a boomerang effect. It was Ms. Lester who was being blackmailed.

I watched this curvaceous blonde stub out her cigarette and utter the name *Matthew* as if wishing it were he who could be so easily deprived of oxygen. "We met at one of those New York parties frequented by rich, middle-aged widows and attractive young men."

"They have their counterpart in Palm Beach," I informed Ms. Lester.

With a toss of her head that said either she knew this or couldn't care less, she continued, "We hit it off, Matthew and I. You might say we went together like Stoli and caviar. Believe me, I had no illusions about our relationship. There had been other Matthews in my life, but none more endearing or lasting as with Matthew Harrigan. If you're thinking H–A–double R–I–G–A–N spells Harrigan, go right ahead."

I must say the lady had a sense of humor. I don't usually get comic relief during an initial interview.

"I provided entrée to the better restaurants and the crowd that frequents them, good theater seats and the occasional hundred-dollar bill for cab fare home. Matthew was handsome, witty, young and energetic, thereby providing value for my money. Cutting to the nitty-gritty, I allowed Matthew to read my diary. It amused me and inspired him. It was his idea to turn it into a book with no-holds-barred. I went along with him because it was fun to plot our best-seller and, as you insist on honesty, because it kept him interested in me."

When Claudia realized that Matthew was serious, boldly refusing to abandon the project when she insisted he do so, she flatly refused to continue the ruse and sent Matthew packing. "I still see many of the old crowd and enjoy all the perks of that privileged world. I had to choose between courting their wrath or dumping Matthew, and poor Matthew came in a distant second.

"Forgetting I had given him a key to my apartment and the fact that the doorman knew him as a frequent caller, he paid me a final visit when I was out and took the diary."

"Breaking and entering is a felony," I said.

"He didn't exactly break the lock, but he did enter and help himself to my property. Two days later, I received a call from him. He was here, in Florida, and ready to return my property for fifty thousand dollars."

"Why did he come here?" I asked.

"I have no idea, but a guess would be that it added drama to the intrigue and made it very inconvenient for me. That's when I talked to Vera, and she suggested that I speak to Deci, as I'm a stranger in your paradise. Deci has remained on friendly terms with all his wives, you know."

Alimony being the chain that binds, I thought, then said, "Blackmail is also a felony."

"What these things are called, Mr. McNally, does not interest me. Getting back what is mine does."

"And just how do you intend to do that?" I asked.

"Pay him, of course. And that's where you come in. He's staying in a motel not far from here. The exchange is to take place there at nine this evening."

"And I'm to be the courier," I stated.

"That is why I'm here, Mr. McNally."

"He's had more than enough time to make a copy, you know. The fifty thousand could be only a down payment," I reminded her.

"I know that, but it's a chance I must take. However, I don't believe Matthew would have the nerve to double-cross me. He knows the people who owe me favors."

I was looking for a reason to bow out of this deal, and she had just provided it. "Then why don't you call in your mark and have them take care of Matthew?"

"I don't want them to know the diary is gone missing. In fact, I don't want them to know the diary exists," she explained. "I know making Matthew privy to the diary jeopardized my position, but prudence is not the trump card of a woman in love."

"And why don't you deliver the ransom and pick up your diary?"

"I don't want to see him," she said, seemingly annoyed at the questions. "More important, I want him to know he is no longer dealing with only me. He has a vivid imagination and will take the money and run."

Remembering I had no place to run, I said, "Get yourself another messenger boy, Ms. Lester. This one is not interested in the assignment."

She started as if my words were a blow to her jaw, not her ego. "Why, may I ask?"

"Because I refuse to take part in a blackmail scam and because I don't intend to be a target for the people who owe you favors," I answered.

"As the Bard said, Mr. McNally, what's in a name? This thing you insist on calling blackmail can also be construed as a business deal between consenting adults. I made Matthew believe I was going to allow him to write the book. I deceived him, you see, taking up his time and, if you'll excuse the analogy, his energy. I owe him something."

"Fifty thousand bucks is a lot of something," I noted.

"I can afford it. As for my friends, let's say I was exaggerating a wee bit. After tonight I'll forget we ever met."

"I'm ready to forget that right now, Ms. Lester."

My hand lay on the table, and she covered it with hers. The flesh was warm, the gesture seductively reassuring. She obviously hadn't lost the touch. "I'm at the Ambassador," she said. Before I could repeat my resolve not to take the assignment, she put a finger to my lips. "Don't say no. Think about it. Seven this evening, if you agree."

2

• For reasons that will soon become clear, I now digress to the events leading up to my meeting with the enigmatic Ms. Lester on this sunny September morn in Palm Beach, Florida, USA. The day began at the McNally abode on Ocean Boulevard as it did most mornings, with nary a harbinger of the capricious escapades in store for this Discreet Inquirer in the week ahead.

The sire, Prescott McNally Esq., had breakfasted early, as was his wont. For my father, there is no such thing as "business casual," and today was no exception: he appeared at the table in his traditional garb, a custom-made vested suit in banker's gray; a white-on-white French-cuffed shirt; a rich silk tie, in a regimental stripe he was not authorized to wear except on our side of the Atlantic; and Cole-Haan loafers in leather as soft as a newborn's patoot.

After breakfast he mounted his iron steed—a silver Lexus—and made his way to the McNally Building on

Royal Palm Way to preside over McNally & Son, Attorney-at-Law. Father is the attorney of this for-profit enterprise, where he controls both the purse strings and the ambience within an edifice whose modern exterior belies its stuffy old-fashioned heart.

Unlike the House of Windsor (née Saxe-Coburgs via the Hanoverians), the House of McNally is descended not from kings, but court jesters. My grandfather, Freddy McNally, was a Minsky circuit comic who took a break from prat-falling long enough to invest in prime South Florida real estate when a thousand bucks—ten percent down—could get you an acre of oceanfront property.

Today, the Hearst mansion in lovely PB is on the market for twenty-nine million and is classified as a "distress sale": it is assumed that Veronica, Randolph Hearst's widow, will feel a bit pinched financially thanks to the family code that prevents Hearst money from being inherited by any but blood relations. In the meantime, Howard Kessler just paid thirty-nine million for an oceanfront mansion and Janet Annenberg Hooker's beach house went for a mere fifteen, but it's rumored the new owners will spend another fifty to renovate the joint.

Last season's real-estate news was all about the old Addison Mizner house in Manalapan. Zillionaire Gary Ross bought it, divided it into three parts like Caesar's Gaul, and then had the pieces "floated" by barge to Palm Beach, where they were reassembled on the Palm Beach lot he had acquired from cosmetic queen Estée Lauder. Alas, the old house couldn't withstand even that brief sea voyage and is now destined for demolition. Truly a titanic gesture, if you'll forgive the pun.

My mother, the lovely Madelaine McNally, had taken her juice, toast and coffee with His Nibs, then departed for the greenhouse to minister to her beloved begonias. Metro-Goldwyn-Mayer once boasted that it had under contract more stars than are in the heavens. If this is so, mother has more varieties of begonias than MGM had stars.

That leaves the Dark Prince, yours truly, to journey to Yale in search of the Holy Grail—that would be erudition and a law degree—only to return with a variety of silk berets and his tail between his legs. The reason I was "sent down" from Yale has never been made public, but, like the identity of Jack the Ripper, it has been etched in bronze and stashed away in a time capsule to take the edge off future shock.

As the son of McNally & Son, I occupy a wee office in the McNally Building where I have been dubbed a discreet inquirer. A private investigator in a town whose inhabitants shun private investigators, they'll flock to me when ruffled feathers need smoothing and indiscretions demand a coat of whitewash. I've managed to take on the odd murder investigation without courting publicity or the attention of nosy policemen.

I had overslept, as Dark Princes often do, and was now in the kitchen of our faux Tudor abode enjoying a not-so-petit-déjeuner of cinnamon French toast prepared by our housekeeper-cum-chef *magnifique,* Ursi Olson. The butter-crisped bread was lapped with Ursi's own delectable honey-maple syrup. The morning's only surprise came from Ursi's husband, our houseman, Jamie Olson, who divided his attention between the morning newspaper and sips of his wife's bracing black coffee. The usually laconic Jamie suddenly blurted, "Your friend got his name in the paper."

This gave me pause, but did not prevent my fork from making its way to my mouth. Just who could it be? All my pals are year-round Palm Beachers and all are members in good standing of the Pelican Club, of which I am a founder. We Pelicans are a less eclectic group than those who frequent the Bath and Tennis and the Everglades Clubs. Aside from appearing in a little black book titled *Palm Beach's Most Eligible Bachelors* or being mentioned in the society columns, we tend to shun more common coverage in places like the police blotter.

The days when nice folks' names appeared in the paper just three times—when born, married and last when they died—are as passé as long engagements and longer marriages. Therefore the field was wide open. So who had managed to make the early edition of Jamie's tabloid?

" 'Sergeant Al Rogoff,' " Jamie read aloud, reading my thoughts as well as any psychic, " 'assigned to the Palm Beach burglary strike force, was on duty last night when his attention was drawn to a light in an upstairs window of the Beaumont mansion on Dunbar Road. As the house has been closed and secured with hurricane shutters for more than twenty years, Sergeant Rogoff pulled over to investigate when he spotted two men climbing over the three-foot brick wall that surrounds the house.' "

Well, Al Rogoff was one I counted as a friend, but I was so startled by Jamie's sudden loquaciousness I actually put down my fork, and even Ursi stopped puttering about the stove to stare at her husband. As Jamie continued, it was the song, not the singer, that held our rapt attention.

" 'Burglary, however,' " Jamie continued, " 'was not the motive of the suspicious duo. One of the men was dressed in a skirt and wore a blond wig above a face liberally powdered and rouged. When confronted by Sergeant Rogoff, the men admitted that they had climbed the wall in search of privacy to engage in sex.' "

What a scream! And what a sight for my still-sleepy eyes. I let out a chuckle at the image of Al, who looks like Smokey the Bear in a police uniform, confronting the romantic couple.

"'Sergeant Rogoff called for assistance and charged Thomas Mitland, twenty-nine, and Bruce Bennett, twenty-four, both from West Palm Beach, with trespassing. Before backup arrived, Mr. Mitland tossed his purse into the bushes, which was later found to contain a cocaine pipe and a plastic bag filled with crack cocaine. Mitland was then charged with possession of an illegal substance.'"

What? No credit for the designers of the skirt and wig? And what about a detailed description of the purse filled with contraband? Both a Palm Beach news item taboo. If we wanted just the facts, ma'am, we'd read the *Times*. *Woman's Wear Daily,* even.

"'Mr. Bennett was released after posting a five-hundred-dollar bond. Mitland is still in custody,'" Jamie concluded.

Imagine waking up in jail still dressed in last night's street wear! I made a mental note to call Al to see if anyone had shown up to bail out poor Mitland, or at the very least to bring him a change of clothes.

"What's the world coming to?" Ursi wondered aloud as she refilled my coffee cup.

"I don't think it's much different now than in the days when the Beaumont mansion was the jewel in Palm Beach's crown," I answered. "All the news that's fit to print now seems to be all the news, period."

"Still," Ursi complained, "it's a travesty to read that the Beaumont lawn is being used as a lover's lane."

"By the odd couple," Jamie quipped without taking his eyes off his newspaper. My word, he was feeling his oats this morning. Was this a harbinger of things to come? Recalling that thoughts have wings, I suppressed the notion, but, alas, the gods will not be fooled and were already looking down at Archy with malice aforethought.

From what I have heard about Madison "Mad" Beaumont, I would think he would have invited the odd couple into his home for a game of backgammon after posting bail for Mr. Mitland. Ursi, of course, would disagree: a leader among the domestics along Ocean Boulevard, she was also a bit of a prude, always lamenting the good old days when those they served confined their high jinks to something you did in the dark, or in Europe, and when family skeletons and odd couples were kept behind locked closet doors.

"I'm sure croquet wasn't the only game played on the Beaumont lawn in the good old days," I mused aloud. "No doubt a wide variety of contact sports were offered as an option for the more agile houseguests." (Come to think of it, I would have enjoyed witnessing some of the Beaumont high jinks for myself, had I been of age.)

"Tennis?" Ursi said, either not knowing that tennis is not a contact sport or purposely deflecting my innuendo with a vapid response. If I were a betting man, I would set the odds at twelve-to-seven in favor of the latter. I was certain that Jamie, who continued to sip, read and take in every word spoken, knew of what I spoke.

The Beaumonts were as close to royalty as families are permitted to get in our supposedly classless society. Descended from presidents—hence the given names of Madison, Jefferson and Rutherford—they were as entrepreneurial as the Astors, Du Ponts, Mellons and Morgans. Like *the* Mrs. Astor, the Beaumonts did not socialize with the new rich Carnegies, Rockefellers, Vanderbilts and, for political reasons, Roosevelts.

Madison "Mad" Beaumont broke with family tradition in the second half of the last century when he lowered social bars his forebears had kept so rigidly intact. To the family homes on Manhattan's Fifth Avenue, Southampton's Gin Lane, Maine's Bar Harbor and Florida's Palm Beach came café society, Hollywood society, dethroned royalty, presidents and their first ladies, gangsters and their molls. "Mad" was a blue-blooded Gatsby whose Twelve Days of Christmas celebration was a coveted invitation not meant for the timid.

As you may have already guessed, each day featured a living tableau of the popular Christmas carol, including the ten ladies dancing and the eleven lords a-leaping, compliments of the New York City Ballet. How he handled the three French hens a-laying and the eight maids a-milking I haven't a clue. It was all as amusing as could be until, some two decades ago, on the thirteenth day of that Christmas, the lights went out in the Beaumont mansion—permanently.

"What happened to the family?" I asked Ursi. "Around the time I left for New Haven they closed the house and never returned."

"Terrible tragedy," Ursi said, joining us at the table. "Madison Beaumont had twin boys, Madison Jr. and Tyler. Like two blond angels, they were. So cute the press referred to them as the Beau Twins. It was just after the big Christmas party that year when one of them—I believe it was Madison Jr.—died. That was when the family closed the house and just picked up and left."

"How did the boy die?" I asked.

Jamie, clearly having exhausted himself in the telling of the saga of the impounded purse, made no comment re: Madison "Mad" Beaumont, but I'd bet my collection of

Cracker Jack prizes that he knew more than his wife about the sad story of the Beau Twins.

"Well," Ursi said, just warming up, "the house had a huge curved marble staircase that rose from the reception hall to the second floor. Very impressive. Mrs. Beaumont, one of the last great ladies to employ the couturier Mainbocher to create all her dresses and gowns, used the staircase to make a grand entrance at her own parties." As an aside, Ursi added, "You know, Archy, Mainbocher made the dress the Duchess of Windsor wore the day she married the Duke."

Ursi's knowledge of the great and near great never ceased to amaze me. She was a walking encyclopedia of opulent trivia who could spot costume jewelry from ten paces and detect a phony accent quicker than 'enry 'iggins. No detail was too grand to bedazzle, and certainly even the smallest wasn't to be overlooked.

"Where was I?" Ursi wondered.

"Descending the marble staircase in a Mainbocher original," I offered.

"Yes. And what a scandal that was," Ursi stated.

"The gown?" I ventured.

"No, Archy. The gowns were lovely. I mean that Mrs. Beaumont was always the last to appear at her own fancy dress balls. She waited for all her guests to arrive before she descended the marble staircase, but not before the staff had managed to usher everyone into the reception hall to watch the show."

Like the eleven o'clock number in a Broadway musical, I thought, as Ursi castigated the theatrical hostess. "If one can't receive her guests properly at the front door, one should stay in bed," Ursi proclaimed with a profound nod of her head.

Ursi's story had all the complexity of an oater with a cast of thousands. Somewhere among the shoot-out at high noon, the chase and the barroom brawl there existed a plot. One simply had to persevere to discover what it might be.

"What happened to the boy?" I persevered.

"He fell down them marble steps and never got up." Jamie spoke to his newspaper.

Insisting on the last word, Ursi said, "That was the rumor at the time. The papers reported only that the boy's death was accidental."

And given the influence wielded by the Beaumont family, that was all the public was ever likely to know.

A glance at Mickey's hands signaled that it was time to shift gears and move on, as idle gossip does not pay the rent. True, my three-room garret suite comes compliments of *mon père,* which makes the aphorism a non sequitur, but one should make the effort. In fact, I did have an appointment with a prospective client at eleven and had just enough time to kiss mother's cheek—a chore I would not defer even if it did make me late before climbing into my Miata and making my way to the salt mines.

The sight of mother bending over her potted plants in the dappled light of the greenhouse would make an apt subject for an impressionist master. I never approached the scene without placing it in a gilded baroque frame in my mind. Title? *Woman in Her Potting Shed.* And what a lovely woman she was. Even the smudge she always managed to get on her cheek when at her labor of love served to enhance her comely features.

Mother had become a bit forgetful in her golden years. Like the high blood pressure that gave her cheeks a rosy glow, this was a matter of concern to father and me, but happily both conditions were mitigated by the combination of medication and understanding by those who loved her.

"How nice you look, Archy," she said, and smiled.

"How clever of you to notice," I replied, bending to kiss the offered cheek.

Some say my mode of dress is rather theatrical—my father being among my most vocal critics. If my attire is theatrical, it is meant to please an audience of one, Archy McNally—and more often than not, I succeed. As a rule, I shun ties because my favorite wit, O. Wilde, remarked that *"a well tied tie is the first serious step in life."* I, of course, refuse to take that step. When things, like love affairs and chest colds, become serious, they lead to marriage and pneumonia.

Love, especially, should be treated like a vintage port. A few sips are enchanting. Empty the bottle and you get a headache. In this, my light-o'-love, Consuela Garcia, vehemently disagrees and is threatening to close the door on our "open" relationship. It appears she may give in to the ardent courting of one Alejandro Gomez y Zapata—whom I will think about tomorrow on the off chance that tomorrow will never dawn.

Alejandro is a rebel with a cause—to oust Mr. Castro from his island paradise. In this quest Alex is at the end of a very long line and has about as much chance of succeeding as he has of ousting me from Connie's affections. He has positioned himself in Miami as the Great White Hope of our Cuban brethren with much fanfare and—aside from invading Palm Beach to conquer Connie's heart—little action.

"Archy, you must make an effort to get up early and leave for the office with your father," mother scolded gently.

"Did he ask for me this morning, mother?"

"He asks for you every morning, Archy."

Our canine sentinel of blended heritage, Hobo, looked out of his gabled home, sniffed at my approach and withdrew therein. I wonder if among the blend Hobo doesn't have a turtle in the woodpile. When a man is ignored by his own best friend, it's questionable as to who is occupying the doghouse.

Alone with my thoughts, the trip to Royal Palm Way was disquieting, to say the least. I drove with the top down. An ocean breeze ruffled my hair. A hint of autumn floated on the salty breeze. All should have conspired to lift my spirits. Maybe it was those shuttered Beaumont windows that had me believing the hurricane season had arrived early, with Archy in the eye of the storm. Suddenly, I was being attacked on all fronts and threatened with insurgency within my own camp.

Had I for too long taken too much for granted? Was my secure and sublime existence in danger of extinction? If I had been as snug as the proverbial bug in a rug, I could now hear the roar of a vacuum cleaner the size of a steamroller, headed straight for my nest.

Last night Connie had the audacity to dine in public at—of all places—the Pelican Club, with Alejandro Gomez y Zapata. Our crowd knows that Connie and I enjoy the kind of relationship that allows me to play the field and her to keep a light in the window. If you think that's chauvinistic, you're correct. I have cheated on Connie more times than I have fingers—or toes, come to think of it—but, like a gentleman, I conduct my affairs covertly, sparing Connie any embarrassment and the trouble of rendering me a capon. True, our romance is a delicate balance, but it's one I have managed to juggle without ever dropping a ball—till now.

I was at the bar of the Pelican as the aforementioned Cuban couple munched the special of the day and drank Cuba Libres in honor, no doubt, of Alejandro's pledge to *libre* Cuba from Castro, not from Spain, for which the odious drink got its name, as well as a hit single for the Andrews Sisters.

The Pelican is located in a clapboard house with the first floor serving as bar and dining room. Given the givens, it ain't spacious enough to pretend you can't see who's tête-à-tête with whom after one quick glance around the room. To add to my discomfort, everyone made a point of stopping at the bar to ask me, "Who is the guy with Connie? What a hunk—like a movie star."

I will admit, even though it hurts, that Alejandro does resemble a screen idol. Think Tyrone Power in *Blood and Sand.* (But then, I have often been likened to Jeffrey Lynn, so there!) Alejandro is a second-generation Cuban with boatloads of charisma who has inflamed Miami's Cuban population (which is most of Miami, in case you haven't noticed) by vowing to raise an armada and invade Cuba; raise an army and invade Cuba; raise an air force and invade Cuba; all of the above and invade Cuba. He speaks at political rallies, marches in parades, organizes youth groups and does a mean tango—think Valentino in *The Sheik.*

There is talk of Alejandro running for political office, and to that end a pretty *mujer* with the right credentials (Connie is a Marielito) would go a long way in securing votes. Connie's cousins, who alone comprise half the Cuban population of Miami, are devoted followers of Alejandro, and on her last visit there the two met and indulged in a tango or two. Alejandro is now smitten and Connie is issuing thinly veiled ultimatums: name the day or *adiós,* Archy. Connie has made similar threats, veiled and otherwise, and I have prevailed by turning the other cheek and ordering another martini.

Alejandro is also several years younger than Connie, making him several-plus several years younger than I, a fact that inflates her ego and pricks mine. I would rather be intimidated by Connie's knife than Alejandro's good looks and youth.

Is it any wonder I awoke with a headache? Once again I missed breakfast with the family, which caused father to comment, mother to scold and Hobo to withdraw. I depend on father to maintain my lifestyle and on Connie to contain my libido. To alienate either would cause me pain; to estrange both would be suicidal. And right now my generous benefactors were politely cautioning me to shape up or ship out. Out? I have no place to go except, perhaps, to share the digs of my friend Binky Watrous, late of a mobile home in the Palm Court. Pass the hemlock.

But before anything so repugnant is passed my way, let's look at the situation in the bright light of day. Was I being a bit too pessimistic? Had the sight of Connie flaunting her relationship with Alejandro put me in a funk out of all proportion to reality? The answer to both is a resounding Yes!

There was method to Connie's madness. She was manipulating me and I was reacting like a puppet pulled by strings. What was called for was retaliation, not capitulation. There were any number of young ladies—*young* being the operative word—who would be more than happy to give Archy's ego a boost in these trying times. All I had to do was pick and choose. Those who came immediately to mind had me thinking that Consuela Garcia was doing me a favor. Things were looking up.

As for my parents' concern for my future, well, it was only natural that they longed to see me settled. And perhaps one day I might do just that—but not right now.

So it was with a light heart that I sped down the A1A on this glorious South Florida morning for my meeting with Claudia Lester.

I should have known better.

3

Later, in my office, I could still feel the touch of Claudia's finger on my lips and see the look in those blue eyes promising that all things were possible. I remembered, too, the warmth of her hand covering mine. What is the old adage? Cold hands, warm heart? It was the converse, warm hands, cold heart, that gave me cold feet. Our parting was a standoff. When I said goodbye, she said, "Till later," with a confidence born of prior experience.

As Binky, preceded by his mail cart, entered my monastic cell, I filed Ms. Lester in that area of my brain labeled "Do Not Open Till Christmas," where she was cheek-to-jowl with Alejandro. Perfect positioning for a spirited tango, and the pounding in my head told me they were already going at it. Well, at least I hope it was the tango.

"Not one with a first-class stamp," Binky greeted as he placed a pathetically small packet of envelopes on my desk, unnecessarily bound in a rubber band.

Binky Watrous is our mail person, a position he holds thanks to my advocacy. It was a show of beneficence I was beginning to rue, but then there is so much to rue in the life and times of Binky Watrous. "Your job," I reminded him for the umpteenth time, "is to sort, collate and deliver the mail, not scrutinize the postage and return addresses."

"I take an interest in my work, Archy. It's the secret of my success."

If Binky had had any success during his tenure in numerous previous positions, it was the best-kept secret since the location of Amelia Earhart's last pit stop.

"Al got his name in the paper," Binky now said with great relish.

Did I mention that Binky is a Palm Court neighbor of Sergeant Al Rogoff, his trailer being but one removed from Al's? It is not a happy pairing, when one considers that Al's WELCOME mat has been replaced with one that reads GO AWAY. I told Al to practice the good-neighbor policy and give Binky time to exhibit his more comely qualities. "He grows on you," I told Al. "So does fungus," Al replied.

"He caught two guys bonking on the lawn of the old Beaumont place," Binky informed me.

Bonking? Now, that was a new one on me. Binky's colorful vocabulary was largely self-created. "To bonk," I said, "is to collide."

"I guess that was their aim," he remarked with a giggle. Binky is the most enthusiastic fan of his own wit. "One of them was wearing a skirt. What do you suppose he was wearing under it?"

"I have a very delicate stomach this morning, Binky, and would rather not think about bonking or undergarments. Good day."

"I guess it's a result of all those olives you consumed last night."

I could see that the gods were not going to give Archy a break anytime soon. It's said there is a time and place for everything, and this was a time to keep my mouth shut. Due to the couple Fred-and-Gingering in my medulla oblongata, I didn't heed the warning. "And how do you know how many olives I consumed last night?"

"I ran into Tommy Ambrose this morning, and he said you were popping olives last night like there was no tomorrow."

Tommy Ambrose is a hooligan whose father gives him carte blanche at the club, an indulgence enjoyed by too many errant youths in this affluent beach town. I noticed young Ambrose at the Pelican bar last night in the company of a girl who was no better than the kid deserved. "And here it is tomorrow, so I guess I was wrong. Goodbye, Binky."

Not the type to be discouraged by a door slammed in his face or a mat stamped GO AWAY, Binky inquired, "Who was the blonde you saw in the conference room this morning?"

Is nothing sacred around this office? Not with anchorwoman Trelawney broadcasting newsbreaking stories as they happened. "None of your business, that's who."

Binky shook his head of limp blond hair and rolled his brown doe eyes upward. "You're out of sorts because Connie invited Alejandro to dinner at the club. You don't know how to handle rejection, Archy."

"And, apparently, neither do you."

"What's that supposed to mean?"

"It's supposed to mean that you invited Alice for a drink seventeen times and she turned you down seventeen times." Alice D'Amico is one of our prettier young secretaries, whom I would have invited for a drink were it not my policy to shun office alliances outside of the office. I have no doubt I would have fared better than Binky Watrous.

"I didn't know you were counting, Archy."

"Everyone in the office is counting," I countered.

He began to back himself and his cart out the door, as it is impossible to make a U-turn in my chamber. "Are you on a case, Archy?" he asked.

"I will be on your case if I don't see the back of your head, lad."

"That's not possible in this closet."

"It's a figure of speech," I all but shouted.

"So is bonking," he all but shouted back.

No sooner had Binky departed than Claudia Lester returned to fill the void. She was a hard woman to shake off—or was I reluctant to see her go? I must say her dilemma and its solution had piqued my interest. She was at the Ambassador with a suitcase filled with fifty thousand dollars in cash, awaiting my arrival. A guy named Matthew Harrigan was in a nearby motel awaiting the arrival of the suitcase.

It was the perfect plot for one of those old serial films that ran for fifteen consecutive Saturdays at the local Bijou. In the first episode the hero is in possession of a map that leads to a hidden treasure. The lights go out, there is a scuffle, and when the lights come on again our hero is holding half the map in one hand and rubbing his head with the other. He spends the next fourteen episodes looking for the other half of his map while the villain is looking for the half he left behind.

Both the genre and the Bijou have long been extinct, and I had no desire to carry half the map to its mate in order to shower Matthew Harrigan with gold. There was something that didn't smell right about the setup, and, come to think of it, Ms. Lester didn't smell at all. Unless I was suffering from a bout of anosmia, I would say Claudia Lester wore no scent. Her eyes said it all, and what they said was *I don't believe Matthew would have the nerve to double-cross me. He knows the people who owe me favors.*

Anyone involved with that diary would eventually draw the attention of those who owed Claudia. I resolved, yet again, to forgo the stipend I would have earned as her messenger boy. This day had begun with a headache and had gone downhill from there. I should have left the office, gone home, changed into my beach togs and taken my swim—my customary two miles—before retiring to my room to sulk until the cloud of doom blew out to sea.

What I did was call Connie to make sure a light was still burning in her window for yrs. truly. On a day like this I should have known better.

"Lady Cynthia's residence." Connie, at the controls of a communication system that was the envy of the Pentagon, picked up on the first ring.

Connie is social secretary to Lady Cynthia Horowitz, a septuagenarian of great wealth and little sense. Lady C, who has the face of a hawk and the body of Aphrodite, spends her time and her money giving parties and taking lessons—tennis, swimming, golf, dancing, acting, et cetera—and hires only the best (looking) instructors as her mentors. So determined is she to succeed that she insists the instructor of the moment move into her oceanfront ten-acre spread. Not an unusual arrangement in sunny Palm Beach.

"It's me, Connie. Archy."

"Oh, you."

Or was that "who"? Two words and already it was not going well.

"Did Alejandro go back to Miami?" I politely asked.

"He did," Connie told me.

I couldn't help wondering aloud, "Did he leave last night or this morning?"

"No comment," Connie said as if she were giving a press conference to publicize one of Lady C's charity balls.

"No comment is the most telling comment of all," I lectured.

"Then you have your answer," she said.

Moving right along, I suggested, "Would you like to have dinner with me tonight?"

"I'm washing my hair tonight."

"Fine," I said, "I'll bring over the fixings, and cook dinner, and I'll rent a video for later on."

"I'm not in the mood for your paella, Archy, and even less in the mood to see *What Price Hollywood?,* with what's-her-name."

"Constance Bennett is her name, and the film is a classic." Really, Connie could be infuriating. There was a time when she would cook the paella and watch the Three Stooges run amok just for the pleasure of my company.

"I know it's a classic, Archy, but after several viewings it wears thin, like other things I could mention."

Good grief, what was she referring to? Unless I was mistaken, it had a slightly risqué connotation, at my expense. "I guess you don't want to see me tonight, or any other night," I whined.

"Don't get your ego in an uproar, Archy. I just need some time alone to think."

"Think? About what?"

"My future. Now I have to go, my entire board is lit up. Call me tomorrow, Archy."

Tomorrow? My life was in shambles, and I doubted if the pieces would all come together by the morrow. However, if I had reached the nadir of existence, what had I to lose by showing up at the Ambassador at seven this evening? Seek and you shall find, and I had just found the rationale to do what I had intended doing since eleven o'clock this morning.

• H. W. Longfellow wrote, *"Between the dark and the daylight, When the night is beginning to lower, Comes a pause in the day's occupations, That is known as the Children's Hour."* At the McNally house that time of day is better known as the cocktail hour. In the drawing room El Padre mixes, stirs and pours two martinis that are as dry as the rain forest. Mother, smart woman, drinks only sauterne. We then fill one another in on what course our lives had taken that day and impart our thoughts on current and sometimes future events. Our motto: Families that drink together, think together.

Father reports on his rich clients, mother on her begonias and her clubs, while Archy relates his latest case as long as it is not too macabre or bawdy for mother's ears. I assiduously avoid mentioning my love life, or lack thereof, and pass around pictures of my sister and her three lovely children when cornered. It satisfies their grandparental urges and gets me off the hook. Dora, the sister in question, resides in Arizona, which is near enough for an annual visit and far enough for anything more frequent.

When summoned, we march into the dining room for one of Ursi's culinary delights.

If my occupation as a discreet inquirer I owe to father, my bon vivant ways go back to what I learned at my mother's knee. "Archy, live as if every day may be your last, and always wear clean underwear." Tonight, I would do both. On covert operations, such as delivering the ransom loot, I dress in black. Jacket, trousers, turtleneck, socks and shoes. Plus a clean pair of heather-gray briefs and matching T-shirt.

I once added a black mask to this ensemble and went to one of Lady C's costume balls as Zorro. I spent the evening brandishing a sword with a black Crayola tip and marked many a costumed behind with my trademark. Although I did not win a prize that evening, I did precede the graffiti craze by a decade.

Tonight I would have to forgo both the vermouth-laden martini and Ursi's minty loin lamb chops, garlic and herb roast potatoes, arugula, orange and fennel salad and chilled raspberries topped with a dollop of vanilla-bean-scented whipped cream. Yes, I snooped in the kitchen when telling Ursi to make my apologies to them who bore me, stressing the fact that I was off to a business meeting. "Business before pleasure" was one of Prescott's favorite edicts, and I aimed to please.

Perhaps Ms. Lester would offer me a drink, and when I returned with her precious diary would invite me to the Ambassador Grill for a late supper. That presumption was my first mistake of the evening. My second was not renting a more nondescript set of wheels, as my red Miata is both easy to spot and easy to remember. My third mistake was ogling the lady who opened the door to her Ambassador suite, thereby giving her the opportunity to comment with a mocking smile, "I knew you would come."

She wore what I believe is often referred to as a little

black dress. It began with spaghetti straps at the shoulders and ended with a slight flare above her knees. In shimmering black, the little that was betwixt and between the straps and the hem clung to Ms. Lester to accentuate the positive and resembled madam's undergarment once, and perhaps still, known as a slip. There was little doubt what was beneath: nothing.

Eyeing my outfit, she quipped, "Who died?"

"I am in mourning for my life," I said.

We were in the suite's sitting room, which contained comfortable chairs, two side tables with lamps and a desk. The few pictures on the walls were hotel art of the finest quality. "As bad as all that?" She spoke as she walked to the desk, upon which was a black attaché case I would guess was labeled "Crouch and Fitzgerald, Madison Avenue."

"My favorite brunette refused to dine with me tonight." Not knowing if she could handle the fact that she was aiding and abetting my suicide, I let it go at that, grossly underestimating the lady's ability to tolerate suffering in those she employed. Ms. Lester would find *Les Misérables* amusing, but once again I get ahead of myself.

"How lucky for me," she exclaimed, "and you should never fret over a lost love, Mr. McNally. Like trains, there will always be another."

I wondered if I should ask for her timetable as she opened the executive tote bag and said, "Count it."

"Is that necessary?"

She focused those blue eyes on me and stated, "Very necessary. I don't want Matthew moaning that I came up short."

"Do you think I'm a crook?"

With a shrug of those creamy white shoulders, she informed me, "I think everyone is a crook, Mr. McNally, and am seldom disappointed."

"You speak of Matthew Harrigan?"

"I speak of *Homo sapiens.*"

That's when I should have left. Instead I counted the greenbacks. They were arranged in stacks of fifties and hundreds. There was a time when the culprit would have demanded tens and twenties, but times do change. "If it's legal tender," I said when finished, "it's all here."

"Oh, it's legal, believe me. The Crescent Motel. Number nine. Just off the main drag as you approach Juno Beach. He knows your name. I'll expect you back directly after you've made the exchange. If you have any problems, call me here."

And I was dismissed, thinking myself lucky that she didn't handcuff my wrist to the handle of the attaché case. Having lured me into doing her bidding, she saw no reason to waste her time or charm on a hooked fish. Only professional civility prevented me from reneging on the deal.

Florida has more motels than you can shake a stick at—whatever that means. The Crescent was a convenience motel, if you get my drift, with one carport for each of the attached units, which were laid out in, what else, a crescent shape. Not being a resident, I pulled into the visitors' space at the far end of the complex. Very neat. People could come and go without attracting the attention of the office—again, if you get my drift.

To fortify myself for the chore ahead and kill time, I had stopped at the Ambassador's bar for a bourbon and branch water. The black cloud that had been hovering over me all day had grown to encompass most of southern Florida, threatening rain. It was pitch dark and the hotel's small community parking area was lit by a single flood atop a ten-foot pole. I could just make out a few other cars parked in the convenience area. Meaning no disrespect to the management, I locked the Miata before trudging to number nine.

I knocked and the door, still on its chain, was opened a crack. "Yeah?"

"Archy McNally," I announced.

"You alone?"

"The last time I looked, I was."

He had to close the door to unhook the chain. When he opened it again, I stepped into a room that was more shadow than substance owing to the one lamp aglow with the standard motel sixty-watt bulb. As expected, Matthew Harrigan was a good-looking guy who displayed his wares in a pair of tight jeans and tank top. If I wasn't mistaken, his hair was beginning to thin, and were the light brighter I might detect the onset of wrinkles below his dark eyes.

I could see why Matthew had chanced the blackmail scheme to pocket fifty thousand. He was nearing thirty, which is tantamount to death in his profession.

He held out his hand, and I gave him the case.

"Do I have to count it?" He had a pleasing voice with just a hint of a New England accent. Had he at one time aspired to be a crooner? I wouldn't doubt it.

"It's all there. She won't screw you."

"You don't know how many times she's screwed me," he said, and laughed. On a small dining table was a package wrapped in plain brown paper and tied with a string. "And this is all here." He undid the string and opened the package.

It wasn't a book bound in white velvet with a tiny clasp lock and engraved with the words MY DIARY. I was looking at a stack of perhaps three hundred eight-by-ten sheets of white typing paper. As he ruffled them for my inspection, I could see that some pages were typed and others written in longhand.

As he rewrapped the package he said, "I would offer you a drink, but room service is experiencing delays and I know you want to be on your way."

For the second time this evening I was being given the boot by my inferiors. I took the package and headed for the door. Matthew and I had exchanged all the words we were ever going to say to each other. There is something about a seedy motel room that makes its occupants act like characters in a B gangster film, and I feared it was catching. I had taken the job because I was feeling sorry for myself, and now applauded the decision. My encounter with Matthew Harrigan reminded me of the corny platitude *I cried because I had no shoes until I met a man who had no feet.*

I left the Crescent feeling a hell of a lot better about myself and ready to take on any and all who threatened to rock my boat. It just shows to go you, don't it?

I could hear Matthew bolt and chain the door behind me. It was a ritual he would be doing for the remainder of his life. Outside it had begun to drizzle. Holding the diary close to my chest, I took the crescent route to my car. I fumbled a few moments trying to unite key and lock in the semidark. When I finally got the door open I tossed the diary onto the passenger seat. As I bent to enter the car I felt a hand on my shoulder.

I turned with a start, and that's the last thing I remember.

4

I had accepted this assignment because I believed I had reached the nadir of existence and, my ego taking on the guise of a punching bag, had nothing to lose by showing up at the Ambassador at seven this evening. When I awoke sprawled across the seat of my Miata, legs dangling over the paved ground of the parking area and being rained on, I recalled the comforting maxim *There's always one step further down you can go.*

I had tripped over that step and, highlighted by the merciless glare of the parking area's floodlight, found myself the centerpiece of what might very well be the tawdry cover art for a pulp fiction periodical. Life, as it were, imitating art. I also learned that a bruised head hurts more than a bruised ego. Rising slowly, I placed my right hand over my left breast. No, I wasn't feeling for a heartbeat, but for my wallet. It was there. Next, I reached across to the passenger seat, feeling for the diary. It was not there.

When I got to my feet I almost welcomed the rain, heavy now, cascading down on me and helping to clear my head, although it didn't take much cogitating to know that I had been mugged and my client's diary stolen. Rubbing the bump on my wet head, I leaned against the car until I was sure my legs would obey me before starting to walk the path back to number nine. Need I say that the Crescent Motel was as silent as a cemetery at midnight? Not a creature stirred behind the windows that showed a crack of light between the drawn blinds. The Crescent regulars minded their own business in the interest of self-preservation, but that's not to imply that my faltering meanderings went unobserved.

The car that had been parked in the space reserved for number nine was gone. I tried the door and found it was locked. I knew I wouldn't get any sympathy from the management—nor did I want to explain my presence in their hotel—so had no recourse but to go back to my car and flee while I still had the wherewithal to do so. Like many who live in close proximity to the ocean, I keep a beach towel in the trunk of my car and now used it to dry my hair, checking to see if the miscreant had drawn blood. He, or she, hadn't. When finished, I laid the towel across the driver's seat to protect it from my now soaking posterior. Without a pang of guilt, I went into the glove compartment and pulled out the English Ovals I keep there should the need arise, for the need had quite obviously arisen on this accursed night.

For those who are counting, it was my third of the day. Breakfast, lunch and now, which should have come after dinner but thanks to Claudia Lester and her purple prose there was no telling when or if I would be able to take nourishment this evening. As scheduled, I had arrived at the motel at nine, and it was now a few minutes after ten. As it wasn't a powder puff that had raised a welt on my noggin, this case had gone from a routine exchange of cash for merchandise to assault with a lethal weapon in one hour. Neither in appearance nor mind-set was I now capable of marching into the Ambassador and demanding to see my client, so I headed out of the Crescent Motel and made for home, where I could both literally and figuratively lick my wounds.

How ridiculous that this day was to end the way it began—with a headache.

To keep my mind off the throbbing pain and vexing humiliation, I tried to figure out who was doing what to whom, and why, with Archy as the fall guy. My first thought was that Claudia's "friends" had got wind of the missing diary and its contents and decided to apprehend it—not for ransom but for extinction. How did they know? Could be Matthew tried to hit them up before approaching Claudia. His type usually had more brawn than brain. But if they knew where to find the diary, why didn't they just march into number nine and take if from Matthew? These guys weren't in the least shy.

If they had found out about the missing diary via Matthew, it was possible they also knew that Matthew was holding it in exchange for fifty thousand bucks and that one Archy McNally was the go-between. Perhaps the "friends" told their hired hands that if they got to the Crescent after me they could keep the loot in payment for their trouble and pick up the diary from the departing courier. In fact, such a scheme would be nothing more than business-as-usual for Claudia Lester's wheelers and dealers.

Next I focused in on Matthew Harrigan. Had he followed me out of the motel room, clobbered me and repossessed the diary? Reason? He now had the fifty thousand and was looking to sell it again for another fifty to either Claudia or her "friends." Why not do it in the motel room? Because he didn't have the mettle to attack me one-on-one and because he didn't want to take the chance of me being found in his room, thus linking him to the crime.

Last, *cherchez la femme.* Was everything Claudia Lester told me pure blather? If so, what was the truth? She had no reason to attack me in the parking lot, because I was about to deliver what she would have taken from the seat of my car. Was it absurd to think she did it to avoid paying my fee? That last supposition told me I had run out of viable ideas. With an aching head full of foolish thoughts and a belly void of sustenance, I drove through the pouring rain to my sanctuary.

My parents retire early, so I was certain they would be abed by the time I arrived home, saving me the indignity of having to explain my appearance, which would only worry mother and cause father to look at me askance. With luck, both Ursi and Jamie would be in their quarters over the garage watching the telly, as they did most nights. Our sentry, Hobo, would be in dog dreamland—besides which, he never comes out in the rain. My intent was to enter unseen, raid Ursi's well-stocked refrigerator and carry the pickings to my penthouse suite, where I could munch in peace.

All went as anticipated, which was a pleasant change on an evening full of surprises, including the one that had me prowling around my own home like a mouse in search of a crumb of bread. The crumb I selected was attached to half a loaf of French baguette, which I filled with thick slices of roast ham and a Brie Ursi has the good sense never to refrigerate. I also found a pair of kosher dills, ripe olives void of pits (they leave no trace) and a bottle of chilled St. Pauli Girl. For dessert, a brownie made from scratch.

I reserved my feast until I had undressed, showered and examined my bump with a shaving mirror held over the back of my head as I peered into the bathroom mirror. It was the size of an egg, for which I swore revenge. For the present I medicated myself with aspirin, thinking I was far from finished with Ms. Claudia Lester. I had a score to settle with the woman, and as R. Kipling wrote, *"Nothing is ever settled until it's settled right."*

I called the Ambassador and learned that Ms. Lester had checked out a few hours ago. I expected as much, but it was early days and I refused to plot my counterattack on an empty stomach. Wrapped in a comfy terry robe, I sat at my desk and dug into my cold victuals. On a scale of one to ten I would rate the meal a six. Not bad for leftovers. I decided to raise it to a seven by finishing the evening with a small marc savored with an English Oval—bringing my total for the day to the allotted four.

Then to bed and perchance to dream—but of whom? Claudia Lester? That only brought back my headache. Connie? That only reminded me of the Cuban liberator who wanted to liberate me from my favorite girl. Did I, deep down in some dark crevice of my subconscious, want to be free of the lovely Connie? Of course not. Then all I had to do was pop the question, and bye-bye Alejandro and hello Mrs. Archibald McNally. The title sent tremors through my exhausted body, and I feared it would cause the bump on my head to erupt like Vesuvius.

Did I or did I not love Consuela Garcia? There are those who live for love, those who die for love and, on numerous occasions, those who murder for love. I live for life, have no intention of dying before my time and will not murder Alejandro, drawing the wrath of the entire Cuban population of Miami. If I lost Connie, as Rudolfo had lost Mimi, would I lament in a flawless tenor, *"Farewell to sweet mornings, waking up together"*? Truth is, I seldom spent the night with Connie because I rather liked waking up alone. I am not at my best in the morning, and, so I've observed, neither is Connie. Familiarity breeds not only contempt, but divorce.

Ergo, to save our relationship, Connie and I must avoid the M word at all costs and keep whatever quo is status. Now all I had to do was sell the proposal (wrong word, perhaps?) to Connie, banish Alejandro and track down Claudia Lester—then to bed and perchance to dream. . . .

• I awoke with a head as clear as the September sky that hung over southern Florida like a canopy of shimmering lapis lazuli. I was not concussed by the sneaky pimpernel of last night's adventure, or misadventure, and the only reminder of the evening was the bump on my head that caused me to wince when I combed my hair. I am not complaining, for to retain a full head of hair places me in a minority of American males for which I would gladly suffer a wince or two.

Out of a sense of duty, or perhaps fear, I arranged the rest of me for breakfast with the lord of the manor and his lady fair. Being in a conciliatory mood, I had to select my wardrobe carefully if I wanted to avoid a scowl from father. Miracles being as rare in Palm Beach as bread lines, I knew nothing I chose would be rewarded with a nod of approval, so to thwart disappointment I strove for the least offensive rather than aspiring in vain to the most pleasing.

Lightweight cord and seersucker are two of my favorite fabrics. However, up north, one must never wear either, or anything in white except a dress shirt or underwear, before

Memorial Day or after Labor Day. In tropical climes like ours, one can be seen in full summer regalia every month of the year. Hence my love affair with Palm Beach.

I avoided my post-preppie togs, fearing they would put father in an Eli frame of mind and remind him of my fall from grace. I finally selected a pair of summer-weight gray flannels, a lilac dress shirt with open collar, a somber navy blazer and black wing tips. But beneath was pure Archy—red briefs and blue T-shirt emblazoned with a capital S in yellow.

The McNally establishment is rather pukka, giving the impression of old family wealth, but it's more facade than fact. We usually breakfast in the family kitchen, where the housekeeper and her mate often sit down with the family for coffee and a sweet roll. All except Jamie were at the morning meal when I arrived. Father raised his face and patted his bushy guardsman mustache with a napkin at my entrance. "Well, Archy," he remarked, "to what do we owe the pleasure of your company at this ungodly hour of the morning?"

"Good morning, Archy," mother said, her greeting as sincere as father's was acrimonious. For this I kissed her florid cheek before sitting.

"I have a full day ahead, sir, and thought it best to get an early start."

"That's very good of you, Archy," mother quickly put in, "especially as you had to work so late last night."

Ursi had delivered my apology for missing cocktails and dinner last night, but it seemed only mother had remembered that I was away on business, not diversion.

"What can I get you, Archy?" Ursi called from her position at the range.

"A cheese omelet with a rasher of bacon would be nice," I ordered.

"It'll have to be cheddar," she answered. "My Brie seems to have melted overnight, and I'll toast you an English muffin, as the baguette I was saving for breakfast went the way of the Brie."

"I missed dinner and helped myself when I came in," I announced, looking for sympathy. I was beginning to wonder if I should tell them whom I intended to call upon this morning but decided to hold on to my trump card until father played his ace.

Mother, bless her, responded with, "You should never miss meals, Archy. You must make this clear to your clients before you agree to help them."

Father, in blue serge and rep tie, looked the quintessence of a defender of the law, and it wasn't all veneer. I think he truly believed that right makes might no matter how often history has proved the aphorism wrong. He was Judge Hardy of the old flicks, but, alas, he had sired Archy, not Andy. His tombstone could justifiably bear the inscription "He never jaywalked."

"You're on a case, Archy?" he asked.

"I am, sir."

"On behalf of Claudia Lester?" was his next question.

Father's clairvoyance comes by way of anchorwoman Trelawney. "Yes," I told him. "I met with Claudia Lester last night and then represented her in a business transaction." Ursi placed a glass of fresh squeezed orange juice before me—the nectar of the gods to my parched throat as well as the Sunshine State's prime export. Next a cup of steaming coffee was placed to my left, and I could now smell the bacon sizzling in Ursi's iron skillet—things were looking up, but not for long.

"And the nature of her business?" father continued to interrogate.

I could sense Ursi and mother pricking up their ears in anticipation of my answer and disappointed them with, "I'm afraid, sir, I'm not at liberty to reveal the nature of my work for Ms. Lester."

Father nodded thoughtfully, knowing that my answer was our code for stating that the case was not a fit topic for mother or for Ursi's ears, where it would wend its way along the domestic grapevine that stretched the length and breadth of Ocean Boulevard.

I was presented with my golden omelet and crisp rasher just as father inquired, "And how is Connie, Archy?"

In all fairness, I think he did it more to divert the conversation from Claudia Lester to one he knew would pique mother's interest. That it ruined my appetite was not noted.

Mother looked at her favorite son as if I were the poet laureate of our dominion about to recite his "Ode on a Cheddar Cheese Omelet." Ursi stopped puttering and turned, wielding a spatula in one hand with the other on her hip. Thanks to that never-wavering line of communication—Watrous to Trelawney to father—Alejandro Gomez y Zapata's invasion of Palm Beach, and his intended target, was common knowledge. My love life is currently the most discussed soap opera in the McNally household.

"She's well," I informed my audience.

"Have you seen her recently?" I assumed father was the designated spokesperson for the household on the subject of Archy versus Alejandro. The squire reads only Dickens, and in his heart of hearts he hopes I will slap Alejandro's face with a glove and challenge him to a duel on the Esplanade. With Binky as my second I would probably be handed an unloaded gun.

But I was only fooling myself. What father wanted,

what they all wanted, was a marriage. A ring would repel Alejandro much as garlic sends Dracula packing. All happily married couples think it their duty to recruit on behalf of the institution. This does not mean that my progenitors and Ursi and Jamie Olson exist in pure marital bliss. Ursi is verbose, Jamie as taciturn as a clam. Discourse between the two has all the vivacity of a Sunday sermon.

Mother and father can never agree on the temperature setting for their bedroom air conditioner. He scolds her for drinking sauterne with meat and fish, while she thinks he's nuts to demand starched collars and cuffs on all his shirts. Once, I recall, she referred to him as "father" and he bristled, telling her that as he was not her father she should not call him father. However, on numerous occasions he has referred to her as "mother." Go figure.

If one did become formally engaged, how long before one had to take the next step? Now, that was something to think about. A countermove to stall for time. But how much time? Next March? April? May? May the first or may it never happen? I could enter a Trappist monastery, but brown is not my color.

"In fact, I talked to her just yesterday," I said, spreading Ursi's homemade beach plum jam on my liberally buttered muffin.

"Is Alejandro still here?" mother asked rather timidly. "I hear he's a very brave young man."

"Talk is cheap," Ursi announced, saving me the trouble of doing so.

"He's gone back to Miami," I answered mother.

"For good?" Ursi spoke the thought aloud and startled even herself.

"I don't know the liberator's travel plans," I said, weary

of being grilled by those I loved, "but I doubt if Cuba is on his itinerary."

"You should think of settling down," father advised. "Remember, *tempus fugit.*"

Tempus was not fugiting fast enough this woeful breakfast hour. "I don't think I'm unsettled, sir." I spoke in defense of my right to life, liberty and the pursuit of happiness. How much did one have to surrender in return for room, board and an open relationship? A great deal, I was beginning to learn—but don't count me out. Where there's deluxe accommodations and fringe benefits, there's Archy McNally.

"The guest suite has a lovely sitting room and a commodious dressing room and bath," mother reminded me.

I put down my fork for fear of choking. Connie move in with the in-laws? She would rather parachute into Cuba with Alejandro's flying tigers—and so would I.

"More coffee, Archy?" Ursi offered, hovering over me.

"No, thank you, I really must toddle."

"Would you like a lift to the office, Archy?" Father played his ace.

"No, thank you, sir. I'm not going directly to the office." Striking a blasé air, I put a finger to the bump on the back of my head and laid down my trump. "I have a business meeting with Decimus Fortesque at his place."

There is nothing like dropping the name of a millionaire potential client to get father's rapt attention. Prescott McNally is a man of honor, but that does not deter him from being a man of business. Upon learning my destination, he stroked his mustache contemplatively, a sure sign of his approval.

"I've met him," mother cried. We all three looked at her as if she had confessed to having had tea with J. D.

Salinger. "Well, I did," she insisted. "He lectured at the C.A.S. just last month."

The C.A.S. is the Current Affairs Society, of which mother is a devoted member. Over the years the group has honed in on such diverse topics as the dwindling ozone layer, the increase in single-parent parenting and the bias encountered by transgenders in upscale boutiques.

"He spoke," mother told us, "of his mania for collecting."

"Did he bring his collection of wives for show-and-tell?" Ursi asked.

"No," mother answered, "but he brought a snuffbox that belonged to the king of France. I don't remember which one."

"What's he like?" I wanted to know. I had no visual image of Decimus Fortesque. I knew I had never met the man, and if I had ever seen a picture of him it had left no lasting impression. If I was going to his home uninvited, the more I knew, however peripheral, the more confidence I would have in my mission.

Mother sat quietly, her head tilted in deep thought. Then her eyes lit up and she exclaimed, "He looks like Mischa Auer."

Mother and I often describe people, their look and manner, in terms of bygone film personalities. However, in her euphemistically labeled golden years, mother's recall is far from total. Thus, I had to prod to see if she had named the correct film actor of yore. "Tall and thin," I stated rather than asked, "prominent eyes and a black mustache that looked as if it had been drawn on with a fine pencil point."

"That's him," mother cried with joy at her lucky guess.

Father's stroking turned to tugging, a sure sign of his growing displeasure at our game. The sire does not cotton to those he respects being likened to character actors. "You will see me directly after your meeting with Mr. Fortesque," he ordered.

"I will, sir." I rose, kissed mother, said ta-ta to Ursi and left in triumph. Now, if I could only grand-slam Alejandro.

5

• Jamie was in the driveway hosing down mother's wood-bodied Ford station wagon. The classic car would see duty this morning on one of three errands: a shopping expedition to the Publix for groceries, a tour of the nurseries in search of orphaned begonias in need of adoption or a run to transport mother's prize specimens to a flower show. My Miata was where I had left it last night, on the graveled turnaround in front of our three-car garage, not blocking the left-hand bay that housed father's Lexus. Even nearly concussed, wet, angry and hungry, I knew better than to thwart the Don from his appointed rounds.

Hobo ran happily through the puddles created by Jamie's labors and stopped only briefly to sniff the cuff of my trousers before returning to his footbath. "Decimus Fortesque," I spoke the name to Jamie.

Without a pause he mumbled, "The collector."

"That's the one," I said.

"Sam Zimmermann is his houseman. He was hired by the first Mrs. Fortesque, outlasted her stay and the seven that followed."

If the domestics of Palm Beach were formally organized, our Jamie would be the union boss. He knew them all intimately and therefore knew as much as they did about their employers—which was more than the employers knew about their respective spouses, significant others and blood kin. Jamie was often an invaluable source for my discreet inquiries.

"Maybe he should have married Sam," I speculated aloud but did not get a laugh, or even a smile, from the guy with the hose. "Where does he hang out, Jamie?" I asked.

"Fortesque or Sam?" Jamie responded in short, clipped grunts that did not get a laugh from me, nor, I imagine, were they intended to.

Rather than spend the morning watching Jamie playing fireman and Hobo splashing about the gravel, I stated my need in more pragmatic terms. "What's Fortesque's address, Jamie?"

Because God put more millionaires in Palm Beach than he made oceanfront lots, it was necessary for some moneyed folks to reside inland, which, on an island, is never very far from water, be it the briny or the Intracoastal Waterway, aka Lake Worth. Jamie told me that Fortesque's digs were on the Intracoastal down toward South Palm Beach. I slipped Jamie a tenner, which, if he knew it, would outrage my father. The Olsons are handsomely rewarded for keeping us McNallys in the comfort to which we were not born, but as dispensing classified information was not in their job description I thought it only fair to recompense my informant with the extra quid or two.

I put the Miata in drive, lit an English Oval and headed

south on the A1A, never thinking that I was taking the first step into a maze of deceit, chicanery, backbiting and murder most odious—but then one never knows, do one?

Chez Fortesque was a genuine Mizner. A pile of white-washed stucco with red trim that I appraised at five mil—give or take a mil. The iron gates that separated the driveway from the road were wide open, and if there was an alarm system it was neither evident nor announced by one of those dreadful metal disks attached to a stake and bearing the security company's logo. I'm afraid the likes of these were becoming more and more in vogue on our once pristine island in the sun.

Sam Zimmermann, who had seen eight wives come and go, greeted me at the front door almost before I had a chance to announce that I wished to gain entrance. In appearance Sam was every inch the English butler, but his accent bespoke Brooklyn rather than Berkeley Square. He wore a gray suit and black bow tie. "Good day, sir," Sam said.

"Good day to you," I responded. "Archy McNally here to see Mr. Fortesque."

"Very good, sir." Sam bowed from the waist. "He's expecting you. Right this way, please."

Expecting me? Did Sam mistake me for an invited guest? Could be, but that wasn't going to stop me from having a word or two with Decimus Fortesque. In my line of work, gaining entrance by subterfuge was an accepted business practice. As I followed Sam from entrance foyer to drawing room I surmised the place was furnished in what I believe is called Mediterranean, but whether that made its provenance Barcelona or Beirut was Greek to me.

Thanks to mother I recognized Fortesque immediately, but even forewarned I was more than a little amazed at his likeness to the late Mischa Auer. Tall and lanky, he had a razor-thin mustache that must have been tedious to maintain and could have been a testimonial to the tonsorial talents of Sam Zimmermann. All Fortesque needed was one of my berets and a pad and pencil to take your order for the *prix fixe grenouille* Provençal. From the moment I entered the room, Fortesque's striking eyes stared at me with such apprehension I feared he was about to upbraid me with, "Who the hell are you?" He did indeed pounce, but his words were, "Well, where is it?"

Had I entered a loony bin whose inmates masqueraded as deceased character actors reciting lines from imaginary scripts? Standing between Jeeves and Mischa I had no place to run, so I joined the cast. "Where is what, Mr. Fortesque?"

Eyeing me like a Boston bull pup who was expecting a bone and got a pat on the head instead, he moaned, "My manuscript, man, my manuscript."

Clearly, it was time to end the charade. "Mr. Fortesque, you and your butler have mistaken me for someone you were expecting this morning. I have nothing for you."

Fortesque took a step back and looked at me as if I were daft. "You are Archy McNally?" he asked.

"I am, sir."

"The Archy McNally that woman hired to deliver the fifty thousand in return for the manuscript?"

Woman? Fifty thousand? *Mazel tov!* "May we sit down, sir, and talk about this?"

"Of course. Of course," he muttered. "I was so intent on getting my hands on the manuscript, I seem to have forgotten the basic civilities. Please, do have a seat." With a wave of his long arm he addressed his servant. "Sam, why don't you get us some coffee."

The room was slightly smaller than an airplane hangar, with floor-to-ceiling windows for a west wall that opened to a balcony and a majestic view of Lake Worth. The day being one we Floridians like to think is typical, and isn't, a profusion of pleasure crafts and catamarans, with colorfully billowing sails, lazily traversed the sparkling waterway. All the scene lacked was a sound track rendering the haunting refrains of Offenbach's *Barcarolle*.

The vast space was divided into several sitting areas, some obviously designed for reading, others for a game of cards or, in the case of the grouping featuring an antique captain's chest bookended by a pair of comfortable club chairs, for polite chitchat. I took one of the clubs as my host settled into the other. Leaning across the chest that separated us, he sighed. "I gather you don't have the manuscript."

"Before we go any further, sir, may I know if the woman in question is Claudia Lester?"

"But of course it is, man. When she asked me to recommend someone she could trust to close the deal—actually a bagman, but no offense, I'm sure—I recommended you."

Bagman? Insult had just been added to injury. I felt the bump on my head quiver. Claudia Lester deserved to be hanged by the thumbs, and I was ready to donate the rope. "And who recommended me to you, sir?"

"I won't say," he snapped, "and in your profession I'm sure you understand why."

Not certain he didn't mean the bag profession, I let that one go and had my say. "Claudia Lester hired me to deliver fifty thousand dollars she said was hers, to a man in a motel she said was her ex-lover, in return for a diary she said was hers."

Fortesque grinned like a schoolboy who has just been told a naughty story. "Is that what she said? Clever minx,

I'll say that for her. What she was doing, you see, was keeping our business all in the family, as they say. The less people knew, the better the chances of getting our hands on the manuscript. With something like this, you don't want a lot of avid collectors with deep pockets bidding on the item, not to mention the tabloid press."

"Will you tell me what this is all about, sir?"

Fortesque waved a finger at me. "Oh, no. Not just yet. First tell me what became of my fifty thousand and the manuscript."

"Gladly," I began. "In fact, it's the reason for my visit. I delivered the fifty thousand to the Crescent Motel, unit nine if you care to know, and gave it to Matthew Harrigan, Claudia's ex-gigolo."

"Never heard the name," Fortesque informed me. "Did he give you the manuscript?"

"Harrigan showed me a stack of bond paper, some covered in type, some in script, which I believed to be the lady's diary because I had been told that's what it was. He rewrapped the package in brown paper tied with string and handed it to me. Naturally, he kept the fifty thousand."

"So where's the bundle of brown paper tied with a string?" Fortesque interrupted.

"I'm not finished with my story, Mr. Fortesque," I protested.

"Sorry, man. Do go on."

"I carried the package out into the rain and to the motel's guest parking area to retrieve my car. Here, I was attacked from behind—hit on the noggin with a rock or lead pipe, is my guess. When I awoke the diary was gone. Meanwhile, back at unit nine, the door was locked and the carport reserved for number nine empty. I assumed Harrigan had done me in and absconded with Claudia's loot and the diary."

If I thought I was going to get a bit of solace from Decimus Fortesque, I was wrong. Instead of asking after my noggin, he reminded me that "it was my money and my manuscript, man. Does Claudia know about this?"

"I called the Ambassador to report in and was told that Ms. Lester had flown the coop. I'm here because she told me you had steered her my way, which makes you my only link to the lady. As you can imagine, I'm most eager to have a word with her."

"You think she stiffed you," he quipped.

"If it was your fifty grand, Mr. Fortesque, I would say it was you who got stiffed. When was the last time you spoke to Claudia Lester?"

"Last night," he confessed, "just before you arrived at her hotel. She told me that she had hired you to make the exchange, so when you showed up on my doorstep this morning I assumed you had come to deliver the manuscript."

At that moment Sam came into the room wheeling a tea cart burdened with a carafe of coffee, bone china cups and saucers that I was certain bore the logo of the potter Josiah Spode, and an array of delectable-looking miniature pastries. My connoisseur's eye spotted napoleons, babas au rum, cream puffs and biscuits *à la cuiller,* or ladyfingers to the common folks.

As Fortesque poured he explained, "Sam is a Cordon Bleu with a specialty in French pastries. He makes them by the dozens, freezes them and then pops them in a warm oven, never a microwave, for ten minutes before serving them up. Help yourself."

I did as ordered. A cream puff, light as air, and a rum

baba, equally palatable. It was no wonder Sam had not gone the way of his master's harem. "He's a find," I said, reaching for a napoleon.

"He also sings," Fortesque confided. "Says he's related to the great Broadway star."

I couldn't imagine which one but didn't challenge Sam's claim. I was here to trace Claudia Lester, not the butler's family tree. The possible loss of fifty thousand big ones didn't seem to affect Fortesque's appetite, but then a loss of fifty thousand to a man like Decimus Fortesque was like Joe Blow taking a hit for fifty bucks at the track. "How do you keep your figure with these goodies crowding your freezer?" I asked.

Fortesque shrugged. "Metabolism is my guess. I can make a meal of these things and drop five pounds in the process."

Bully for you, I thought with envy. Knowing I would gain five pounds if I had one more, I stopped reaching for the specialties of the house, pulled in my tummy, and pleaded my case. "As I'm the innocent victim of your dealings with Claudia Lester, I think it's only fair that you tell me what the deuce this is all about, Mr. Fortesque. I might even come up with a clever plan to get back your fifty or this manuscript you seem besotted to possess."

Fortesque put down his cup and nodded sagely. "And I will, but before I do may I ask the extent of your knowledge on the art of collecting, Mr. McNally?"

Collecting, which I doubt is a bona fide art form, is a very popular couch sport in Palm Beach. The more outré the objects of desire, the more zealous the team players. At one time I collected crystal shot glasses, my *pièce de résistance* being a Lalique two-ounce jigger. I then plunged into swizzle sticks and managed to acquire a Stork Club, a Park

Casino, a Romanoff's and a Kit Kat Klub. I was told the latter cabaret existed only in Christopher Isherwood's mind and, were this true, I wouldn't be the first collector to be duped. After hearing Fortesque's story, I knew I wouldn't be the last, either.

One of my favorite musical shows, which I have preserved on vinyl so the music goes round and round, has a very clever song that pokes fun at collecting mania. Some of the coveted items vocalized are, *"A hat that belonged to Wally Simpson before the Prince of Wales was in the bag . . . A shirt with Henry Richmond's laundry tag,"* and even *"A G-string Sally Rand wore at a stag."*

I told Fortesque about my jigger and swizzle-stick combinations but spared him the witty lyrics, as I didn't think he would be amused.

"*Besotted* is the operative word, Mr. McNally," he mused. "Louis Auchincloss—do you know him?"

"I know his work," I answered.

"Louis Auchincloss writes about people like us," he lectured.

Auchincloss writes novels about New York society with a capital S. If by "us" Fortesque meant me, I was a bagman with expectations.

"Auchincloss has written," Fortesque picked up where he had left off, "that collecting is much like a sexual drive much more potent than any love for the baby produced. Very apt in my case, as I've never had children, not from lack of trying, believe me, and perhaps have substituted collectibles for progeny. Like any parent, I want my children to stand out like diamonds in a coal mine. Some collectors, like yourself, focus in on one or two items such as autographs or antique cars. My children are more a rainbow ensemble, but each must be the best of its kind."

Fortesque paused to sip from his cup. "Examples of the avocation's fervor," he went on, "are evident by the anonymous collector who paid twelve thousand dollars for the ruby slippers Garland wore when she played Dorothy in *The Wizard of Oz,* or the one who paid a million for the dress Marilyn Monroe wore when she sang 'Happy Birthday' to President Kennedy. Just recently, Bette Davis's Oscar for *Jezebel* brought five hundred and seventy-eight thousand at Christie's in New York."

The satisfied, almost gloating, look on Fortesque's face made me wonder if his trophy room contained Judy's slippers, Marilyn's dress and Bette's Oscar. No doubt he was rich enough to be the avid Mr. Anonymous.

"Claudia Lester is an agent, or broker, in the sometimes shady world of collecting," he said. "Nothing actually illegal, mind you, but agents like Claudia have a reputation for being able to get their hands on collectibles being offered where the buyer won't ask too many questions about the seller or how he or she came in possession of the article. 'Nuff said, Mr. McNally?"

"More than enough, sir. In the real world it's called the fencing of stolen goods."

"Oh, don't be so unctuous, man," Fortesque chided. "Not necessarily stolen. Let's say legally acquired by Machiavellian tactics."

No doubt *Il Principe* was Deci's favorite tome. "And just what did Ms. Lester acquire, legally or otherwise, sir?"

Fortesque took a deep breath, squared his shoulders and spoke as if he were trying to raise up Beelzebub. What he raised was the hairs on my bump. "Nothing less than the complete text of *Answered Prayers* by Truman Capote," he bellowed.

What I knew of this particular Capote book was that it

was started some years before the author's death and, surrounded by controversy and scandal, never finished. When I reminded Fortesque of this fact he went into a detailed history of the notorious novel.

Capote sold the first chapter of *Answered Prayers* to a popular magazine in 1975, drawing the wrath of his society and celebrity friends whose exploits, mostly sexual, he had written about in detail; some characters were thinly disguised and many boldly named. In retaliation, the beautiful people who had lionized the author (and obviously whispered titillating secrets in his receptive ears) joined forces and labeled Capote persona non grata.

Devastated by their snub, it was believed, Capote never finished the novel, but in 1976 he published two more chapters in the same magazine. Fortesque noted that in his *Music for Chameleons* Capote stated, "I returned to *Answered Prayers,* I removed one chapter and rewrote two others." This had many believing that he did continue working on the book. According to Fortesque, Capote wrote the final chapters at his beach house in Sagaponack, the posh Hamptons community.

"At the time," Fortesque said, "he employed a houseboy who did for him. No pun intended, Mr. McNally. Getting back at his former friends, he wrote with a vengeance, exposing the indiscretions of those who now snubbed him, as well as all he had heard from them about the shenanigans of their forerunners. No holds barred, man.

"The antics at Cielito Lindo here in Palm Beach in the good old days. That was Jessie Donahue's place on South Ocean Boulevard. She was Barbara Hutton's aunt, in case you don't know. It had a tunnel that ran under the highway to the beach and was torn down to make way for mini-estates, but I believe two wings of the old mansion are still standing. If walls could talk," Fortesque lamented.

The old geezer was really getting off on this.

"The Duke and Duchess of Windsor spent more time at Jessie's place than governing Bermuda," the collector rambled on. "Jessie's son, Jimmy, made up the royal couple's ménage à trois, and how I would love to know what they were getting up to, although I understand the poor Duke couldn't get up to very much. Then there's the true story of the late James Dean and . . . "

And on and on he droned like a man possessed. Fortesque was clearly a scandalmonger whose eight wives couldn't compete with the vicarious pleasures a work like this offered. Given his enthusiasm, he was an easy mark for unscrupulous brokers of collectibles. After listening to Fortesque drop names about those who dropped their clothes, he finally got back to our central theme—Ms. Claudia Lester.

Again, according to Fortesque, Capote went to California in '84, leaving the manuscript at his home in Sagaponack and the boy in charge of the house. Capote died in California eight years after the second installment of *Answered Prayers* was published.

"One can spew a lot of rancor on paper in eight years," Fortesque noted with glee. "The boy kept the manuscript, not knowing its value. Now a man of some fifty years and in need of money, the former houseboy called an auction house in New York, telling them only that he had an original Capote manuscript.

"The auction house sent a representative to Florida—the houseboy now lives in Key West—to look at the manuscript. When the man saw what it was, he quickly decided to make a profit from the discovery. He put out the word of its existence on the collectors' black market, telling the auction house the manuscript was nothing more than a typed version of the published *Answered Prayers.*

"Enter Claudia Lester," I prompted.

"Exactly," Fortesque said. "She's a friend of one of my ex-wives."

"Vera," I reminded him. "Number three."

"Correct, man. But how did you know?"

"Claudia told me," I admitted.

Pop-eyed, he commented, "You and Claudia certainly got intimate rather quickly."

"Not in the biblical sense, sir."

Knowing Fortesque's obsession with acquiring rare objects, especially of the more racy variety, Vera Fortesque put Claudia in touch with her ex-husband—and Archy sees stars on a rainy night.

"And you trusted her with fifty thousand dollars?" I asked.

"Why not?" he challenged. "She's a friend of Vera's, and the name Claudia Lester is not unknown in the collecting trade."

Also, I was thinking, you were so hot to get your hands on that manuscript you would have handed over the money to anyone who promised to deliver the goods. A fact Vera and Claudia must have known. "Who was the guy in the motel room who handed me the manuscript and kept the money, if it wasn't Harrigan?"

Fortesque shrugged. "Don't know. Could be the houseboy who owned it or the rep from the auction house. All I know is that the manuscript would cost me fifty thousand. The details, like how the money was to be divided, I left to her. That's her job."

"The guy was too young to be the houseboy, so it must be the rep. I think the lady skunked you, Mr. Fortesque."

He started at that one. "I don't believe it. She has her reputation in the collecting community to think about. Why would she chuck it all for a lousy fifty thousand?"

Decimus Fortesque was not a quick study, and thus an easy mark for the grifters. "Her reputation is no better or worse than it was before last night," I explained, "thanks to me. She showed me the money and even made me count it. Then I delivered it to the motel and was shown a manuscript. The exchange, as she promised you, was made with me to bear witness to the fact. Once it was a done deal, I'm mugged and the loot and manuscript disappear.

"If asked why she fled, she'll say that when I didn't return with the manuscript she feared a double-cross by the houseboy or the rep and went undercover. I don't think we've seen the last of Claudia Lester, sir. If she wants to stay in business, she'll have to surface and tell her side of the story."

Fortesque looked dismayed, to say the least. I think I had finally made it clear to him that he was the victim of a new twist to the old Ponzi scheme. For fifty thousand he gets a tantalizing look at the dessert cart. For another fifty he gets the charlotte russe—maybe. "If you think you can recover my money or the manuscript, Mr. McNally, I'd like to hire you to represent me in this fiasco."

If I was going to go after Claudia Lester, why not get paid for my trouble? The way I saw it, both the lady and Fortesque owed me big. It took me a nanosecond to stick out my hand and take on a new client. "If Claudia Lester contacts you, and I'm sure she will, you'll let me know before you have any more dealings with her," I cautioned the collector.

"I will," he promised. "If you return my money or the manuscript, I'll be very generous, Mr. McNally."

Now, that's the sort of pep talk that gets me where I live. "I'll do my best to oblige, sir." Rising, I added, "Tell Sam he should open a bakery on Worth Avenue and grow rich off the fat of the land."

"I'll tell him no such thing, and don't you go putting ideas into his head."

He walked me to the door, and there, unable to stop myself, I boldly asked, "Your given name, sir. Is it a family name?"

"Oh, that." He chuckled. "I was born on the tenth day of the tenth month, which was my parents' wedding anniversary day. What choice did they have, man?"

6

I had a lot to think about on the drive back to Royal Palm Way. Based on what I had learned from Fortesque, several scenarios could fit the plot of last night's events, all of them starring Claudia Lester. First, I was sticking to my belief that the lady was defrauding her client and using me to vouch for her innocence. What better witness to the validity of her securing the manuscript with Fortesque's money than the man Fortesque had recommended as a reliable assistant?

She had made up the story of her stolen diary not to keep the deal confidential, as Fortesque had suggested, but to provide an excuse for needing a middleman (or the invidious bagman): she didn't want to confront her ex-lover. It appears intrigue is an accepted business tool in Ms. Lester's line of work. I now believed that the man I met at the Crescent was the representative from the auction house whose name might or might not be Matthew Harrigan.

When Claudia Lester surfaced, she would tell Fortesque that the rep double-crossed her and was holding the manuscript for another fifty thousand. The rep had probably told the old houseboy the manuscript was worthless but he would take it off the poor man's hands for a few hundred bucks.

When I got to Vita Serena I careened west, off South Ocean Boulevard, and continued north on South County Road, heading for the Everglades Golf Course like they were expecting me.

Knowing Fortesque's passion for collecting and his predilection for prurient hearsay, she had no doubt but that the old fool would hand over another Crouch and Fitzgerald attaché case filled with greenbacks. And who, I extrapolated, but a former wife would have such intrinsic knowledge of Fortesque's obsessions? Vera Fortesque had put Claudia in touch with the old lech, so one had to wonder if Vera also had her hand in the till.

If it was all an elaborate scheme to separate Fortesque from his money, it was doubtful that such a thing as the complete text of *Answered Prayers* truly existed. Thinking I was being shown the lady's diary, I didn't bother to check a single word of the manuscript revealed to me. Of course, anyone could have typed the chapters of the book already published, and passed it off as Capote's original. I would have to visit the library and do some research, though any references to the additional chapters of the book would be pure speculation. If someone wanted to pull a sting, I couldn't think of a better lure than the wily author's most infamous work.

Finally, giving both my clients the benefit of the doubt, one had to acknowledge that such a manuscript could exist, however improbable, and that Claudia Lester had been duped by her contact. After all, the lady did have her shady but reliable reputation to consider, and if that isn't an oxymoron I'll eat my berets. The point being, it was too early in the game to rule out anything. Where money is concerned, all things are possible.

Speaking of money, I got off South County and drove up Worth Avenue to assure myself that conspicuous consumption was alive and thriving in our humble realm. The shops, the strollers, the pets being aired and the chauffeurs being kept waiting served to remind me how pleased father would be when I told him Decimus Fortesque was now a client of McNally & Son. I turned north on Coconut Row and onward to Royal Palm Way, where I would powwow with the chief and, I hoped, share a peace pipe.

• As I drove into the McNally Building's underground garage our sentinel, Herb, gave me the thumbs-up sign from his glass-enclosed kiosk to warn me that Mrs. Trelawney was inquiring as to my whereabouts. However, even if father's secretary did not want to see me, Herb would call up to announce my arrival. In this way our girl Friday could keep abreast of everyone's coming and going without the bother and expense of installing television cameras in strategic places. To break the Herb/Trelawney connection one had to give up using the company garage.

I wanted to call Connie and see if she would lunch with me at the Pelican. To stifle the rumors making the rounds, thanks to her dinner with Alejandro the other night, I thought it prudent to be seen breaking bread with my girl at our usual corner table. Be that as it may, I thought it more prudent to report to Mrs. Trelawney before making my lunch date. I took the elevator directly to the executive suite and, upon arriving, said, "You wanted to see me, Mrs. Trelawney?"

She shook her gray head of pseudohair and sassed, "Not really, but your father does and so does Sergeant Rogoff of our police department."

"Al Rogoff called?" I asked, not masking my amazement. Al and I see each other socially and we have worked together on a number of cases, in a complementary rather than competing fashion, to both our advantages. We keep both aspects of our relationship as low key as possible in chatty Palm Beach, because the police and private investigators are far from bosom buddies. For this reason, we seldom contact each other at our respective places of business and confine our work meetings to such places as the parking lot at the Publix and a popular juice stand in PB. Our social meetings are confined to the Pelican Club and Al's trailer home.

"Is he free?" I asked, with a nod at our CEO's door.

"He is, and he's expecting you, but I think you had better contact Sergeant Rogoff first. He called twice and both times said it was urgent that you get back to him ASAP. You can use the phone in the conference room—it's not in use at the moment."

I went to the room where I had first encountered Claudia Lester, without asking if Al had left a number. No matter the urgency, he would never call me from the palace—Al's sobriquet for the police station, which looks more like the home of a French nobleman than a hangout for the men in blue—but before punching out Al's home number I put a call through to Connie.

After telling me I was in communication with Lady Cynthia's residence, I asked Connie if she wanted to have a burger and suds with me at the Pelican.

"You paying?" she asked.

"Of course I'm paying. Would I ask you if it wasn't my treat?"

"Sure you would," she shot back.

That hurt, but hurting Archy seemed to be in vogue this week. "About two," I said. "I'm sorry I can't make it any earlier."

"Two is fine, Archy. Will you pick me up or meet me at the club?"

"I'll come for you, Connie." I'm sure that's what Alejandro would do.

"Gotta go," she suddenly cried. "See you at two. Bye."

In the past, when Connie cut me off with an abrupt "Gotta go," I always believed I was being usurped by an incoming call for her boss. Now I had to wonder if the call was for Connie from her Cuban conquistador. Paradoxically, the green-eyed monster makes the heart grow fonder as it fosters distrust. But having secured my lunch date, it was an optimistic suitor who called Al Rogoff.

"It's about time," came that gruff voice. "I pulled the graveyard shift and ain't had no shut-eye waiting on your call."

"I trust you didn't intrude upon any romantic interludes during your nocturnal rounds."

"Oh, you read about that, did you?"

"Indeed I did, and so did most of Palm Beach and vicinity," I goaded him. "Was Tom Mitland able to raise bail and go home to get out of that skirt and into a suitable morning frock?"

"Some fancy lawyer from Jupiter sprung him, but the counselor ain't saying who put up the moola."

"I'm glad to know chivalry is not a lost virtue," I offered, "but if a guy in a blond wig doesn't inspire gallantry, who will?"

"Funny thing about that light in the old Beaumont place," Al told me, "is that we've been getting reports from people who thought they saw one in an upstairs window, but we never paid no attention to 'em. Now I would swear I seen it myself."

You may have noticed that Al Rogoff assassinates the King's English, but don't be lulled into a false sense of superiority. Al's mind is as sharp as his grammar is wanting, and his leisure pursuits include ballet, opera and string quartets. He's been known to fly to New York to catch a performance at the Met or Carnegie Hall, a fact to which only I am privy. He tells his cohorts Las Vegas is his destination and lets them fill in the blanks.

"Is that the reason for your urgent call, Al?"

"Oh, I almost forgot. The state troopers have an APB out on your car."

An APB is an all points bulletin, which is police-speak for "We're after you." And the owner, not the vehicle, is what they would be after. "I had a lousy night, Al, and a trying morning, so spare me the police lingo. What's up?"

"Did your lousy night take place at the Crescent Motel out toward Juno?" he asked.

My knees began to buckle, but I refused to reach for a chair. "And what makes you think I was at the Crescent Motel last night?" I asked as if I didn't know.

"Because a resident of that renowned establishment saw a red Miata pull in the guest parking area about nine last night and leave an hour or so later. I'm calling all the guys I know who own a red Miata."

Murphy's Law! As provable as it is unscientific. The

one time I don't rent a nondescript black sedan to work a job is the one time I am seen coming and going as if I were wearing a neon tag flashing ARCHY MCNALLY in cerise.

"So what's the big deal, Al? Was the place raided? Are the vice boys now looking to harass respectable citizens? I was visiting a friend."

"Was your friend in unit number nine, Archy?"

I pulled a chair away from the mahogany conference table and sat. "Who wants to know, Sergeant?"

"Homicide, that's who. They found a body in *numero nueve.*"

"A dead body, Al?"

"Let me put it this way, pal. When they shoved him into the icebox at the morgue, he didn't ask for a blanket."

My forehead was damp, my heart was going thump, thump, thump, and a chill was running up and down my spine. It was either the flu, thrombosis or a panic attack. "I was on a case, Al," I explained hopefully. "And when I left unit nine the man I went to see was very alive."

"Hey, pal," Al groaned, "I ain't looking for no alibi offa you. Tell it to O'Hara."

"Who?" I cried, certain it wasn't Scarlett.

"George O'Hara. The officer on the case," he explained. "Look, Archy, when I got off duty this morning I saw the APB and figured it was you they was looking for. O'Hara must have already contacted the motor vehicle people and will have a list of all the red Miata owners in Florida. You should be hearing from him within the hour. I'm calling as a favor to a friend."

"Thanks, Al. It's appreciated," I assured him.

"No charge. I'm a public servant."

"I guess I should call O'Hara. It'll show him I want to cooperate."

"It can't hurt, Archy. But remember, it's usually the guy what done it that volunteers information."

"That's encouraging," I said. "So who found the body?"

"Don't know. You'll have to ask O'Hara. All I know is it was reported about fifteen minutes after ten. If you didn't ice the guy, Archy, you were the last person to see him alive."

"You're all heart, Sergeant. Do you have O'Hara's number?"

Reaching for a pad and pencil, I took down the number and told Al to get some sleep. Instead of George O'Hara I got a brash young man who identified himself as Trooper Swathmoore. When I told him who was calling, he said, "You just saved the state of Florida two bits, Mr. McNally. I was about to call you."

"I understand Officer O'Hara would like to speak to me," I told him.

"You understand correct. Georgy isn't here right now, but if I contacted you I was told to request that you come in at two this afternoon for an interview."

"Request?" I ventured. "Does that mean I have a choice, Officer Swathmoore? You see, I have a conflicting engagement."

"It's your call, sir. You can come here at two or we can come to pretty Palm Beach and bring you in."

Swathmoore was a barrel of laughs. "Where is here?" I surrendered.

His directions placed their barracks not far from the Crescent Motel. It told me why they were first on the scene. I said goodbye to Swathmoore and without putting down the phone called Connie. If she was heartbroken over not seeing me for lunch, she spared me her sorrow. "I'll be sensible and share a fruit salad with Lady C."

"I hate to do this, Connie, but I have to see a policeman about a murder."

"Sounds like more fun than a burger and suds at the Pelican. Anyone I know?" she questioned.

"It's not a cop from Palm Beach," I said. "He's a state trooper."

"I didn't mean the cop, Archy. I meant do I know the person you murdered?"

Everyone was a comedian—at my expense. "It's not a joke, Connie. I'm a suspect."

"Dearheart, you have always been suspect," she countered.

Quitting while I was behind, I asked if she was free for dinner.

"I'm washing my hair tonight," she said.

"You washed your hair last night," I reminded her.

"Did I? I forgot. Now I must go. Do keep in touch."

When I emerged from the conference room, Mrs. Trelawney did a double take and said, "Are you all right? Your tan seems to have faded since last we met."

"I've felt better, but unfortunately I think I'll live. Is father still free?"

"He is. And he's expecting you." Never able to stem her curiosity, she asked, "Did Sergeant Rogoff have disquieting news?"

"You might say that, Mrs. Trelawney, and I'm sure you'll read all about it in the morning papers." Leaving her to seethe over that one, I knocked once and entered the inner sanctum and the nineteenth century. Father's office looks as if the furnishings came from the capricious shops on South Dixie Highway in West Palm, an area that has gone through urban gentrification and been christened Antique Row. It included a rolltop desk but not Queen Victoria looking down accusingly from a framed portrait. Father did once refer to Palm Beach and West Palm as "a tale of two cities."

"Well, Archy?" he said as I took my chair.

I began with the good news and worked my way down. Father looked pleased when I told him we could now place Decimus Fortesque on our billing roster; pensive when I told him all that had transpired since taking on Claudia Lester as a client; concerned when I reported being attacked at the Crescent Motel; alarmed when I told him what I had learned from Al Rogoff.

"Murder?" he questioned in disbelief. "You're assaulted and the man you went there to see is found dead minutes later? There's more to this, Archy, than two fools chasing after some penny-dreadful novel that may not even exist. I want you to tell the police all you know and have done with both Claudia Lester and Decimus Fortesque."

For those who are not scholars of nineteenth-century literature, a penny dreadful was the pulp fiction of the time—and poor Capote must be turning over in his grave. However, I will say I was elated by father's concern for my safety even at the expense of losing a viable client.

"I appreciate your counsel, sir, and your apprehension regarding the ethics of my clients, but I don't think Fortesque is capable of anything more than vicarious lechery, and I want to stay on the case if only to protect him from himself. I'll reserve judgment on Claudia Lester until I hear her side of the story."

"You think she'll contact you?" father asked.

"Me or Fortesque," I answered. "She has too much at stake to disappear completely."

Father leaned forward and asked, "How much time did you spend in that confounded motel room?"

"Ten—fifteen minutes, at most."

"If you got there at nine and left at ten, or a few minutes after ten, you must have been unconscious for more than thirty minutes." He spoke like a lawyer building his case.

"It was a heavy blow, sir."

"No doubt," he said, "but do you realize the precariousness of your position, Archy? You are seen entering the motel at nine and leaving at ten. The man you visited is found dead—murdered—a short time thereafter. If no one saw you being attacked in the parking area or witnessed another person entering that room, you are the prime suspect."

"My car was seen entering and leaving," I countered. "I don't know if anyone saw me enter and leave unit number nine. The evidence is circumstantial at best."

"If no one comes forth to say you were with them in a different room, and they obviously will not, you can't prove you weren't in unit nine, and I don't want you to attempt any such thing." This was the seasoned lawyer speaking. "The truth is your best defense, Archy, and men have been electrocuted on less circumstantial evidence."

On that cheerful note I pleaded my case. To wit: Let me speak to Officer O'Hara and see what the police know or suspect. I will tell them as much of the truth as I deem necessary at this point without jeopardizing my position. "In short, sir, I think we should play it by ear until we know more about the game and the players."

Father tugged at his mustache. "As you know, Archy, I am not a fan of your dilettante ways—now, hear me out before you shut your mind to my words—but I have always been impressed, and proud, of the way you have conducted yourself on behalf of McNally and Son. Your reputation as an investigator is above reproach and well deserved.

Therefore, against my better judgment and concern for your well-being, I will allow you to continue with this case as you see fit if you keep me au courant, allow me to change my mind—and don't breathe a word of this to your mother."

Deeply touched, I agreed to the terms and left his office feeling more confident than I had when I entered. I didn't cotton to the dilettante label, but then I'm sure he didn't enjoy being thought pompous. What mattered was that beneath the somewhat embellished epithets there existed a common bond between us that was as solid, if not always as transparent, as the glass-and-steel building that bore our family name.

Emerging from his office, I tweaked our executive secretary's prying mind with, "I'll see you in court, Mrs. Trelawney."

"Has this anything to do with that Claudia Lester? I thought she looked fast."

"I refuse to answer on the grounds that it may tend to incriminate me. *Ciao, bella.*"

"The only thing that can incriminate you, young man, is your expense report, and don't *bella* me."

• There were perhaps a dozen desks in the spacious room, all of them manned by men and women wearing the uniform of Florida's state troopers. Some stared at computer screens, others shuffled printed matter from pile to pile and two whispered conspiratorially around the copy machine. The silence was terrifying.

The nameplate on the reception desk told me I was one-on-one with Gary Swathmoore. The trooper sported a crew cut, a pug nose and freckles, a Norman Rockwell painting come to life. Given the somber atmosphere of the joint, I thought it wise to report in properly.

"Archy McNally here to see Officer O'Hara."

Swathmoore gave me a wide grin and displayed his braces. "Glad you could make it, Mr. McNally." He jerked a thumb over his shoulder. "Make a left at the copy machine, then it's the first door on the right."

Not an eye followed me as I traversed the cavernous room, so why did I feel a dozen pinpricks boring into the back of my neck? The pair at the copy machine didn't even flinch as I walked by, made the left turn and arrived at the first door on the right. There was another door farther along, and two more on the opposite side of the narrow hall. None of them bore any identifying markings, so I surmised that the rooms were used by any officer conducting a private interview.

I knocked and heard a mumbled response. I opened the door and entered.

George O'Hara was a green-eyed blonde with a movie star smile and a figure to match.

"You look surprised," she said.

"I was expecting a man," I stammered.

"So was my father. His name is George. Mine is Georgia. Have a seat, Mr. McNally."

7

"So, Mr. McNally, you're a shamus," she stated as I took the visitor's chair.

I hate that word, and I was sure she knew it. Compliments of my relationship with Al Rogoff and some prior experience, I knew the interviewing techniques of the law-enforcement branch of our republic. First the element of surprise, either by word or deed, to throw the guy in the hot seat off kilter. In O'Hara's case, it was neither word nor deed but personal appearance that had achieved that goal, and I don't think it was the first time the officer had taken advantage of this ploy.

Swathmoore had referred to her as Georgy, as she was probably called by her friends and colleagues. The name came, no doubt, from the film *Georgy Girl,* which was a few years before this Georgy's time but popular with her parents' generation. Al Rogoff had glanced at the APB fax bulletin after a long night on duty and, more interested in the red Miata than the issuing officer's name, read Georgia as George. Given her career choice, I will go out on a political limb and call it a logical mistake.

After surprise came demeaning the suspect, as in calling a prestigious investigator a shamus. When people are demeaned they are apt to respond with malice and say things they would not say when thinking clearly. I kept my cool—but not for long.

"I'm the investigative arm of a law firm," I informed her with all the pride I could muster given the reason for my presence.

O'Hara glanced at a sheet of paper on her desk that might have contained my life history or the lunch schedule for the Juno barracks. "Yes," she nodded, "with McNally and Son in Palm Beach. Are you the father or the son?"

She was getting to me in leaps and bounds. "Do I look old enough to be the father?"

She shrugged as if she couldn't care less. "You're certainly old enough to be a father." She referred again to the paper on her desk. "But I forgot that you are one of Palm Beach's eligible bachelors. I have the book."

"Are you looking for a husband, Officer O'Hara?"

Her emerald eyes sparkling mischievously, she responded, "Are you applying for the position, Mr. McNally?"

That fictional Georgia belle with the same family name was not a beautiful woman, but, her creator tells us, men seldom realized this when looking into her green eyes. This modern version *was* a beautiful woman, and real to boot.

Going along with the breezy repartee, I quipped, "I'm flattered, but we just met." Then, pointing at the printed page on her desk, I said, "But you seem to have found out a lot about me on very short notice."

"We have our methods," she said. "And you seem to know a lot about our inquiry in the same space of time. Swathmoore told me you called him. How did you know we were looking for you?"

"I have my methods," I retaliated.

She shook her head of blond hair that was pulled from her face and fastened from behind with a simple silver clip. The sun coming through the window behind her chair highlighted every strand, giving a specter-like appearance to her fine features. Did she let her hair down to dance in the moonlight like Terspichore or, given her calling, did she worship Diana, goddess of the hunt? Whichever, these were not the details a man should notice about his tormentor.

"Let's stop shadowboxing, Mr. McNally, and see if we can't help each other. I take it you were at the Crescent on a case."

After surprise and demeaning came comradery. Befriend the suspect and lull him into a false sense of security. "Don't be hasty, O'Hara. I may have been there on pleasure, not business."

"In and out in one hour? You're a fast worker, Mr. McNally." Now she was actually flirting.

"Fast but thorough, I'm told."

"Who did you visit at the motel?" she demanded, going from flirt to interrogator in one giant step.

"Matthew Harrigan."

She arched an eyebrow. "For business or pleasure, Mr. McNally?"

The comeback was so swift, so filled with innuendo, I could feel myself blush. If this was a ball game, I had just made the first out. "Okay, I was on a case," I admitted.

"And what was the nature of your case?" she pitched.

I caught it and tossed it back. "For now I will plead client confidentiality, and remember, I came here voluntarily."

"And saved us the trouble of coming for you. Did you see this Matthew Harrigan in unit number nine of the Crescent Motel?"

Remembering that I couldn't prove I wasn't in unit number nine, I followed father's sage counsel and admitted to seeing Harrigan in that room. I had said I would play it by ear but now feared I was going deaf and had no idea where I, or she, would go from here. How much did O'Hara know? Did the person who had witnessed my Miata coming and going see me enter unit nine and leave ten minutes later? That, however, was now a moot question. Did anyone see me getting clobbered and the person who did it? "I was in the room no more than ten or fifteen minutes," I told her in case she already knew.

"What was your business with Harrigan?"

"My business with Harrigan is the crux of my case, and I still ain't saying," I answered. "I will tell you that I went to the Crescent to make an exchange with Harrigan on behalf of my client. When the exchange was made, I left."

"Now, that's interesting," O'Hara said. "May I know what was exchanged for what?"

"No, you may not," I informed her, trying not to sound like a hostile witness. "We're going round in circles, officer, and I'm getting dizzy. I gave Harrigan something, he gave me something. I left. That was my visit to the lovely Crescent Motel."

"I'll take an educated guess and say you paid for something your client wanted. A late-night exchange in a one-star motel has blackmail written all over it." This not-so-clever deduction seemed to please her.

"There you go again, jumping to hasty conclusions." I

wagged a finger at Officer O'Hara. "I repeat, I conducted my business with Harrigan and left." Almost as an afterthought I added, "Oh, yes, he was very much alive when I departed."

There was a large crystal ashtray on the desk, which O'Hara now pushed toward me. "You may smoke if you wish," she invited.

Yet another inquisitor's ruse used primarily for two reasons, the first being that she wanted a smoke. Should I comply with the thoughtful gesture, she hoped I would offer her one of mine. In this way professional interviewers got more than they gave in more ways than one. Second, it was to stall for time. She didn't know what to ask next, meaning she knew as much as I did, or less, about the murder at the Crescent Motel. This I took to be a good omen.

I had stopped at a lunch counter on my way here for a burger and a cup of decaf. A far cry from one of Leroy's delicious quarter-pounders and a draft drawn by Leroy's father, Simon Pettibone, at the Pelican.

Having had my after-lunch ration of tobacco, I declined without explanation and the ashtray was withdrawn.

"You know about the murder," O'Hara finally said.

"That's the reason I'm here, isn't it?"

"It wasn't in the papers or on the local news, so I strongly suspect you have a friend in the Palm Beach Police Department. What else did he tell you?"

"How do you know it's not a she?" I quickly got in.

"Because a female officer would have the common sense not to prep a possible suspect before an interview."

I bowed my head in disgrace. "Forgive this possible suspect," I apologized. "Harrigan was alive when I went into the room and alive when I left."

"Was there anyone else in the room?" she asked.

"Not unless they were hiding in the bath or closet," I told her.

The green eyes widened, hinting that I may have given her the first matching piece in the puzzle. "You got there at nine, spoke to this Harrigan for ten minutes, give or take, and left the motel at ten. We're missing a significant number of minutes."

"Did your witness have a stopwatch?" I complained, like a defense lawyer on the offensive.

Her lips curved into a tantalizing smile. Did I mention that Officer O'Hara wore no makeup? A soap-and-water girl who needed nothing else. "He was just sitting down to watch his favorite television show," she explained. "It goes on at nine. He heard a car drive by, looked out and saw the red Miata heading for the public parking area. When he heard a car again, the show had just ended. He took another look out and saw the Miata drive away. As you may have guessed, it's a one-hour show."

Having no rebuttal for that, I again obeyed father's orders and told the truth. "I was mugged in the parking lot. Zonked out for half an hour."

"Did you report it?"

"To who—or whom?" I asked her. "The management of the Crescent?"

"No, Mr. McNally. To the police. Did he or she take your wallet?"

My, how gender conscious we were these days. "No, ma'am, he or she did not."

"And you didn't report it to the police because the perpetrator took whatever Harrigan gave you and the item might prove an embarrassment to your client." Without waiting for a confirmation, she went on, "Did Harrigan follow you out and take back the prize?"

"That was my guess," I said, "but when I came to my senses and went back to the unit, it was locked and the room's carport was empty. If Harrigan is dead, as you say he is, he couldn't have zapped me on the head and then driven merrily on his way."

"Now who's jumping to conclusions?" she mocked. "I didn't tell you Harrigan was dead."

"Then who is?" I begged.

"First tell me what this Harrigan looked like."

I thought a moment before answering. "About six feet. Good-looking if you like the boy-next-door type." Recalling the jeans, I said, "Dressed for cruising in South Beach. Close to thirty, but with a little makeup and good lighting he could pass for younger."

She picked up a large brown envelope, opened it and withdrew a black-and-white photo. I knew I was about to get a sample of the scene-of-the-crime boy's photographic skills. She handed it over and I was looking at a torso shot of a man who had seen his fiftieth birthday a few years ago and would never see another. Near his head was the base of what I believed to be a toilet bowl.

"He's not the man I saw in unit number nine of the Crescent Motel," I said.

"His driver's license tells us he's Lawrence Swensen with an address in Key West. The room was registered in his name. We contacted the police down there but have no word back as yet."

His age and home address told me he could be the houseboy who was selling Capote's manuscript. "I take it you found him in the bathroom." When she nodded, I said, "He could have been there when I was talking to Harrigan."

It made sense. Harrigan, the rep from the auction house, met Swensen in the motel to get the manuscript—if the houseboy and the manuscript actually existed—oversee the deal and collect his and Claudia's share of the loot. Being greedy, he does in Swensen, puts him in the bathroom and waits for me to come with the fifty thousand. I deliver, leave, and Harrigan goes after me, takes back the manuscript and beats it with the cash and the cash cow. The script had one flaw, which I voiced aloud. "The empty carport. If Harrigan left in his car, where was Swensen's car?"

"In the parking lot," came the answer. "You may have parked near it. Swensen seems to have left his space free to accommodate his guest. Thoughtful, don't you think?"

No, I didn't think any such thing. He left the space free so his guest wouldn't attract attention by having to drive the length of the crescent route to the parking lot like yrs. truly. And, come to think of it, the creep that attacked me could have been hiding in Swensen's car—but that was a long shot. Now that I knew Harrigan wasn't dead, I again fingered him for my nemesis.

"I can tell you," O'Hara was saying, "that Swensen was heavily sedated and then strangled." She took a deep breath before reading me the riot act. "Now we have to get down to the nitty-gritty, Mr. McNally. As you can see, we have to find this Matthew Harrigan. If you're telling me the truth, he's our leading contender for the role of the heavy. If we don't find him and you can't come up with a better alibi than being asleep at the time of the crime, we award you the blue ribbon.

"Your client is our only lead to finding Harrigan, so at the risk of making you dizzy once again, I must ask your client's name and the nature of your case. Blackmail often leads to murder, as I'm sure you know." To bring home the point, she threatened, "You can tell me now, or I can subpoena you and get it from you later."

In a bid for time and to get as much information from her as I could before baring my soul, I asked her who found the body. She consulted the paper on her desk, which I now believed contained everything she knew about the murder—and me.

"One Rodney Whitehead," she said, "from New York, New York. He called us at a quarter after ten."

And another county is heard from. But his hometown did link up with Claudia Lester. The only thing unit number nine at the Crescent Motel lacked was a turnstile. "Did he say how he got into the room?"

"He said the door was open."

This was a lie. Whitehead got there literally minutes after I had tried the door and found it locked. Someone let him in. If it wasn't the corpse, it must have been Harrigan who went back after mugging me. No. The carport was empty, so Harrigan must have driven away. But that was pure conjecture. Let's say *someone* drove away—and enter Rodney Whitehead. This was beginning to resemble a box of Kleenex—pull out one and up pops another.

Without my asking, O'Hara volunteered, "Whitehead said he went to see Swensen on business. When we asked the nature of his business with the dead man, Whitehead clammed up. Said he wouldn't say anything more without a lawyer present. He's staying at a motel in West Palm. We told him not to leave town without our permission. Now tell me what I want to know, Mr. McNally."

I didn't want to involve Fortesque until I had found Claudia Lester. I had to see if she would corroborate what Fortesque had told me and maybe shed some light on what took place at the Crescent last night now that everyone's cards were on the table. As I saw it, I could shield Fortesque, for a time, without actually lying to the police.

O'Hara wanted to know what I was doing at the Crescent Motel last night, and I told her the truth. "My client, Claudia Lester, hired me to retrieve something that belonged to her. She said a young man named Matthew Harrigan had stolen it and would return it for a certain sum of money. Harrigan would be at the Crescent, unit number nine, at nine o'clock last night to make the exchange. The rest you know."

"What did he have that belonged to the lady?"

"Her diary," I said.

"A diary that could prove embarrassing to this Claudia Lester and therefore a motive for murder," O'Hara concluded.

"But it wasn't Harrigan who got done in," I reminded her.

"If the man you spoke to at the Crescent was Harrigan," she shot back. "You didn't ID him, did you?"

"We're on that merry-go-round again, officer. Can we hop off, share what we know and see if we can't make some sense of this charade?"

"That's what I've been trying to do, Mr. McNally. Are you telling me everything you know?"

"I'm telling you everything that transpired between my client, Claudia Lester, and me, including what happened in the execution of my duties—so help me Sam Spade."

She looked at me as if I had told her the dog ate my homework, but she didn't challenge my testimony. I think O'Hara, too, was playing it by ear and didn't want to tread too heavily until she knew more. My position exactly.

Then came the inevitable. "Where do I find Claudia Lester?"

"She was at the Ambassador in Palm Beach. She checked out last night and left no forwarding address. I'm waiting to hear from her."

Looking puzzled, O'Hara asked, "Why do you think she beat it?"

"I thought the bump on my head had something to do with it. When I didn't get back to the Ambassador after the time it should have taken me to make the exchange, she suspected something went amiss and ran. I don't know why, but Swensen's murder makes the cheese more binding, as they say. It's clear that Ms. Lester had reason to run and that she was less than truthful with me. I'm as eager to speak to the lady as you are."

O'Hara shook her head. She wasn't buying it, but she wasn't calling me a liar, either. "That must be one hell of a diary the lady kept," was all she said.

I felt guilty not telling her all I knew and wondered if I would have felt the same if she were a sturdy male trooper rather than a beautiful female trooper. "Once upon a time," I began, "there lived a beautiful actress named Mary Astor. She kept a diary that fell into the public domain, causing important men in Hollywood and New York to blush from coast to coast."

"I think it had something to do with the prowess of a famous director during a long, long cab ride around Central Park." She spoke with all the panache of one of the guys telling tall tales in the locker room. "My reading habits are less than Proustian," she confessed with nary a tint of crimson in her flawless complexion.

Good grief, she sounded just like someone I knew—myself. Had she also read *Answered Prayers*? No doubt she had, and I, for one, admired her unabashed honesty. Yes, I liked Officer O'Hara. I liked her a lot but wasn't unaware of the dangers inherent in my esteem. As a possible suspect in a murder case, the accusing goddess could easily prove to be a Venus flytrap posing as one of the boys.

"Do you think this Claudia Lester will contact you again, Mr. McNally?" she then asked.

"I'm sure she will. I was the last person to have my hands on her precious diary. She'll want to know what happened to it and to her money."

"How much was she paying to get her property back?"

Again protecting Fortesque, I let it go at, "It was a hefty sum."

"She told you there was only one person involved in the theft of her diary. Matthew Harrigan. Now we have two other people on board. The victim, Swensen, and the man who found him dead, Rodney Whitehead, who's from New York. Did you say Claudia Lester is from New York?"

"I didn't say, but, yes, she told me she was from the Big Apple. And, yes, there could be a connection."

"We'll check with the police in New York as well as the Ambassador down here to see if we can get a lead on her," O'Hara said. "If you get to her before us, you *will* call me immediately." It was an order, not a request. "And don't leave town, Mr. McNally."

This hunk of masculine flesh was being used as bait to snare Claudia Lester. Apparently, O'Hara believed most, if not all, of what I told her. No fool she, but I'm not complaining. I needed time to catch up with Lester—and I had offered myself up for less noble causes.

"I will do just that," I promised, "on one condition."

"What's that, Mr. McNally?"

"That you call me Archy."

"Get out of here before I have Swathmoore put you in a holding cell."

On that note my first meeting with Georgy O'Hara came to a close. It wasn't to be my last, so as they say on the soaps, stay tuned.

8

This was the first case I had ever worked where I was to report to my father not only as a member of the firm and the family, but as one who might be in need of a lawyer. My interview with O'Hara was strictly at the honeymoon stage of her investigation—and how she would love that metaphor. And why, pray tell, did the metaphor pop up as I mulled over my meeting with Georgy O'Hara on my ride back to the office? Connie, that's why. Her game of brinkmanship with a church aisle as the dividing line and Alejandro Gomez y Zapata as her dare had me seeing a bride behind every palm tree. Connie would be sorry when they led me away in handcuffs. Or would she?

Without Harrigan I was the only person who could be placed at the scene of the crime during the crucial hour before Swensen's body was discovered. I don't believe I was seen entering and leaving unit nine, but I had admitted to spending enough time in the room to spring Swensen from this vale of tears. And why was he drugged before he was strangled? To make the murderer's job less arduous? And let's not forget father's cheerful account of what a good prosecuting attorney could do with a dollop of circumstantial evidence.

Could I retract what I had told O'Hara? Had I been taped? Doubtful. I believe they have to tell you if you're being recorded, and they have to read you your rights. Not having done either, I would guess O'Hara was on a fishing expedition, and what better fish to hook than the investigator (shamus, indeed!) who was working the case that led to the murder? She had hauled in Claudia Lester and Matthew Harrigan with her first casting, and she had given me Rodney Whitehead.

Dare I hope that together we would solve the crime and live happily ever after—or for a short while thereafter? One mustn't rush into things like burning buildings and love affairs. I would suggest putting our heads together over drinks at her place and show Consuela Garcia how the game was played. Of course, when O'Hara learned that I was holding back Decimus Fortesque and the elusive manuscript from our *noir* drama, I imagine she would feed me to the sharks.

Another all-time first for this discreet inquirer was taking on a client, Fortesque, to keep a watchful eye on another client, Claudia Lester. I think it's called playing both ends against the middle. Last night I was amazed, if not chagrined, when a simple hire to make a switch turned into assault with a deadly weapon. Less than twenty-four hours later, the assault is upstaged by murder.

If Swensen is the houseboy who was bartering the manuscript and Harrigan is the auction house rep, who in Hades is Rodney Whitehead and what was his business with

Swensen? Or was Swensen also playing both ends against the middle? And look what happened to him. *Oy vey!*

Not caring if Al Rogoff had had his beauty rest, I called him from my cubbyhole the moment I got back to the McNally Building. He was having his coffee (probably a beer), and in the background I could hear Siegfried warbling to Brunhilde. I prefer Fred and Ginger, but to each his own.

"First of all," I griped, "her name is not George, but Georgia. He's a she, and she practically called me a murderer."

"Keep your shirt on, pal," Al answered. "You're overreacting. It ain't good for the blood pressure. Did you tell her everything you know?"

Spoken like a cop. "I did a Scheherazade, if you know what I mean."

"Can you keep it up for a thousand and one nights, Archy?"

His inadvertent double entendre was too good to let pass without a smart retort. "With Officer O'Hara I could."

Pause—but a brief one, as Al is a quick study—followed by a burst of raucous laughter. "Good, pal. Real good. For a guy on his way to the electric chair, I'm glad you ain't lost your sense of humor. I take it the dame's a looker?"

"A Georgia peach, Al, with all the charm of an ice goddess."

"I never seen a policewoman that was a peach, Archy. Maybe you need specs."

Al was being pursued by policewoman Tweeny Alvarez. Tweeny's idea of a romantic evening was watching wrestling on the telly while quaffing down beer and pretzels. More discouraging, poor Tweeny doesn't know one Wagner who pronounced the name with a V.

"I told her just what I knew last night, but omitted—"

"Can it, Archy," Al bellowed. "I don't want to know what you told her and what you didn't tell her. Me and O'Hara work the same side of the street and we're obliged to share."

You had to admire the man, but his stance caught me off guard. I suddenly felt bereft of those I loved and counted on for support when needed. First Connie and now, albeit for a more noble reason, Al Rogoff. In an effort to deflect the blow to my cause I moaned, "Whoever would have thunk it—an honest cop—and just when I need a rogue in blue." In self-defense I pushed on, "Honest injun, Al, I have no intention of holding out on O'Hara. I was on a case when I stumbled into this mess, and I'm trying to locate my client to nail down a few facts before I pass on what I know to Georgy. I have my client to consider, remember."

"Georgy, is it? Ain't that sweet. What does she call you, Snooky?" Al grumbled. "And what do you mean you're trying to locate your client? You mean he disappeared?"

"She, Al. She disappeared. But I have another client, a he, who's also looking for the she. If you would just let me explain—"

"Archy," he cut me off again, "I think you are in deep doo-doo, and until you're ready to cooperate fully with the trooper in charge I think we should limit our conversation to things in general, like death and taxes. Does she know I called you about the APB on your car?"

"She knows I was cautioned, so she knows I've got a contact with the Palm Beach police, but your name wasn't mentioned. Can I buy you dinner at the Pelican tonight? We can discuss taxes, but death is not a topic I care to dwell on right now."

"I'll take a rain check, pal. I don't think you and me

should be seen fraternizing—it may give Georgy ideas. No hard feelings."

My feelings weren't hard, but they were certainly hurt. More so because Al was right. He had gone out on a limb to alert me to the APB, and I had repaid him by not being aboveboard with the police. The loss of Al's shoulder and his expertise only sparked my determination to find Lester and Harrigan so I could hear their stories before turning them over to O'Hara and maybe redeem myself. Furthermore, I didn't see how I could keep Fortesque out of it. Bottom line: I was in deeper than even Al Rogoff suspected.

I could still count on Binky, I theorized when Al rang off, but I wasn't about to bring him within firing range of a murder investigation. Binky had proved helpful in the past, but he did have his limitations. Right now the boy was besotted with finding a roommate of the opposite sex to share his trailer. Binky has arrived at the age where his unsurpassed collection of Victoria's Secret catalogues no longer does the trick. I understand he now gets more of a kick trading them on eBay than ogling them. eBay being as relevant to me as Einstein's calculations, I can only hope that Binky is trading up.

The ringing telephone jarred my already taut nerves. I looked at the instrument as a harbinger of more bad news and was tempted to ignore it, but, having parked in our underground garage, Mrs. Trelawney knew I was in situ. My line defaults to hers in my absence, and eschewing the need to explain my negligence to duty, I picked up the transmitter of ill tidings and identified myself. "Archy McNally here."

"Deci Fortesque tells me you wish to speak with me."

She didn't have to identify herself. Claudia Lester had the voice of an actress audiences immediately recognize as the tough babe with a heart of gold. "That, Ms. Lester, is the understatement of the new millennium. And I am on the end of a long line of those wishing to have words with you, among them the state troopers who patrol our highways and byways."

"You mean that unfortunate business at the Crescent Motel? I had nothing to do with it, Mr. McNally."

Unfortunate business? Was this lady for real? "Neither did I, Ms. Lester, but thanks to you and the parcel of lies you fed me, I am being considered a suspect in that unfortunate business. If you talked to Fortesque, you know that I am aware of what you and Harrigan were up to."

"I'm sorry, but things got out of hand, as I'm sure you know." This was tossed out as if she were talking about a soufflé fall. "Matthew has fled with the manuscript and the money. I want you to find him."

I didn't know whether I should laugh, cry, or jump out the window. As my closet is equipped with an air-conditioning duct in lieu of a window, my choices were limited. To spare the lady a salvo of expletives I chuckled stoically, but, as the old song had it, I was laughing on the outside and crying on the inside.

"Ms. Lester, you couldn't hire me to watch paint dry at double my usual fee. I was seen at the motel last night and have already been questioned by the police. I told them only that I was acting on your behalf, and what you told me your business was with Harrigan. They are most eager to speak to both of you. This unfortunate business is looked upon as a grievous offense here in Florida, with the accompanying dire consequences. You, Harrigan, and by association, me, are the chief suspects in a murder investigation."

"I would like to explain my position, Mr. McNally," was her response to my tirade.

"First explain why you checked out of the Ambassador last night," I said.

"I was scared, that's why. When I heard about the murder—"

"You heard about the murder last night?" I interrupted. "How?"

"Why, Rodney Whitehead called me, of course."

Claudia Lester had a way of socking you with the improbable as if it were the obvious. I couldn't hide my amazement when I asked, "You know Rodney Whitehead?"

"He's the representative from the auction house in New York," she said. "Or was the representative. If this brouhaha goes public, poor Rod will be looking for work."

Unfortunate incident. Brouhaha. What other cozy euphemisms did she have for murder? "I think we had better sit down and talk, Ms. Lester. The sooner, the better."

"Good," she said. "It couldn't be too soon for me. I'm at the Bradley House on Sunset. Do you know it?"

I assured her I did. It was now near five and I wanted to have a word with father before leaving. I told Claudia Lester I would be there in half an hour. "And, Ms. Lester, you know I will have to tell the police where they can find you."

She laughed. "I'll try not to stray, Mr. McNally."

I will say the lady had good taste when it came to lodgings. From the Ambassador to Bradley House. The latter was born the Algomac Hotel more than seventy years ago and founded by Col. E. R. Bradley, who also ran the famous Bradley's Beach Club. For convenience the hotel was situated directly across the street from Bradley's Casino, another winter oasis for the colonel's pals. Metamorphosed into Bradley House, it became a first-class apartment hotel with all the amenities and a short stroll to the ocean.

* * *

"We all have to be good, and we all have to prosper. God grant you never have to choose," was Claudia Lester's toast as she handed me a bourbon and water.

If I wasn't mistaken she was quoting Moll Flanders, an apt role model for my lovely hostess. Was I going to hear how she had to kick and claw her way to Sutton Place without noticeable damage to her manicure? The mannish business suit she had worn for our previous meeting was abandoned for jeans, rather tight around the shapely hips, sharply pointed high heels and a white silk blouse that showed a lot of décolleté. If the outfit was intended to mix casual informality with a hint of feminine allure, it had succeeded admirably.

She had taken an efficiency apartment, but it did contain a kitchenette. The modest bar setup was no doubt furnished by the occupant, not the management.

"The sun is not officially over the yardarm, Mr. McNally, but under the circumstances we can dispense with the formalities," she said as she mixed our drinks, joining me in a bourbon and water more, I suspected, to prove her mettle than out of a fondness for the sour mash. I say this because she sipped it gingerly, never emptying her glass during my stay. It also occurred to me that Ms. Lester did not want her thoughts beclouded by the brew. The sign of a serious orator or a crafty liar?

When we were settled into comfortable chairs she opened the meeting with, "Deci told you of our business arrangement."

"He did, but he said he was dealing only with you. He didn't know Matthew Harrigan or, I imagine, Whitehead or Swensen."

She nodded. "That's true. Collecting is a very competitive business and often unscrupulous, as you've just learned. The less the customer knows, the less worry that he will try to negotiate a better deal with one of my associates the moment my back is turned. And not everything I told you was a lie, Mr. McNally. My CV was accurate, including the keeping of a diary. However, I wouldn't be foolish enough to let the likes of Matthew Harrigan get his hands on it."

"Was Harrigan your boyfriend?" I blatantly asked.

With a coy smile she answered, "I'm not saying. We met on the New York fringe circuit. My name for those who have no visible means of support other than their ability to oblige those who can afford to buy. What gets traded would make the bazaar in the Casbah look like a Wal-Mart. Matthew was in a position to gain the confidence of rich women—and men; your sex is not immune to the Harrigans of this world—and learn what collectibles they might possess and not know it, and be induced to part with for a price. He's a good contact for my operation, so I took him on as an apprentice, a position he was happy to accept as time was running out on poor Matthew.

"I got into the business," she went on, warming to her topic, "when I admired a glass paperweight in a friend's apartment. She told me it was an old family piece made by the Mount Washington Glass Company. Later, at a dinner party, a man who collected paperweights had been to an auction at Sotheby's and recounted how amazed he was when a Mount Washington Glass Company paperweight went for thirty thousand dollars. I asked him how much he would be willing to pay for a similar paperweight. He said ten thousand. Knowing my lady friend was a bit hard up for cash, I bought the paperweight from the unsuspecting woman for a thousand and, as they say, the rest is history."

Fortesque had the right take on her operation. Not illegal but not exactly kosher. After the paperweight sale it was onward and upward for our modern Moll. She gained a reputation with the fringe crowd, whose tentacles stretched from the lowest of the low to the highest of the high. When Rodney Whitehead, the representative from the auction house, stumbled on the Capote manuscript he decided to stop playing middleman for his boss and get in on the action. Who else to contact but Claudia Lester, a broker of collectibles who didn't ask too many questions about the provenance of the acquisition?

When Claudia told her Sutton Place neighbor, the third Mrs. Fortesque, what was afoot, Mrs. Fortesque told Claudia about Deci's passion for collecting esoterica. Thus, Swensen is strangled, Harrigan is on the lam, Whitehead is out of a job and Archy is suspected of murder. Only Claudia Lester is sitting pretty in her Bradley House bed-sitter on Sunset Avenue in posh Palm Beach. Didn't Moll end up going to the New World? If so, I think I have found her direct descendant.

"Is the manuscript fact or fiction, Ms. Lester?" When those blue eyes shot daggers at me, I added, "The truth, please."

"Rodney is an expert in the field of old manuscripts. That's why he was sent to investigate the claim. It's real, Mr. McNally. Trust me."

Trust her? To comment would only legitimize the request. "I take it Swensen is Capote's former houseboy who kept the manuscript."

She took a cigarette from her pack. "Should I offer you one?"

I shook my head. "Not until after dinner, thank you."

"I admire your fortitude, even in the face of murder," she said as she struck a match.

I inhaled secondhand smoke, gladly, and almost lost my fortitude. "You fed me the story of the diary to protect Fortesque and keep as few people as possible from knowing about the manuscript, because it might not have been Swensen's to sell, as he wasn't Capote's heir. Correct?"

"Correct," she exhaled along with an aromatic cloud of smoke.

Now for the jackpot question. "But why did you hire me to make the exchange?"

Without missing a beat she said, "Oh, didn't I explain?"

"No, ma'am, you did not."

"Well, as the buyer, Deci Fortesque, was in Palm Beach, Swensen came here with the manuscript, checking into the Crescent. Matthew would take him the money and pick up the manuscript. Later, Rodney would go to the Crescent and get his share from Swensen. I don't know what that amount was to be. I would get my percent directly from Deci.

"Before we finalized the plan, Rodney advised that we should use caution. He didn't know Swensen very well, you see. What if Swensen was planning to take the money without handing over the manuscript? What if he pulled a gun on Matthew or was holed up at the motel with a gang to do his bidding? Matthew is not the hero type, as you may have guessed. Heeding the warning, I hired some muscle to take Matthew's place and ensure no one got hurt."

So a man got iced and the muscle got whacked on the head. I quickly reminded her, "But I was expecting to see Matthew Harrigan, a young man, and I did see him. What if it had gone as planned and I walked in to find Swensen, who did not answer the description of your ex-flame?"

She shrugged this off with a wave of her cigarette, giving me another snort. "Come, come, Mr. McNally. Where are your gumshoe smarts? Before leaving the Ambassador, didn't I tell you to call me if you encountered any problems? I would have told you there was a change in plans and the gentleman in room nine was acting for Matthew Harrigan. When you didn't call is when I began to smell a rat, if you'll forgive the cliché."

I forgave her the cliché but not the misnomer—and her story was plausible, nothing more.

"Matthew was also at the Ambassador, at my expense. Of course, he knew I had hired you," she said with ire. "When Rodney called and told me Swensen was dead and no sign of either the money or the manuscript was in the room, I called Matthew and was told he had checked out. I knew then what had happened."

So did I. Or at least I thought I did. "Matthew went to the motel, did in Swensen, made the exchange with me and then followed me out to the parking lot, zonked me on the head and made off with the manuscript."

She looked startled. "Is that how he did it? I wasn't sure. When I didn't hear from you in a reasonable amount of time I knew something was wrong. After Rodney's call and Matthew's disappearance, I panicked and ran. Who knew what else Matthew had in mind? I expect he had help when he came after you. Matthew has some very rough friends."

If it was sympathy I was after, I would get it only from my mother and I wasn't permitted to show her my boo-boo. "Have you heard from Matthew?"

"No. And I don't expect to. That's why I want you to find him and get back what is mine."

I didn't know if she meant the manuscript, which wasn't hers, or the money, which also wasn't hers, but in Claudia Lester's fringe world the words "legal owner" were a mere formality if not a nuisance. I was on Fortesque's payroll to find Lester, and now I was being offered the job of finding Harrigan on Lester's dime. If I wasn't careful I would end up chasing myself.

"I think the police will do a better job of that than I can, Ms. Lester—with your help, to be sure. I'm going to give you the phone number of Officer O'Hara. I suggest you call as soon as I leave."

I had written O'Hara's name and phone number on a piece of notepaper before leaving the office. Not wanting to take away Georgy's shock appeal, I purposely omitted her first name. This I now placed on the glass-topped coffee table we had been talking across.

Picking it up, she said with a lot of attitude, "I will. And am I to assume you are now out of my employ, Mr. McNally?"

"Yes, ma'am. Case closed."

I got that mocking smile and, "Deci told me you were now working for him. It seems we are two of a kind, Mr. McNally—both for sale to the highest bidder. Case closed."

9

The murder at the Crescent Motel made the local TV news that evening. It's a program my parents view religiously before the cocktail hour, but much to father's relief, my name was not mentioned. The police were not giving away even what little they knew. What they had released to the press was strictly S.O.P. for a murder case.

The victim was identified as Lawrence Swensen from Key West. The Key West police reported that Swensen managed a guest house there that catered to an all-male clientele. He had checked into the Crescent yesterday afternoon and his body was discovered by a business associate that evening shortly after 10 P.M. Swensen had been strangled. One person had been questioned in connection with the crime, and two more were being sought for questioning.

The report did not state that Swensen had been drugged, nor did it say where the body was found. This would save having to check out all the kooks calling to confess to the crime who couldn't accurately describe their modus operandi. The two sought for questioning were not named for fear they might flee, and I was not named because I was associated with those wanted. Like I said, this was still the honeymoon stage of the case. The finger-pointing and hard sell would follow.

Mother's only comment was to reiterate her lament for the good old days when there was no need to lock the front door or fear strolling the beach at midnight. Terror was not solely a foreign import. All the above was reported to me by father that evening over a glass of his best port after mother had retired.

I missed the news and the cocktail hour due to my harangue with the lovely Ms. Lester. After getting in the last word, she showed me to the door. Our parting was less than affable. In fact, I don't remember ever leaving a former client so indignant at my refusal to continue working on their behalf. But then, I seldom had clients who called murder an unfortunate business and whose only interest in apprehending the assassin was in taking from him that which did not belong to them.

And if Harrigan had made off with the cash and manuscript, as she claimed, he would be as far from Palm Beach tonight as a plane could take him in twenty-four hours—which was very far indeed. I hadn't the resources to trace Harrigan's movements since last night, but the police did, and I wished them luck.

My obligation now was to my remaining client, Decimus Fortesque. He had taken my advice and directed Claudia Lester to me, but I had no idea what Lester had told him. Unless Deci was lost in a lurid account of some movie star's shenanigans, he would have heard about the murder by now whether Lester had given him the news or not. As the rich did not like to see their names in the press unless pictured bestowing largesse, Deci would be in a dither. I would have to call him in the morning to report that Lester was talking to the police, and his name was sure to come up in their conversation. In short, Deci, the jig is up and *Answered Prayers* will once more make headlines.

To make sure that Lester would be talking to the police, I pulled up to the first public phone I came to on my way south and called the Juno barracks. Covering my tail, I gave the officer on duty my name and left a message for O'Hara stating that I had seen Claudia Lester, that she was staying at the Bradley House apartments, and that she had promised to contact O'Hara the soonest.

I had missed the early news and cocktails, but I was on time to enjoy one of Ursi's masterpieces. Dinner at eight was a fact, not a clever comedy, in the McNally abode. Served in the formal dining room, the meal was accompanied by damask, Sèvres, Sheffield and stemware that exploded if foolishly put in the dishwasher. When it came to the culinary arts and its proper service, Prescott McNally did not stint. When it came to portraying the squire enjoying the comforts of the Hall, father had no peer, because he didn't see it as an act but as his due.

I think, therefore I am. Conversely, I am whatever I think, and Prescott McNally thinks he is a nineteenth-century squire trapped in a twenty-first-century body, screaming to be freed.

When Ursi's fare is not strictly American, it tends toward the French with a definite Scandinavian touch; in other words, dieters beware. Tonight she treated us to grilled veal chops served with a red Bordeaux reduction, fingerling potatoes sautéed in lemon and garlic and baby green peas accented with the tiniest of pearl onions and fresh chopped dill. The *pain* was Ursi's own sourdough served with room-temperature plugra butter, and the wine, from father's cellar, was a white Hermitage from the Rhône Valley.

With espresso brewed from freshly ground beans, Ursi brought in her famous chocolate mousse served with whipped cream and a handful of fresh berries. Being the true scion of a faux squire did have its perks. Table conversation was confined to the weather, mother's begonias and father's lunch date with a new client. Archy's love life was neither mentioned nor alluded to, thus enabling me to declare the evening banquet a modest, if not a roaring, success. At this point in my life, less roar and more modesty is okay with me.

Knowing father and I would rally in the den as soon as mother bid us good night, I delayed my after-dinner smoke until I had poured out our port, while father carefully snipped off the end of his cigar and began the lengthy business of putting torch to tobacco. Sinking into a comfortable chair covered in Morocco leather, I lit my English Oval and knew contentment on a day sorely lacking in compassion for the oppressed.

Before my meeting with Claudia Lester I had given father a brief account of my interview with Officer O'Hara. Now I reported in detail on my meetings with both O'Hara and Lester. He listened attentively while stroking his mustache, and when I finished he nodded thoughtfully and asked, "Do you believe the Lester woman?"

"I have no reason not to believe her, sir, but past experience tells me not to trust her. I would like to hear Harrigan's side of the story, but that doesn't seem possible at this juncture."

"If Harrigan is gone," father said, "it would appear he ran off with the money and the manuscript, as the lady stated. Why else run? What I don't understand is why he murdered Swensen. If Harrigan did drug Swensen and put him in the bathroom to get him out of the way for your visit, all he had to do was follow you out, get the manuscript back and take off. Why kill the poor man after rendering him senseless?"

It was a point that had long preyed on my mind. Why drug a man before killing him? To render the victim unable to defend himself was the only logical answer. Now father had posed an even more interesting enigma. Why kill the man after drugging him? If all Harrigan wanted to do was get away with Swensen's money and the manuscript, a drugged Swensen was as incapable of stopping him as a dead Swensen. Not even a hardened criminal, which I was certain Harrigan was not, would leave himself open to a murder charge when he could achieve his goal without resorting to that most abhorrent of crimes.

Why was Swensen drugged *and* murdered? That was the rub. But as Sigmund liked to say, "Once we know the problem, the solution is easy." And as Archy likes to say, "From your lips to God's ear, Ziggy."

Puffing away happily, I couldn't help but envy the length of father's cigar. My English Oval seemed to be shrinking at an alarming rate.

"The answer to that, sir," I expounded, "would go a long way in solving the crime. One reason for murder is to silence the victim. Did Swensen know something Harrigan, and perhaps Claudia Lester, did not want made public? If so, it would have to do with the manuscript. What Swensen's murder does tell us is that we don't know diddly-squat about these people, their game and how far they would go to win."

Father stroked his mustache. "While I find your language unnecessarily colorful, Archy, I do get the point, but what if this Whitehead, the unethical auction house representative, wanted to silence Swensen? How do we know Swensen wasn't alive and conveniently drugged when Whitehead arrived on the scene?"

"I hadn't thought of that," I answered truthfully. "But, yet again, it doesn't make sense. If the money and the manuscript were gone, why kill Swensen after the fact? It wouldn't save Whitehead's job if the story of the manuscript fiasco went public. And don't forget, he didn't have to call the police. He could have beat it when he saw the body and left it for the cleaning lady to trip over the next morning. Fact is, Whitehead put himself in jeopardy by reporting the murder."

"He also put Harrigan and you in harm's way," father added. "Remember, Whitehead said he found Swensen dead. The murder was committed earlier, when both you and Harrigan were in the fatal room. There's no honor among thieves, Archy."

Silence followed. I took a final puff and doused my cigarette in the ashtray as father tapped ash off his cigar that still had more miles on it than there are minutes in an hour. I would overcome, but there was little joy in the resolve.

I sipped my port. Father, seated behind his desk and perhaps eager to begin his nightly voyage back in time, fingered a beautifully bound copy of Dickens's *A Tale of Two Cities*. "I don't think the police consider you a likely suspect," he said, as if the thought had just popped into his head. "But that doesn't put you in the clear. You're still the only person they can place in that room before the body was discovered. Harrigan's presence there depends on your testimony. They could build a case against you, but it wouldn't be easy."

If that was a pep talk, it missed the mark, but knowing

that father was thinking one step ahead of the police was reassuring. "Thank you, sir. But even being an unlikely suspect is too close for comfort. If Claudia Lester tells O'Hara the true story, and I believe she will, Fortesque is going to be pulled into the charade, which will lead right back to me. O'Hara is going to know I was holding out on her. She asked me why Lester hired me to go to the Crescent, and I told her the truth as I knew it last night."

Father shook his head woefully. "The police consider the sin of omission more mortal than venial, I'm afraid."

Knowing it would please him, I said, "I did it to protect Fortesque. I didn't know anything about the murder when I talked to Fortesque. I wanted to consult with my client before I handed him over to Officer O'Hara. That's my job."

"So it is," father answered, "and you did the right thing, but doing what is right is not always in our own best interest. All we can do is hope that justice will triumph. What's your next move, Archy?"

"I want to sit down with Fortesque, tell him everything that's happened and see if he can shed any light on the situation. Then I'm going to see O'Hara and throw myself at the mercy of the court."

I was rewarded with a smile. "Very good, Archy. Now pour us a tad more of the port and then off with you. I have work to do."

Over the tad of port father commented, "By the by, Archy, if Capote was commissioned by his publisher to write this book and given an advance on the work, I believe they are the rightful owners of the manuscript."

"A Voice from the Grave" was what I dubbed my latest discreet inquiry. It was a clear reference to the late

Capote's ability to stir up trouble and speculation for a second time with his notorious peek into the life and times of the rich and famous. The inquiry, I'm afraid, was going to be less than discreet when the tabloids got hold of this story, and subsequent events, unrelated to the case, would give an eerie relevance to that ghostly title.

I keep a journal of my cases not for the IRS or with any thought to publishing, but as a relaxing means of viewing the events of the day and perhaps seeing something I had missed along the way. Academics are told to publish *or* perish. Were I to go public with my journal, it would be more a matter of publish *and* perish. People come to me because they don't want to bare their souls to the police, as that route is usually one step away from a tabloid headline.

Ignominy being the prevailing atmosphere of my trade, I had picked up more tales of sex, lies and betrayal during my years of pounding the Palm Beach beat than Capote had amassed over all those lunches at La Côte Basque. However, I knew better than to shake down the hand that picked up the tab, a lesson poor Tru had not learned in time to save his career, which, like many artists of his volatile temperament, would be indistinguishable from his life.

I listed my dramatis personae in the order I had encountered them either in person or, as with Rodney Whitehead, by word of mouth, which put Georgia O'Hara next to last. Simply writing her name caused me to pause in my work to light my fourth and last cigarette of the day before continuing to pen my memoirs.

When the reverie—which I refuse to relate, thank you—drifted languidly toward the ceiling along with the last cloud of blue smoke from my English Oval, I recorded the events of the last twenty-four hours and felt the bump on my head. I closed by listing the questions that needed to be addressed and those that needed better answers than had been given.

Why did Claudia Lester hire me as her "bagman"?

Why was Lawrence Swensen drugged before he was strangled?

Why was Lawrence Swensen strangled?

Was Lawrence Swensen dead when Rodney Whitehead entered unit number nine at the Crescent Motel?

Was Lawrence Swensen dead when I exchanged the money for the manuscript with Matthew Harrigan?

Who knocked me out and relieved me of the manuscript?

Did Fortesque know more than he had told me?

Did Claudia Lester tell me all she knew?

Those were the problems, but, Ziggy notwithstanding, I foresaw no easy solution.

I washed my puss, brushed my pearlies, got into my X-large T-shirt, which I wear as a nightie, got into bed and contemplated my potential captor.

Georgia O'Hara was a lovely lass, in spite of the uniform—or was it because of the uniform? No doubt but that I was quite taken with Officer O'Hara, and unless I was very mistaken I think my feelings were reciprocated. She said she knew my vital statistics from the silly eligible-bachelors book, and so had probably anticipated our meeting with more than just a lawman's curiosity in getting a first look at a possible suspect.

Did I live up to her expectations? Well, when I asked if she was in the market for a husband she responded by asking if I was applying for the job. Not exactly a brush-off. Was I reading too much into foolish banter? I think not, because, as someone said, many a true word is spoken in jest.

You may ask how I dare entertain such thoughts while

actively committed to beseeching Connie Garcia, on bended knee if necessary, to abandon her Cuban freedom fighter and return to me, body and soul. Well, as always when pondering intangibles, I turn to the sages of our age who, with a word or the turn of a phrase, can tickle our funny bone, tug on our heartstrings, kindle our emotions and, ultimately, soothe the savage beast. Need I say I speak of our tunesmiths?

I ran through my vast repertoire of sheet music, passing Berlin, Hart, Porter and Gershwin, before coming upon the solution to tonight's quandary in the person of the master of the witty lyric, Jerry Herman. Jerry reminded me that in man's quest for romance he should waive propriety in favor of variety. Bless you, Jerry Herman.

My need to court the raven-haired Connie while seeking the affections of the blond Georgy was not an aberration. It was the norm. More proof? Herman also advises *"Instead of one dandy dish, pass him the candy dish."* With that, I am exonerated of all charges of caddishness. I can stretch, yawn, stroke my cheek and greet the Sandman who comes to me humming "Georgia on My Mind."

• The next morning, when I drove into our underground garage, Herb signaled me to approach his glass cage. When I got there, he handed me an envelope. "A man brought this first thing this morning. He said to give it to you as soon as you came in. I told him you don't always get here at nine and sometimes you don't get here at all."

Taking the envelope, I thanked Herb and said it wasn't necessary to give my itinerary to messengers who didn't know enough to use the front door. "I am often on covert business," I reminded him.

With a wink, Herb replied, "Mrs. Trelawney says you're more often on monkey business."

If I had someplace to go, they would all miss me when I was gone. Not wanting to read my mail before Herb's prying eyes, I went back to the Miata and opened the envelope. The note was handwritten and brief.

"If you want to know what happened at the Crescent Motel the other night, check out the fresh vegetables at the Publix supermarket on Sunset Avenue before noon."

Zounds!

10

I gave Herb a toot as I sped out to meet my mysterious informer. Unless a new recruit had joined our troop, I believed I was on my way to meet with Rodney Whitehead in the produce section of the Publix market, but why the cloak-and-dagger sham was beyond my ken. I said that when Al Rogoff and I felt the need to meet clandestinely our venue was often the Publix parking lot; however, I had never set foot in the popular emporium and hoped I was properly dressed for my debut.

Plotting my revenge for Connie's open liaison with Alejandro, I had chosen jealousy as my strategy and Georgy O'Hara as my secret weapon. Not wishing to camouflage my mission, and as a precursor of coming events, I had stepped out rather smartly this morning in my dress greens. Forest-green twill trousers, Nile-green polo shirt of Sea Island cotton, bottle-green ultrasuede jacket, and a green felt porkpie hat. My combat boots were tassled white loafers with no socks, of course. To be sure, this garb was strictly for parading. I had a duffel bag full of togs for when we went into the trenches.

The Publix offers valet parking (really!), which I eschewed, commandeering one of the many empty spaces. I entered the complex with great apprehension. Would I meet anyone I knew, like our Ursi? Lord forbid. Connie? Even worse. And what about Georgy O'Hara on the prowl for melon squeezers? A moment later I found myself in a fluorescent-lit horn of plenty. Aisle after aisle stacked with edibles in tins, boxes, jars and colorful plastics met my gaze. Ladies in capri pants, men in shorts, housekeepers in uniform, blue collars, white collars and collars trimmed in mink maneuvered their carts without the aid of traffic signals or crossing guards.

So this is it, I thought. The great American leveler, where the classes in our classless society come together to see, be seen and forage. Being the most public of all public places, I could see why my informant had chosen a supermarket for a surreptitious meeting. The best place to hide a book is in a library.

The produce section was big and lush. Freshly washed fruits and vegetables glistened with beads of moisture like the flora in a rain forest. Except for the occasional grape tomato, I am not a crudités enthusiast, but I will admit the display made me think about lunch, which was the rationale for the bountiful presentation. You may think it strange for a gourmand like myself not to be a habitué of food markets, but would a concert violinist hang around a catgut factory?

A pint-sized monster riding shotgun in a cart glided past me and pointed: "Look, mommy, there's the Jolly Green Giant." Impudent little bugger. Children should be neither seen nor heard, was my credo. Perhaps that was why I had not been blessed, as the blessed liked to say. Funny, I always thought it was because I was lucky.

As the imp moved up the aisle, I saw a familiar face coming down the aisle. Was this possible? When Matthew Harrigan approached and said, "You remember me?" I knew it was.

Matthew looked a bit worse for wear. He hadn't shaved this morning, and his clothes, jeans and a white Lacoste, were not exactly April fresh. He was actually pushing a cart that contained a can of baked beans. With a toss of his head he ordered, "Let's look like we're shopping," even before I had a chance to reply to his greeting. I have never seen a man look and act more like a fugitive.

Still not giving me a chance to speak, he blabbed as we began to stroll aimlessly, "I didn't kill Swensen, if that's what she told you."

Enough being enough, I stopped walking and put a restraining hand on his cart. "First," I began, "is your name Matthew Harrigan and are you an associate of Claudia Lester, doing business in Palm Beach with Decimus Fortesque?"

"So she told you everything," he said, looking around as if in search of a hidden microphone or camcorder. "Okay, I'm Matthew Harrigan and I'm Claudia's patsy, that's what I am." He tugged on my arm. "Keep moving. I know you're here alone, because I've been watching you since you came in, but let's not attract attention by blocking the aisles." He removed a box of cereal from the shelf and put it in the cart.

This was all inane and pointless, but I figured the best reaction to his hysteria was to go with the flow and hear him out. "Why didn't you call my office and meet me there? Don't you think this is a bit dramatic, to say the least?"

"I was going to do just that," he answered, adding two cans of tuna fish to our collection while ignoring the sign that said TODAY'S SPECIAL 3 FOR $5. "Then I heard about Swensen on the news last night, and it's in the morning papers. I'm wanted for murder, mister—and keep moving."

"You're wanted for questioning," I said. "There's a difference. And why didn't you keep running after you accosted me in the Crescent parking lot? Why did you come back if you knew the police were looking for you?"

This time he stopped in mid-aisle. "Accosted you? What the hell are you talking about, mister? I never laid a hand on you or Swensen. What's Claudia saying?"

"Excuse me, gentlemen," came the irate voice of a matron trying to get by us.

"Sorry, ma'am." I tipped my porkpie in apology. "Can't we go someplace where we can talk quietly?" I pleaded with Harrigan. "Why did you pick the Publix?"

"Right now I feel safe in wide-open spaces with a lot of people around, and this suits the need. I'm also new in town, and it's the only market I saw when I was cruising around. If you prefer the A and P, I'm sorry." He pulled a box of raisins off the shelf.

All the P&V that he had exhibited the other night at the Crescent was drained from Harrigan's demeanor, as was the blood from his cheeks. I had thought the sleazy motel setting might have tainted my initial opinion of the man, but watching him furtively tossing groceries into his cart while looking over his shoulder confirmed my first impression of Matthew Harrigan.

He was a part-time gigolo and a small-time wiseguy who had got himself tangled in a big-time crime and was coping like a TV hood on the lam. I would place the odds at twelve to seven that his favorite film featured a couple of CIA and KGB moles exchanging atomic secrets while trying to decide which softener to soak their undies in.

Physically restraining him from removing a five-pound canned ham from the shelf, I said, "Before you get all puffed up over visualizing your picture on display in the Palm Beach post office, I think you should know that I am also a suspect in the death of Lawrence Swensen, as is your associate, Rodney Whitehead. We all seem to have been in the wrong place at the right time."

That did the trick. He stopped shopping and looked at me with what I believed was hope in those watery blue eyes. He who said misery loves company knew of what he spoke. Harrigan was so happy to have a cohort aboard the paddy wagon to the electric chair, he gave me a welcoming smile.

"Now, if we're going to help each other," I continued, "let's begin by getting out of this place and go where we can talk quietly and in private—like my car, which is in the lot outside."

Without a moment's hesitation he said, "Let's go."

With a nod toward our groceries, I asked, "Aren't you going to put those back where you found them?"

He pushed the cart to an area where it wouldn't block traffic and answered, "One of the clerks will do it."

"You've done this before?"

He shrugged. "I used to work in a supermarket in the Village. Greenwich Village, that is."

"Is that where Claudia found you?"

Reverting to type, he said, "Yeah, in the meat department."

I was very much at home chatting covertly in the Publix

parking lot. Rogoff usually chewed on a cigar during these conclaves, so I told Harrigan he could smoke if he wanted to. He refused, saying he didn't smoke. That dashed my hopes of sneaking in an extra one before lunch, but you can't say I didn't try.

"Have the police questioned you?" was the first thing he wanted to know.

"Yes, but before we get into that, tell me whose idea it was to mug me and take back the manuscript."

He ran a hand through his hair. "I told you, I never laid a hand on you and I don't know what you mean about the manuscript. No one took it back. You delivered it to Claudia."

"No, I did not. I was mugged in the Crescent parking lot and the manuscript was taken from me."

"Look, mister, one of us is nuts or lying, and it's not me. When I got back to the Ambassador, Claudia had the manuscript. The one I gave you and you were hired to deliver to her."

There was no doubt but that he was sincere. He believed I had delivered the manuscript to Claudia at the Ambassador. "Before we go any further, Harrigan, tell me what you and Claudia Lester were plotting and why I was hired to pave the way."

"What did Claudia tell you?" was his comeback.

"You first, Harrigan. Then I'll tell you what she said and what I told the police. Trust me, the information will help your cause. You don't want to sit down with the police and look wet behind the ears."

"Who says I'm going to sit down with the cops?"

"I do, but we'll save that for later, too. Now let's have it, verbatim."

It didn't take much coaxing. Like a man falsely accused, Harrigan was bursting to tell his side of the story.

The guy had been seething for two days and his time had finally come. Sparing no one, he let it all hang out. "Claudia told you how we heard about the Capote manuscript?"

"She did. From Whitehead, the auction house rep."

The beginning of Harrigan's tale corroborated what Claudia Lester had told me. Whitehead came to her with his supposed find, and she contacted Fortesque on the advice of his ex-wife Vera Fortesque. Here their stories parted ways.

"On the plane ride down here we decided to pull off a G.S.O.," Harrigan boasted.

"Translation, please," I interrupted.

"A Grand Sting Operation," he said. "It was really beautiful. Fortesque gets his manuscript, and we go back north with the fifty grand."

It didn't take much to conclude that Swensen and Whitehead got the shaft, and I said as much.

"Only Swensen," Harrigan explained. "Whitehead was in on the deal. You see, Claudia was to get her ten percent from Fortesque, five G's, plus expenses like plane fare and lodging."

Harrigan went on to say that Whitehead was to get his share directly from Swensen, but that Claudia Lester didn't know how much that share was. Whitehead told Claudia that Swensen had heard about the big prices being doled out at auction sales and hoped to make a hundred thousand on the deal. Once Claudia Lester had contacted Fortesque and ascertained that he would pay as much as fifty thousand for the manuscript, she passed Fortesque's offer on to Whitehead.

Whitehead told the ingenuous Swensen that no matter how high the bid went for the manuscript, after the auction house and Uncle Sam took their cut he, Swensen, would be left with the short end of the stick. But if he sold the manuscript on the black market he could clear fifty thousand in cash, less a small stipend for Whitehead. Also, he could have the money in a few days and not have to wait for the auction house to authenticate the manuscript and prove provenance. In short, he scared the bejesus out of Swensen, who jumped at the chance to take the money and run.

Bored with Delta's box lunch and no-smoking policy, Claudia twitted away the time by concocting a scheme to hijack the fifty thousand and split it three ways, with guess who getting the lion's share.

Once in Palm Beach, Claudia went to see Fortesque to get the cash. She, at the Ambassador, had the money, and Swensen, guided by Whitehead, was in unit number nine at the Crescent Motel with the manuscript. What Claudia proposed was to get the manuscript from Swensen without surrendering the money.

"When we got here," Harrigan said, "the three of us, Claudia, Whitehead and I, sat down for a war council." The guy talked like a prince of the Mafia. With a name like Harrigan he should have known better. "Remember, Swensen's only contact was Whitehead. He didn't know Claudia and I existed. As far as Swensen knew, Whitehead was dealing directly with Fortesque."

"Did Whitehead tell Swensen that Fortesque was the buyer?" I asked.

"Sure," Harrigan said. "Thanks to all those marriages, Fortesque is one famous millionaire. The Fortesque name was the bait to lure Swensen into accepting Whitehead's offer."

I was beginning to see why their G.S.O. needed a bagman and Harrigan went on to confirm my suspicion. Swensen's addiction to booze and funny cigarettes was so outrageous that Whitehead picked up on it shortly after his first meeting with the man. Hence, the conniving trio decided the easiest way to part Swensen from the money and the manuscript would be to slip him a mickey. (Harrigan's locution, not mine. Honestly!)

Whitehead was supposed to deliver the money to the Crescent and come away with the manuscript, but Swensen knew Whitehead and Whitehead's employers. If Whitehead administered the mickey, Swensen would run to Fortesque (or the auction house or the police) the moment he awoke to find he'd been duped, so Whitehead had to be made above suspicion—and here comes Archy.

It was Claudia's idea to hire a disinterested party, preferably one recommended by Fortesque himself, to count the money, deliver it and pick up the manuscript. When Swensen went crying to Fortesque, or anyone else, Archy McNally himself would vouch that the transaction had taken place. In short, it was a respected Palm Beach PI's word against a pothead manager of a glorified male brothel.

"Clever, right?" Harrigan gloated.

Real clever, I thought, rubbing the bump on my head.

Whitehead called Swensen at the Crescent and told him he (Whitehead) had to fly back to New York on business immediately. Mr. Fortesque was sending his own man to the Crescent to look at the manuscript. If all was in order, the man would call Fortesque and shortly thereafter another of Fortesque's people would arrive at the Crescent with the money.

"So I got there," Harrigan said, "and Swensen was already three sheets to the wind, if you know what I mean. He thinks I'm Fortesque's man and invites me to share a vodka and soda. I put the dope in his drink and he passed out. I put him in the bathroom and waited for you. Claudia made up the story of the diary and the ex-boyfriend. Clever, right?"

If Swensen had lived and talked, Claudia Lester would say she made up the diary story to protect her client, which Fortesque believed was the case. "But," I said aloud, "if Swensen talked, I would say I had given the money to a young man, not to Swensen."

"We thought of that," Harrigan said, "but in Swensen's line of work what would be more natural than a good-looking young guy being with him in a sleazeball motel?"

Aside from Harrigan's inflated opinion of himself, he was probably right. Poor Lawrence Swensen didn't stand a snowdrop's chance in Beelzebub's parlor. Harrigan said he followed me out of the room, got into his car and left the Crescent with the money.

"Is your car a rental?" I asked.

"Yeah. I picked it up at the airport as soon as we landed."

"You were parked in the space reserved for that room. I learned Swensen's car was parked in the visitors' parking area. How come?"

Harrigan looked at me askance. "How should I know? Whitehead told me Swensen was in number nine, and I took the space outside the room. It was vacant."

"Did you lock the room's door behind you?"

I got the same puzzled stare. "I didn't have a key, if that's what you mean. I just closed the door behind me. If it didn't lock automatically, I left it open."

It was an old motel, so metal keys and not the newer plastic cards worked the door. Those ancient locks had a little lever on the inside knob that controlled the lock mechanism. In fact, many modern bathrooms still employ such locks. If Harrigan had opened it to let me in he could very well have left it in the open position, but it was locked when I tried it after I was mugged. In the time I was unconscious anyone could have entered the room, killed Swensen and locked the door when they left.

But Whitehead, who got there after I left, told the police he found the door open. How was that possible and whom should I believe—Harrigan, Claudia Lester or Whitehead? My head was spinning with questions as Harrigan droned on.

"Like we planned, I rode around long enough for you to get back to the Ambassador to give Claudia the manuscript. When I got there, Claudia had the manuscript."

"Did you actually see it?" I questioned.

"No. What for? Claudia told me you had delivered it and she had it in a briefcase ready to take to Fortesque the next day. I went to my room to pack and get ready to check out, leaving the money with Claudia. When I got back, she gave me the attaché case and I took off for Fort Lauderdale, where I had a reservation for a flight back to New York."

"And where was Whitehead at this point?" I cut in.

"Him?" Harrigan groaned. "I thought he had left for New York that afternoon. Now we both know he was at the Crescent Motel viewing the remains." Harrigan took a tissue from his pocket, blew his nose and dabbed at his eyes. "When I got to the airport I turned in the car rental. Because of the new stringent security checks all carry-on bags have to be searched, so I had to transfer the money to my suitcase. Turns out it wasn't necessary. The money had become a stack of magazines. You see, mister, the G.S.O. had boomeranged and got me right where I sit." He again combed his hair with his fingers. "I trusted Claudia, and look where it got me."

Not to mention where it got Swensen. Harrigan spent the night at the airport and the next day wondering what he should do. He took a motel room in Fort Lauderdale and heard about Swensen on the evening news. This morning he remembered my name, hired a car and motored to Palm Beach.

His story, like his associate's, was plausible and nothing more.

As is now the custom, I thanked Matthew Harrigan for sharing and then told him how I had fared at the Crescent Motel the other night. His response was disbelief, insisting that Claudia Lester had the manuscript at the Ambassador.

"She had a briefcase," I told him, "which was probably used to stash the money in while you were in your room packing."

"So who has the manuscript?" he wondered aloud.

That being a no-brainer, I replied with confidence, "Whoever raised a bump on my head in the Crescent parking lot."

"It wasn't me, mister. I got out of there before you reached the parking lot, and Swensen was sleeping, not dead, when I left."

"So who strangled him?" I asked.

Harrigan thought a moment before saying, "Whitehead?"

"Then reported it to the police?"

"No. That doesn't make sense," Harrigan said.

"Nothing makes sense," I assured him. "If the guy who mugged me wasn't the guy who did in Swensen, we had more men running around the Crescent that night than appear in a French bedroom farce."

"You don't think it was Claudia," he reflected hopefully.

"No, I don't. Why should she rob me of what I was about to bring her?"

"Yeah," he agreed, "but why should she say you delivered it when you never did?"

Round and round it goes, and where it stops nobody knows.

"Is the manuscript authentic?" I asked. "Is it the complete Capote work never published?"

"Beats me, mister. Whitehead is supposed to be the expert. I went on the ride for the money. Whether it's real or phony is Fortesque's problem." He reflected a moment and added, "Do you think Fortesque is the wild card? Maybe he hired some thugs to get the manuscript and return his money at the same time."

I thought of the pop-eyed Fortesque and his comfortable life with the pastry maven, Sam Zimmermann, and nipped that theory in the bud before proceeding to tell Harrigan what Claudia Lester had told me. "Which, I am certain, is the story she told the police today."

"It's a lie," he protested. "One big lie. She's telling the police that I killed Swensen and ran off with the money and the manuscript."

"She's certainly hinting that you did," I said, "which is why you have to go to the police and tell your story. Claudia has had her say, and I imagine Whitehead will be tooting his horn next. You had better tell the police your side. If you're a no-show, your partners win the day."

He looked out the car window, and for a moment I thought he was going to make a run for it. "They won't believe me," he said, like a man who has been down that road.

"The longer you keep trying to evade them, the less they'll believe anything you say. If you don't turn yourself in, they'll pick you up and treat you like a fugitive. I'm with a law firm," I said to reassure him, "and I can arrange for you to speak to a lawyer."

He was silent, his face turned from me. "The officer in charge is Georgia O'Hara," I continued. "She's with the state troopers at the Juno barracks. Is your car here, in the parking lot?"

He nodded, his chin sagging to his chest. "Follow me out and I'll take you there," I ordered.

"They got me, mister. Claudia and Whitehead got me good." He opened the door, not bothering to mop his eyes with a tissue.

• I treated myself to a celebratory lunch at the Pelican Club. My victory, which had more to do with my love life than with my professional life, will be made clear anon. Simon Pettibone was behind the bar, his eyes glued to the television screen, which was tuned to the floor of the New York Stock Exchange. The Dow tape with its hieroglyphic markings ran across the bottom of the screen. The resulting scene was slightly less baffling than the antics of an ant colony.

Our bartender/manager is a Wall Street wizard, and whether his "buys and sells" or "puts and calls" are sheer luck or founded upon a perceptive knowledge of the financial markets is a moot question. What matters is that those Pelicans who play along with Simon have fared better than those who are guided by their brokers or their favorite seers' crystal ball.

It being a few minutes after high noon and too early for

the hard-core lunch crowd, I was able to take possession of my favorite corner table in the bar area. Priscilla advanced upon me, menu in hand, almost before I had settled in.

"You look like a Lime Rickey on the hoof," she sassed.

"Sticks and stones, Miss Pris, will not pierce my armor, and neither will your sharp tongue. Now, what does Leroy have to tempt us with this afternoon?"

"For starters, we offer a Cuba Libre followed by the Cuba Salad. The entrée is a spicy Cuba Chile that is definitely not for the *cobarde*. It's prix fixe at thirty bucks, with a sawbuck going to the bookies."

After that not very clever spiel I knew I was asking for a kick in the kimono when I responded, "What bookies?"

"*The* bookies," she snapped, hands on hips. Our Priscilla is an African American beauty in the mode of the young Diahann Carroll who caused a sensation on Broadway when she bowed in the musical *House of Flowers*. Today Priscilla wore jeans that showed nary a ripple nor a wrinkle and a patriotic red, white and blue striped tank top that made one want to enlist in whatever cause Priscilla spearheaded.

And how odd that I should liken our Priscilla to the ingenue in a show written by Truman Capote. It seems that voice from the grave will not shut up.

"The bookies," she repeated, "who are taking bets on who will win the hand of Consuela Garcia. Come on, Archy, you must know the place has been buzzing with rumors since Connie dined with Alejandro at this very table the other night while you got sloshed at the bar."

I did not get sloshed at the bar, and the place was always buzzing with rumors. I admit that I had often buzzed with the rest of 'em when it wasn't me ducking the potshots. Now that I was the fish in the barrel I found idle gossip a bore and a danger to national security. There *oughta* be a law.

To acknowledge the talk would only give it credence. However, I had to know, "Who is favored in this bit of illegal gambling on our hallowed premises?"

"Alejandro is the odds-on favorite. You're the long shot at a hundred to one. We're talking big money, Archy."

Hiding my chagrin behind a yawn, I asked, "And why am I pegged as the also-ran?"

Priscilla took a deep breath that went a long way in raising the colors. "Because Alejandro is younger than you, handsomer than you, sexier than you, braver than you, and may just be the next mayor of Miami. And remember, you asked."

I could not take this sitting down. Pride forced me to hint at coming events while not giving away my battle plan. To wipe that smug look from Priscilla's pretty face, I confided, "Heed this handicapper, missy, and reserve this table for me tonight at eight—and put your money on the long shot. With those odds it will finance your way out of the prêt-à-porter league and into a Worth Avenue boutique."

As hoped, this got her attention. If Priscilla put out the word at lunch that something was afoot, the Pelican regulars would storm the doors this evening. I had conceded round one to the challenger, but I would even the score when the bell heralded round two of Archy vs. Alejandro—and we would be playing to a full house.

"We don't reserve tables and you know it, so what are you planning?" she demanded.

Putting aside the menu, I said with a dash of ennui, "I am planning lunch. Nothing more and nothing less. Will Leroy make me up a platter of the Potpourri Pelican?"

Annoyed, she said, "Depends if we have the ingredients on hand."

"And you can bring me a Rob Roy," I ordered as she picked up the menu and flounced off.

The Potpourri Pelican was created by Leroy at my suggestion. Based on the Italian antipasto and the French hors d'oeuvres *divers,* it came into being the day I lamented that I could have only one appetizer when, at times, they all appealed. Ordering two or more might prove a bit unwieldy, if not downright gluttonous. The solution was to present a sampling of all Leroy's starters served over a bed of crisp iceberg lettuce and garnished, if desired, with an oil-and-vinegar dressing.

The dish consists of shrimp, hearts of artichoke, roasted peppers, deviled egg, anchovies, a generous sliver of the house pâté, a wedge of Camembert, chickpeas, black and green olives, capers and one king crab claw. With a slice or two of a warm semolina and a glass of white wine (an Orvieto Classico if available), it makes for a satisfying lunch or a fun way to start a dinner date.

When my Rob Roy arrived I drank a silent toast to the happy events of this very busy morning. I had delivered Matthew Harrigan to the police feeling like a bounty hunter, but as there was no price on Matthew's head my reward was not of a monetary nature. Young Swathmoore was nonplussed when I introduced my companion. He immediately got on the intercom with Georgy girl, who came bounding out from someplace in the rear of the building accompanied by two officers of the male persuasion.

Poor Harrigan looked as if he was going to be sick when the two men led him to what I presumed was one of the interview rooms where I had first met O'Hara. As I noted yesterday, the officers in the room hardly gave the activity at the front desk even a passing glance. Computer screens flickered, printed matter got passed from "in" to "out" boxes and the commercial copy machine was collating a column of pages like a robot who had learned a new trick.

Officer O'Hara told me that she had been trying to locate me for the past two hours. I took it her quest had something to do with her interview with Claudia Lester, and I was right. Swathmoore eavesdropped on our verbal volley with keen interest and looked hurt when O'Hara told me to follow her to her office.

After making the left at the copy machine, she took me into a room just opposite the one she had inhabited yesterday. As I had suspected, the four offices were shared by the troopers. Now I noticed a closed door at the far end of the corridor with a shiny brass plate that identified the occupant. This was where the head honcho hung his hat, but from this distance I could not make out either his name or his title. If this case should drag on too long for comfort, I was sure I would know both before the police were done with me.

"Aren't you going to thank me for delivering Harrigan?" I asked when the door was closed.

No, she was not going to thank me for delivering Harrigan. In fact, all she wanted to do was berate me for withholding evidence.

She: "Perjury is a capital offense."

Me: "Perjury? I don't remember taking an oath, and I did not tell a lie. You asked me what I was doing at the Crescent Motel, and I told you why I went there."

She: "Semantics."

Me: "The truth."

She complained because she thought she could trust me. I told her she could trust me with her life. She said I would be foolish to trust her with my life.

"You knew when we spoke that the diary story Lester gave you was pure bunk. You also knew that Decimus Fortesque was a prime player in this case."

I reacted like a mother hen protecting her chicks. "Fortesque hired Lester to purchase the manuscript. He doesn't know Harrigan, and he knows Whitehead only because Lester mentioned him as her contact, but Fortesque never laid eyes on him or the victim. You can't link Fortesque to the murder."

We were both standing in the small room, squaring off face-to-face. Georgy, bristling, folded her arms across her chest and chided, "But of course. You are now working for Fortesque."

I told her how I had come to be hired by Fortesque. Claudia Lester had given her all the facts of the purloined manuscript, telling Georgy the same story she had told me from the time Claudia joined forces with Rodney Whitehead to the night Swensen was found dead in the Crescent.

"She's fingering Harrigan for the heavy, correct?" I said.

Georgy nodded. "Do you think she's telling the truth?"

"I don't think she knows the meaning of the word," I answered without hesitation. "But if you think you've got a puzzler now, wait till you hear Harrigan's story."

"So you questioned him as well as Lester before handing them over to us," she criticized. "I wish you would keep out of this, Archy."

A moment after she had articulated my given name, I could see the color creep ever so daintily from her neck to her ivory cheeks. I gave her a shy smile as she turned from me and went to stand behind the desk.

"I would be more than happy to keep out of this, officer.

It was you who invited me in when you put out an APB for the guy in the red Miata."

Flustered, she barked, "Where did you find Harrigan?"

"In the produce section of the Publix on Sunset," I stated.

Those blue eyes glared at me for an instant, but before she tore into me the pout became a smile and, tossing back her head, she began to laugh with genuine glee. Naturally, I joined in.

"You are crazy, Archy McNally," she hooted.

I assured her I was, but "I'm also infectious. When you get to know me you'll find me hard to resist."

In the civilized world all relationships, especially between the sexes, begin on a formal basis and progress, either quickly or over time, to an easy comradery and then, perhaps, to something more intimate. The flip side being the associations that regress from the formal to the fatuous. The turning point, for better or for worse, often takes place instantaneously with a word, a look or even the touch of a hand. When it happens, the pleased or woeful couple are simultaneously aware that they have been blessed or banished and must act accordingly.

Do I go too far when I say *that* moment arrived for us when she spoke the word "Archy"? Is my conceit showing when I say her laughter was more a release of pent-up emotion than an expression of glee given the venue of my meeting with Matthew Harrigan? Who knows—and who cares? When a beautiful woman tosses you the ball, you are given a choice. You can drop it or run with it, and a butterfingers I ain't.

Many thoughts were hatching in my noodle when I asked Officer O'Hara to break bread with me at the Pelican that evening. Some were naughty and some were nice, but all proclaimed with joy, "If you play this right, you can K two B's with one S." Was I being crass? No. I am a healthy American boy protecting his turf from the interloper. I am George Washington crossing the Delaware, Lindbergh crossing the Atlantic and John Wayne crossing Iwo Jima. If all is fair in love and war, I am the fairest of them all—and Georgy O'Hara is not exactly chopped liver.

She refused to dine on the grounds that I was a suspect in her murder case. I told her that was gibberish in its purest form. I also remembered that when she heard Harrigan's version of the events at the Crescent Motel it would not only contradict Claudia Lester's tale, it would also impugn my story.

If Harrigan insisted that I had delivered that blasted manuscript, it would mean that I was not unconscious in the motel parking lot when people were entering and leaving unit nine like it was fitted with a turnstile. It was imperative that I sit down with O'Hara and convince her that I, at least, spoke the truth.

"After you talk to Harrigan," I said, "you are going to have more questions in the hopper than hairs on your head. Why don't we declare a truce and join forces. Between the two of us we might even start to make some sense of this opus."

She didn't dismiss the idea completely but seemed to think aloud: "It would be helpful to compare notes on what Lester and Harrigan told you and what they reported here."

"Have you ever been to the Pelican Club?" I asked.

"No," she said rather coyly, "but I've heard of it."

"Good or bad?" I prodded.

"It's not the Bath and Tennis." She laughed.

"I'll say it's not," I assured her, "and amen to that. Good

food and grog in a convivial setting, as the guidebooks say. I'll pick you up at half past seven for dinner at eight."

"Why can't we talk here?" she insisted.

"Because you'll be with Harrigan for an hour, at least, and I can't spare the time to hang around. Also, not being a member of the force, I think we should be more discreet in our assignations."

Capitulating, she warned, "This is strictly a business dinner, and don't you forget it."

"Cross my heart and hope to die," I vowed, then repeated, "I'll pick you up at seven-thirty."

"In the red Miata?"

"What else? Do you like the top up or down, madam?"

"Up, please. I'm having a bad hair day."

When I asked where she lived she jotted her address, and phone number, on a piece of notepaper and handed it to me. The drawbridge had been lowered, and Archy, as usual, rushed in where wise men fear to tread.

Leroy did have the ingredients for my potpourri and even tossed in an extra crab claw for my consumption. The wine was from the Orvieto region of Italia, God was in his heaven and all was right with the world according to Archy McNally.

I had several things to attend to before I could head home for my daily swim, take my shower and assume the arduous task of selecting an outfit for my dinner with Officer O'Hara. It had to be something subtle yet bold, something that practically screamed "tasteful." A tall and perhaps paradoxical order to be sure, but with my wardrobe, it would be a snap.

Before leaving, I reminded Priscilla to keep my table free if she had to sit at it herself.

"First come, first served," she said with a shrug.

It's this personal service that makes me so fond of the Pelican.

Sam Zimmermann met me at the door. "What's cooking, Sam?" I greeted the butler/pastry maven.

"I have several dozen mini-éclairs cooling in the kitchen, sir."

"Is a doggy bag possible?" I ventured.

"With Jesus, sir, all things are possible," Sam preached.

I sidestepped that one and asked to be taken to the master of the house. Decimus Fortesque was in his library, another vaulted room overlooking Lake Worth, with towering mahogany shelves crammed with tomes in no discernible order. Beautiful leather-bound volumes abutted cloth and paperback editions, some stacked haphazardly, others properly shelved. There were comfortable leather chairs, side tables, lamps, a marble fireplace and a refectory table of museum quality upon which stood a lovely vase filled with a bouquet of fresh-cut flowers.

There was even a wrought-iron circular staircase mounted on wheels for scanning the upper shelves. In mystery novels of yore, this prop was usually frightfully unsteady and could be counted on to send someone falling to their untimely death.

All in all, it resembled the untidy but homey and comfortable lounge of a gentlemen's club, circa turn of the (last) century, London. A room my father would gladly give his Dickensian collection to possess.

Fortesque was seated, reading. "Ah, man, so there you are," he called when Sam showed me into the room. "I've just been reading the most amazing thing." He held up a small book bound in red cloth and proceeded to dish me the dirt.

"Queen Victoria's daughter, the princess Louise, married to become the Duchess of Argyll. She died in thirty-nine at the age of ninety-one. The apartment she occupied in Kensington Palace was given to the current princess Margaret when she married Armstrong-Jones. Well, it seems the door leading to the lovely gardens had been bricked up for decades. The reason, you see, was to prevent the Duke from slipping out to Hyde Park in the evening, where he would solicit the guardsmen who were domiciled there."

Fortesque's eyes popped with delight as he recounted the story. "What do you think of that, man?"

"I think, Mr. Fortesque, that princesses who marry beneath themselves get what they deserve. I also think that we would do better to turn our attention to the Crescent Motel and let the royals in Kensington palace tend to their own gardens. You have heard about the murder, sir?"

"Oh, that. Yes, Sam told me. I don't follow current events, man." He waved the little red book in my face. "As you can see, I'm a student of history. Did you know King Richard the Lion-Hearted favored boy minstrels?"

I eased into a chair. "Mr. Fortesque, I am here to tell you that you will be getting a call from the police."

He squared his shoulders and gave me the Mischa Auer stare. Thinking long and hard, all he could come up with was, "Why?"

"Why, sir? Because you hired a woman to buy a manuscript from a man for fifty thousand dollars; that man has been murdered; the manuscript and your money are missing; the woman is accusing her erstwhile partner of absconding with both the cash and the manuscript; said partner is accusing the woman of double-crossing him and being in possession of both; the auction house rep who was double-crossing the auction house discovered the body; the bagman who is your employee got crowned; finally, the police want to speak to the man who hired the woman—really, sir, do you want me to repeat—"

"Oh, cool your heels, Archy," he said. "I'm not as dotty as I pretend to be. I'm a rich old man who wants to be left to sniffing out collectibles and delving into other people's dirty laundry. What you're saying is that we're in one hell of a mess."

"Exactly, sir," and I recanted the events that had taken place since last we met and nibbled Sam Zimmermann's delights.

"What's your take on this, Archy?" Fortesque asked.

"I still believe Claudia Lester hired me to witness that she was acting in good faith when she exchanged the cash for the manuscript. Which she did—or I did for her. What happened after that, I haven't got a clue. All I know for certain is that someone killed Swensen, took the manuscript from me and made off with it and the loot."

Mulling this over, Fortesque offered, "This Harrigan is the most obvious candidate."

"Too obvious," I said. "He's a petty con artist out of his element. When the police led him away, he looked in dire need of the gents' room."

Fortesque shook a finger at me. Amazing how he had gone from borderline senility to clever deducer so rapidly, which proves that hell hath no fury like a rich man who thinks he's being cheated. "Listen to me, Archy," he said. "I know the Matthew Harrigan type very well. All my wives had affairs with them. They're always on stage and the curtain never goes down. Don't count him out."

"I'm not counting anyone in or out," I told him. "Are you saying you want me to continue with the case?"

"Damn right I do," he exploded. "I want my money or that manuscript."

"You know," I reminded him, "now that the police are in on this, the auction house is bound to learn what Rodney Whitehead was up to. Who actually owns the manuscript now that Swensen is dead is debatable at best."

That got him where he lived. "If I don't get my fifty thousand back I own it, and don't you forget it. What should I tell the bloody police?"

"The truth, Mr. Fortesque. Nothing but the truth."

"Hell, man. With all that's happened, I forget what the truth is."

I spelled it out for him, and before leaving I whispered clandestinely, "King Richard's favorite lute player was named Blondel."

I got the Mischa gawk and, "Really? How extraordinary."

• On the way out Sam handed me a small brown paper sack.

"For me?" I exclaimed.

"A dozen minis, sir."

I thanked him profusely, adding, "My doggy bag, as requested. You've made my day, Sam."

Zimmermann bowed his head piously. "Beware of answered prayers, sir."

12

It was nearing three when I got back to the McNally Building. How tempus does fugit when you're having fun. Herb gave me the high sign, but Mrs. Trelawney would have to wait as I had to see Binky Watrous on urgent business. I found him in the mail room, a suite twice the size of my claustrophobic firetrap, reading a paperback novel, which he quickly slipped into the top drawer of his cluttered desk.

Binky is a closeted romance novel aficionado who fancies the historic offerings of the genre. I believe he sees himself as the guy on the colorful cover, often named Thor, a Viking with a stomach that resembles your grandmother's old washboard and a chest that is often continued on the back cover. Binky, in the guise of Thor, raids towns and ravishes beautiful women from Ireland to Spain and back again in a century somewhere between the fall of ancient Rome and the rise of the Protestant Reformation. As you can see, this is not healthy reading for a man a dozen years past puberty, but I must say it is a more literate endeavor than his perusal of Victoria's Secret catalogues.

"Binky, my boy, I am in need of your help."

He was immediately on his feet. "On a case, Archy?"

"You might say that," I confided.

"Has it got anything to do with the blonde who came to see you the other day?"

"You might say that, too," I went on, baiting the hook.

"Do you want me to spy on her, Archy?" he asked hopefully.

"No, Binky, I want you to take Connie to dinner at the Pelican tonight."

Binky ran a forefinger across his upper lip, a gesture he picked up after I had convinced him to shave his mustache. Much to Binky's surprise, no one commented on the missing bit of corn silk, mostly because no one knew it had ever existed in the first place. "What's taking Connie to dinner have to do with the blonde?" he asked rather accusingly.

I rolled my eyes in the manner of an irate professor. "How many times must I tell you that in the detective business things are not always what they seem? There are boxes within boxes, masks behind masks and motives within motives. When Hercule Poirot takes a beautiful woman out to dine, half the restaurant drops dead of arsenic poisoning. Who knows what tonight will bring. Live dangerously, Binky, and reap the rewards."

He clapped his hands a few times and said, "Not bad, Archy. What do you do for an encore, 'O Solo Mio'?"

What cheek. It was that damn computer—that infamous information highway that was encouraging the young of the land to castigate their betters. There *oughta* be another law. I was down, but not out, so I looked deep into Binky's soulful eyes and sighed. "Forget it, Binky. And while you're at it, forget the fact that I got you this job, that I sponsored you for the Pelican Club, that I've stood by you through thick and thin—mostly thin—and defended you whether you were right or wrong—mostly wrong. I also, free of charge, apprenticed you in the detective trade. As someone once said, '*Et tu,* Binky. *Et, tu.*' "

Silence. I didn't know if I had brought tears to his eyes, because Binky's eyes always look on the verge of spilling over. Finally, he moaned, "What do you want me to do, Archy?"

"I want you to enjoy a pleasant dinner with a beautiful woman, nothing more. Is that asking so much after all I've—"

"Can it, Archy. I heard you the first time. This has something to do with Connie and Alejandro or my name isn't Watrous."

"Your name is Watrous," I assured him.

Looking me up and down, Binky frowned and said, "Everyone knows you're green with envy, Archy, but don't you think you've gone a little too far this time?"

"You don't know the lengths I will go to defend my honor and come out the long-shot winner. You've heard that we now harbor a betting parlor at the Pelican?"

"I've heard," he answered rather reluctantly.

"Who's running the book?"

Even more sheepishly, he said, "Tommy Ambrose."

"That delinquent? I might have known. Now I'm more determined than ever to break the bank. Who have you placed your tenner on, Binky, my boy?"

"Ask me no questions and I'll tell you no lies." Originality is not Binky's long suit.

"Okay, I'll not ask, but if you take Connie to the Pelican

tonight the odds on the defender will drop radically. Hedge your bet, Binky."

He looked skeptical, which didn't tell me much, as this is Binky's natural demeanor. "What are you planning, Archy?"

"If I told you it wouldn't be a surprise, would it? Now, call Connie and invite her to the Pelican tonight."

"I can't afford it," he objected. "Since I rented my own pad I have to watch my pennies."

Like Bambi, his movie star look-alike, Binky was orphaned at an early age and raised by an aunt, known locally as the Duchess. After Binky's long career as a trainee in multitudinous professions, the Duchess gave up hoping her ward would ever spread his wings and leave the nest. Then along came Archy and the offer of a steady position at McNally & Son. Here Binky was provided with a weekly stipend that enabled him to move into a box car on concrete blocks.

Was the Duchess sorry to see him go? Prostrate with grief, she paid all his moving expenses and wrote out a check for his one-month security fee as well as his first month's rent. She also gave him any pieces of furnishings she could spare and bought him the things she couldn't spare. I ask you, was the Duchess sorry to see him go?

"I'll pay for the dinner," I offered.

"You mean it?"

"Would I lie?"

"Yes," he said.

The boy was infuriating. "Do you want it in writing?"

"No. I'll trust you," he finally agreed.

"Do you know Connie's number at the Horowitz mansion?"

"I know it," Binky answered.

With raised eyebrows I said, "Really? Why do you know it, may I ask?"

After brushing back a drooping forelock, he informed me, "Because I call her several times a week, that's why."

"And what do you two talk about, may I ask?"

"You may ask, but I'm not telling. Now I have to get back to work. Don't you ever work, Archy?"

My parting words were, "Don't forget to call Connie. It's imperative. And whatever you do, don't tell her I instigated the invitation."

"Suppose she's washing her hair tonight?" he grumbled.

"Her hair, Binky, is squeaky clean, believe me."

Ye of little faith will think I had left a lot to chance in my ploy to get Connie into the Pelican this evening. Think again. My move was as calculated as the design for a labyrinth—and twice as shrewd. The moment I was out of the room Binky would be on the horn with Connie, telling her exactly what I had asked him not to tell her and repeating every word of our conversation with great relish and a good dash of embellishment.

I could just hear him bellow, "He made me promise not to tell, and he even said he would pay for our dinners."

Connie would come to the Pelican tonight in her bedroom slippers and her squeaky hair in rollers if need be. Why? Because neither rain nor snow, sleet nor hail, or a Sherman tank, can keep a curious woman from her appointed rounds.

• Mrs. Trelawney was chomping on her tether. "So there you are," she huffed and puffed as I stepped out of the elevator.

"In person, ma'am, and at your service."

She gave me the fish eye and declared, "You look like an asparagus spear that got away. How do you manage it, Archy?"

Never has my attire elicited so many barbs. This went a long way in boosting confidence in my ability to nettle those I love. Experience has taught me that the best way to deal with criticism is to first consider the source and, should the source prove reliable, ignore it. "You've been looking for me, Mrs. Trelawney?"

"Only because it's my duty. Where have you been? The first day in weeks that you arrive here on time, and what do you do? You run off even before you're out of your car."

I could see Herb had reported on my arrival and departure before I had cleared the exit ramp onto Royal Palm Way. I was sure Mrs. Trelawney was itching to know what was in the note Herb had been instructed to pass on to me. Turning the screw, I said, "I had an urgent call. And lest you forget I am not a pencil pusher like some I could name—I cover the town from lake to shiny sea."

Her gray wig appeared to unravel in places, shooting out here and there like corkscrews in search of a bottle of Chianti. She picked up a piece of paper upon which were her jottings in shorthand. Yes, Mrs. Trelawney still takes dictation and translates it on an IBM. One Christmas father gave her a quill pen and a brass inkwell. She was thrilled.

"An Officer O'Hara, from Juno Beach, called three times. She said it was urgent that you get in touch with her." Looking up, she lectured, "Why don't you get a cell phone?"

Listen to Grandma Moses telling others to join the electronic revolution. "I have been in touch with Officer O'Hara," I said, "and I don't have a cell phone because I prefer to stay out of touch, thank you."

Adjusting her glasses, she continued, "Your father has been asking for you."

"I am here to report to him," I told her.

"Well, you'll have to wait. He's with a client and can't be disturbed. Finally, you had a call from New York."

That was the only surprise in her tidings. I could not think of a soul in New York who would call me unless it was someone from Palm Beach off on a spree and in need of a bondsman. When she said the name "Tyler Beaumont" I thought I had heard wrong.

"Did you say Tyler Beaumont?"

"That's what I said. He's coming to Palm Beach, and he wants to set up an appointment to meet with you. Do you know him, Archy?"

"I don't know him, but I do know of him. Did he say why he wanted to see me?"

Mrs. Trelawney shook her head, causing more corkscrews to erupt from the synthetic gray mass atop her head. "No, he did not. He expects to be in Palm Beach tomorrow and will call again when he arrives."

When is a coincidence not a coincidence? When the Beaumont house gets a mention in the local press, and the family gets discussed at our breakfast table, and the scion of the clan returns to Palm Beach after an absence of some twenty years seeking the help of a discreet inquirer—is when a coincidence is not a coincidence. A voice from the grave and a light, real or imagined, in an abandoned mansion. It made me want to run to my bed and pull the covers over my head, but, alas, I had other fish to fry, as the saying goes. I have always prided myself with the capability to put off till tomorrow what I should do today. *Ciao,* Tyler Beaumont—for now.

Even father would have to wait for my briefing. I had

earned my salary for today, such as it is, and had much to do before picking up Georgy girl in the provinces.

Upon arriving home, I presented Ursi with ten mini-éclairs (two had disappeared en route) and told her to be sure to tell father they were made by the Fortesque pastry chef.

Once in my room, I got out of my dress greens and into a simple Speedo of white sateen with green (and why not?) braided piping. I wrapped myself in my hooded terry robe and dashed across the A1A, bringing traffic to a halt. The Florida sun was still warm, even at four in the afternoon, and the sea warmish. I swam my two miles, one north, then back from whence I came, with the sandy beach always a few dozen strokes from my person.

There has been much talk of sharks off our idyllic shore, but, touch wood, I have never met one either coming or going. Once, skinny-dipping with Connie, a crab did nip me in the most embarrassing place—let's say it put a damper on what would otherwise have been a romantic evening—but other than that unfortunate incident I usually emerge from the sea as unblemished as I enter it. I trust this has much to do with the little prayer I offer up to Poseidon before entering the water. I still worship the old gods, because if there is life after death there's no telling who awaits us on the other side of the River Styx.

I showered and washed my hair, blow-dried it with my Turbocharger 2000, then combed it with part on the left. The final touch was to brush it back on both sides of the part in the style of Ronnie Reagan before he left the Brothers Warner for Washington. A dab of my favorite cologne, whose name I will not divulge, on the nape of my neck, and a squirt on each wrist for luck, and I was ready to cover my briefs and T-shirt in—what?

I began with basic black. Black silk trousers and black tropical-weight wool turtleneck. Upon this palette, the jacket would have to carry the sartorial message, something classic but edgy. To this end silk blend glen plaid blazer, black on the barest of beiges, with a slight stubby nub to the fabric—and I was the new Bond. Who could resist? I'd soon find out.

Black captoe lace-ups buffed to a high gloss completed the ensemble, and I was ready for my night of nights. My mirror image said "quiet but elegant," and with that I went downstairs belting out an old Merman favorite—stopped dead in my tracks, hit my forehead with the heel of my hand and shouted, "Ethel Merman was born Ethel Zimmermann."

• It's the guest cottage of the big house you passed coming up the drive," Georgy said as she led me into her charming home.

Approaching it in the early-evening dusk, I thought I had come upon a gingerbread house in the woods and fully expected the Wicked Witch to lure me in. Instead, I was welcomed by a lovely green-eyed blonde who had gone out of her way to dress for a business meeting. She appeared in a straight skirt, just knee length, in crisp tan; a white blouse with a fetching print silk scarf knotted loosely at the neck; a tailored vest in the same color and fabric as the skirt; and black patent heels with squared-off toes.

If the outfit was intended to obscure her femininity it failed on every level, and the presence of an elegant tortoiseshell clip in her cascading golden locks told me she never had any intention of succeeding.

"Only the old lady is left in the manor house, as I call

it," she rambled on. "The children, grandchildren and even great-grandchildren are spread all over the country. When she put it up for rent a dozen people bid on it, but I got it because of my uniform. The poor thing sees a terrorist on every street corner and likes the idea of having a police presence in her backyard."

The front room was comfortably furnished in a fashion that put me in mind of an old Sears Wishbook—pure Americana, cozy and familiar. A galley kitchen and breakfast nook were part of the room, and, I assumed, the bedroom and bath were beyond a darkened doorway.

Having not been invited to sit, I stood and complimented, "It's very nice and unique. It's not easy to find a rental cottage in this neck of the woods."

"Are you in a condo?" she asked.

"I live at home," I confessed.

"You're kidding?"

"Would I kid about something like that? I'm the bat in the leaky belfry. No amenities, but then there's no rent, either, which covers a multitude of drawbacks."

"Lucky you. When my roommate left I practically had to give up eating until I got promoted. Hold on, let me get my purse."

As she went into the darkened doorway I called, "Where did she go?"

"Who?" she hollered.

"Your roommate."

She came back into the room with a black leather Coach bucket bag slung over her shoulder. "Who said my roommate was a she?"

"Ouch. That'll learn me."

"No, it won't," she responded as if she meant it. "Is the club air-conditioned?"

"Only in the winter. In the summer it rests."

She shrugged. "If I need a wrap, I'll borrow your jacket."

I took her by the elbow and forced her to look me in the eye before protesting, "That's the first plain, ordinary, familiar 'he and she' thing you said to me since I arrived. I feel like a salesman taking you out for a demo ride in a used Miata. And in case you haven't noticed, you didn't even invite me to sit."

"I did notice," she wailed. "Archy, this is very difficult for me. I didn't tell anyone that I was seeing you tonight. You are a suspect—yes, you are—and this is a business meeting."

"Did you justify our date by telling yourself you would grill me over the mixed grill?"

"Yes, I did," she blubbered.

"Why, you silly, adorable creature. May I kiss you?"

"If I scream, my landlady will call the FBI."

Well, at least the ice was broken.

Outside we were welcomed by a zillion stars, and somewhere over the vast sea a sliver of a moon would soon be rising. I opened the car door for my lady before slipping around to the driver's seat.

"Tight quarters," she noted, sniffing the air. "And nice cologne."

"My secret blend. Careful, it's aphrodisiacal."

"It's Boucheron," she declared.

13

My entrance into the Pelican Club with a beautiful blonde on my arm was like a strut down the catwalk at a Versace fashion show. If the number of diners and the crowd at the bar were any indication, Priscilla had certainly spread the word. No one was uncouth enough to actually stare, but there was an almost imperceptible pause in the hum of conversation as Georgy and I sauntered in. Several people waved, and I waved back. It was all very much as I had anticipated, and I couldn't have enjoyed it more.

"Well," Priscilla said, rushing up to us, "look what the cat dragged in."

"This is Ms. O'Hara," I said.

"Call me Georgy, please," Georgy said with a smile. "And you must be Priscilla. Archy prepped me on the ride here. He said you were lovely, and I second the motion."

Sizing up my date and returning the compliment, Priscilla cooed, "I love your hair."

"Thank you," I said. "I did it myself."

Priscilla glowered as she led us to my corner table. On the way we passed Connie and Binky, who were also seated in the bar area, and I paused long enough to say, "Fancy seeing you here."

"Fancy indeed," Connie responded, raising her glass. Good grief, it was a champagne glass. And there was a bottle of the bubbly cooling in a bucket of ice beside their table. I stumbled, righted myself and caught up with Georgy just in time to hold her chair.

"Can I get you a drink?" Priscilla asked, depositing two menus on our table.

I could certainly use one and hoped no one noticed. Champagne? Binky never drank anything but Simon Pettibone's drawn lager, and Connie usually had a vodka and tonic before a glass of wine with dinner. Suddenly, on my dime, they develop a taste for champagne. I would have Binky drawn and quartered in the morning. No, death was too good for Binky Watrous. Instead, when he presented me with the bill I would say, "Guess what, Binky? I LIED."

"Can Mr. Pettibone make a negroni?" Georgy wondered.

"Mr. Pettibone can make anything in the bartender's guide to genteel inebriation without so much as a glance at the recipe book." Turning to our waitperson, who was staring at Georgy, I proclaimed, "Two negronis, please."

Georgy looked surprised. "Do you like them, too?"

"Love them," I said, having no idea what a negroni was and thinking how much I admired her courage not to play it safe and go for something more popular. The more one got to know Georgy O'Hara, the more one found to admire.

"So this is the famous Pelican Club," she said, glancing

around the room. "I think I'm going to like it here. Everyone looks very much at home."

"Like I said, good food and grog in the company of friends."

"And who was the lovely Latina lady you stopped to chat with?"

She had a policeman's eye, all right. Or should that be a policewoman's eye? Georgy girl didn't miss a beat. I found myself telling her that Consuela Garcia was Lady Cynthia Horowitz's social secretary and that Binky Watrous was a fellow employee at McNally & Son. Halfway through the briefing I realized that I was telling her more about my private life than I had intended to reveal, but with Georgy it just seemed the natural thing to do. I had to keep reminding myself that this was a business meeting and I was here for show but not tell.

"Lady Cynthia," she gushed. "You do rub shoulders in this town. I once ticketed one of the Kennedy brats. Can't recall which one."

"Would you like me to introduce you to the pillars of our society?"

"No, they might topple in my presence. But I would like you to introduce me to the person who murdered Lawrence Swensen," she requested instead.

"Maybe you're talking to him," I reminded her.

She sighed and focused those green eyes on me with a frown that was more fetching than menacing, but then so was the music of the Sirens. Was the precious frown posed or natural? In appearance, she was every college boy's Homecoming Queen. In reality, she packed a rod and was licensed to kill.

"Archy," she was saying, "three people were in that motel room the night Swensen was drugged and strangled. You were one of them. We have no choice but to keep you in the loop. However, you may as well know that my boss is all for charging Harrigan."

"Your boss being the guy in the corner office?" I put in.

She reared her head and shot back, "Who said my boss was a guy?"

"Ouch, again. Or is that still? I keep shooting myself in the foot," I said by way of an apology for assuming the officer in charge of the state trooper barracks in Juno Beach was a man. "So your roommate was a he and your boss is a she."

She shook her head. "It just so happens my boss is a 'he,' and my ex-roommate is none of your business. And here come our drinks, and not a moment too soon."

Amen to that, baby.

The negronis came on the rocks and were garnished with a lemon twist. This being a business meeting, I raised my glass with a brief nod, said "Cheers," and imbibed. "Campari," I guessed, "and most certainly gin. Not bad." I took another sip. "In fact, I rather like it."

"Campari, gin and vermouth," Georgy said, "and you never had one in your life. Do you ever tell the truth, Archy?"

"Only when it can't hurt his image," Priscilla joined in.

"Do you know, Georgy," I said, "this is the only restaurant in the Western world where the waitperson doubles as a Greek chorus. I would invite you to sit, Miss Priss, but I know duty calls. Right?"

"Right now my duty is to tell you that tonight's special is tournedos of beef with mushrooms and red wine sauce—pricey, but worth it—and the special appetizer is mussels marinated in garlic and olive oil and served as a salad—also pricey. Everything else is on the menu." With that, Priscilla ran off to caution others on the exorbitant cost of the evening's specials.

"She is a vixen," I said.

"An adorable vixen," Georgy modified the noun. "And what a figure, as if you never noticed." Moving aside her menu, she announced, "I want all the pricey goodies, and I won't insult you by saying we'll go dutch, but next time it'll be on me."

The implication was that there would be a next time, which was fine with me. "That makes two for the mussels and tournedos. You won't be disappointed, Georgy girl, our Leroy is South Florida's best-kept culinary secret."

(A discreet glance told me Connie and Binky were also having the tournedos and, no doubt, had already sampled the mussels. My wallet was bleeding to death.)

Getting down to business, I asked, "So, tell me, why does the boss want to charge Harrigan?"

"He's Captain Delaney," she told me, "and right now Harrigan is all we have."

At this point she told me everything Harrigan had told the police, and it jived with what he told me. We also went over the story Claudia Lester was now touting, and, again, it agreed with what Lester had told me. It seemed the two con artists were not only consistent in their accounts of that evening, but also insistent that each was speaking the truth.

I had discussed many a case with Al Rogoff at this very table and, let me be the first to herald, I found Officer O'Hara every bit as professional, knowledgeable and involved in the business of crime and punishment as her masculine counterpart. Don't tell Al, but she's also prettier. Georgy O'Hara could hold her own with any tough guy while never letting you forget she was a beautiful woman.

When I next caught the eye of our Priscilla I ordered two more negronis and told her to bring on the specials *au deux,* both medium rare.

"You see," Georgy now said, "Harrigan admits going to the motel and giving Swensen a generous dose of Seconal to put him to sleep. Then he says he took the money and hightailed it back to the Ambassador, where our Ms. Lester awaited with the manuscript you had delivered. But, according to you, you didn't deliver anything. You were mugged and robbed of the manuscript. Don't let this go to your head, Archy, but the captain is more inclined to believe you than Harrigan."

"Smart man," I said, secretly relieved. "But why should he believe Lester over Harrigan?"

"Because her story agrees with yours. She says you didn't deliver the manuscript. If we agree that you're telling the truth, so is Lester."

Our drinks arrived, and a moment later we were given a basket of warm semolina bread, *pane di casa* and *ficeller,* wrapped in a white linen napkin, as well as a small dish of olive oil for dipping. Gone were the days of doughy supermarket mock-Italian bread and ice-cold butter, and I say, it was about time. I passed the bread before helping myself.

Munching, I told her, "It ain't kosher, Georgy girl." She gave me a puzzled look, and I corrected, "I don't mean the bread, which it probably isn't—I refer to your captain's reasoning. Claudia Lester is telling the truth about the manuscript because she has no choice. It would be my word against hers, and, based on my standing in this town, I would win, a fact poor Harrigan is about to learn. I didn't deliver the manuscript to her, and she says Harrigan ran off with it and the money.

"But did he? And is she telling the truth when she says

there was no conspiracy among these three miscreants to pull a sting on Swensen?"

"The conspiracy is Harrigan's story," Georgy said.

"Correct. So who do we believe? I say Harrigan."

Dipping a crust of bread in the warm seasoned oil, Georgy quickly and correctly reasoned, "Because if he took the money and the manuscript, he would be long gone from our lovely resort and not pushing a cart around the Publix, chatting with Archy McNally."

"There's hope for you, Georgy girl. Also, he had no reason to kill Swensen after he drugged him. And how that bothers me. Drugged and murdered. Why? Nor do I see Harrigan as a killer. If Delaney charges him, he's going to have one hell of a time to convince the prosecution that they have a case. Contrary to common folklore, killers do not return to the scene of the crime."

Looking a bit contemplative, she answered, "I agree. Harrigan's not a killer. Just a bum. He reminds me of someone I used to know."

Taking a chance, I ventured, "The roommate who left you in the lurch with the rent due?"

"You never let go, do you?" she said. "You're like a hound with a bone." When I didn't answer she seemed to give the matter some thought and, with a shrug, opened the door a little further into her private life. "I met him at school in Little Rock."

"Arkansas?" I blurted.

With a sly grin she answered, "Would I kid about something like that? I'm just a little girl from Little Rock. My father was a police officer, a sheriff actually, and I studied criminal justice at college."

"That's right," I remembered. "He wanted a boy, so you did your best to oblige him."

"Sorry, doctor, but he got his boy two years later and called him Sean. I went into criminal law because it was what I wanted and not to please anyone."

"And did Sean become a policeman, too?"

"No," she said, "Sean is a ballet dancer." When I looked rather startled she began to laugh, eyes twinkling and finger pointing. "How I love to tease you, Archy. Actually, he's a lawyer. A defense lawyer, would you believe? Dad arrests them and Sean sets 'em free. We are a close but dysfunctional family."

Her laughter, rather loud I must say, had drawn the attention of several neighboring diners, including Connie and Binky, who seemed to be sharing a joke of their own. Most likely they were adding up their dinner tab. What were they planning for dessert? Baked Alaska flown in from its place of origin?

Georgy's story was about as original as one of Binky's romance novels. She met *him* at school, her first time away from home and on her own. He was tall, blond, handsome and majoring in English lit. He wrote romantic verse, and Georgy immediately applied for the position of Beatrice to his Dante. He seduced her on the third canto, and they moved off campus into a love nest built for two.

After graduation, and much against her parents' wishes, she followed him to Florida, where he had gotten work as a rookie reporter for one of the local newspapers. She joined the force and rose in the ranks. "Actually, I was in the right profession at the right time. The police, the fire department, all those macho trades were falling over themselves recruiting women. You might say I was the beneficiary of reverse discrimination."

Georgy girl was honest to a fault, I'll say that for her. And, I now learned, I was feasting with a lieutenant. Her paramour did not fare as well. The paper folded and, it being a slack season for poets, he went to work as a caddie for one of our many prestigious golf clubs. Being a tall, blond, handsome lad who knew his way around an iambic pentameter, the athletic ladies apparently found him too tasty a dish to pass up.

When a rich divorcée made him an offer he couldn't refuse, he left his Georgy and became a kept man. "A role," Georgy concluded, "he was born to play. In almost five years he never once took out the garbage. Don't ever fall for a gorgeous hunk, Archy."

The arrival of our mussels saved me from promising to heed her warning, but it did not stop me from saying, "If you've given up gorgeous hunks, that puts me out of the running."

She thought that over, picked up her fork and answered, "This looks delicious."

The succulent mollusks had been tossed with a mixture of white wine, lemon juice, shallots, diced artichoke hearts and a blend of herbs and spices before being blended with the garlic and oil marinade. And a splendid marriage it made.

After a forkful my guest said, "So good you could eat the plate."

So good, in fact, it kept us quiet for several minutes, which gave me time to once again observe Connie and Binky. If Connie was upset over my date with Georgy O'Hara, she was certainly keeping it to herself. On several occasions, when caught with a lovely lady on my arm when I was supposed to be at home or out with the boys, Connie had made a scene that would put Emily Post into permanent cardiac arrest.

Tonight, here I was at the Pelican Club, dining openly

with a beautiful woman as Connie sipped champagne and pretended not to notice. But then, hadn't I done just that the night she was here with Alejandro?

I began to wax sentimental with thoughts like, *Is tonight the New Year's Eve of my life as a footloose and fancy-free bachelor?* The end of an era? Goodbye to the old and in with the new? But what would the new bring? I came here tonight determined to make Connie jealous, but the more I got to know Georgia O'Hara the more I sympathized with Connie's intrigue with Alejandro Gomez y Zapata.

Like the plot of a morality play, a stranger had entered both our lives and nothing would ever be the same again. A few days ago it was get married or get lost, but now there were alternatives never dreamed of. Our game might yet end in a draw, with the children, weary but wiser, picking up their marbles and heading home.

"Why didn't you graduate from Yale?" I heard Georgy ask.

"How do you know I didn't?" I replied, not liking where this was leading.

"The bachelor book," she said. " 'Archibald "Archy" McNally attended Yale.' If you had graduated it would have said so. It's like those debutante bios, 'Sara Rich attended Miss Porter's school.' That could mean she sat in on a lecture in deportment one rainy afternoon as an invited guest."

"I got the boot," I confessed.

"Really, why?"

"I have about a dozen set responses to that query. Which one do you want?"

"The true one, of course. I'm a cop."

"None of them are true, Georgy girl."

She put down her fork and touched her lips with her

napkin. "That bad, eh? They say confession is good for the soul."

"I've promised myself that I would reveal all to my bride on our wedding night."

There was that blush again. Georgy O'Hara had one of those rare, and rather lovely, complexions that registered her thoughts like a flashing color chart. And, unless I was reading it wrong, weddings were on the lady's mind. Didn't anyone want to just fool around anymore?

As our plates were removed, I steered the conversation away from binding commitments and toward the more cheerful subject of murder most foul. "You know, officer, there's another party yet to be heard from—namely, the auction house rep, Rodney Whitehead. He refused to state his business with Swensen when you first met him, but now he'll have to fess up. It'll be interesting to see whose side he's on, Lester's or Harrigan's."

"We were unable to get him at his motel today, but if we don't get him tomorrow, we'll send someone to pick him up—and his story is going to sound more like Lester's than Harrigan's," she said. "I mean, the guy is in deep enough without admitting to conspiring to pull a sting on Swensen when we already know he double-crossed his employer."

I was thinking about that door again and verbalized, "He says that door was open, but it was locked when I tried it at ten or a few minutes past. He called your people at a quarter after ten. So who was there between ten and ten-fifteen?"

She shrugged off the question and asked one of her own. "Do you think that manuscript is really Capote's lost novel?"

Priscilla, followed by Leroy, was coming our way with the pricey entrées. I called recess.

Tournedos are more commonly known in our republic as *filet mignons*. The steaks are cut about one inch thick and are three or four inches in diameter. They are wrapped with a strip of bacon and sautéed in a mixture of butter and oil. When done as requested they are removed from the pan—the butter and oil drained—and into the pan go the mushrooms and red wine. As the mushrooms cook they absorb the flavorful cooking juices, binding with the wine to create a rich sauce that is finally poured over the tournedos. The result is to die for.

Leroy's side dishes, served in those charmingly named monkey dishes, were a savory pine-nut studded pilaf and a quick sautée of zucchini and tomato. I ordered a Bordeaux to complement the meal.

Savoring the tender beef, Georgy commented, "Do you eat like this every night?"

"Only when I'm being force-fed."

We honored the repast by limiting conversation to what I believe is called polite chitchat. With coffee we were presented with the pastry tray and agreed to share a napoleon. This brought to mind Sam Zimmermann and his employer. I asked Georgy if she had contacted Fortesque.

"I saw him today," she told me. "He's the catalyst of this mess, but he doesn't have a clue as to who's doing what to whom—or pretends he doesn't. He told me he had hired Archy McNally to find his lost manuscript. I told him a man was dead because of that manuscript and who actually owned the damn thing was open to debate." Recalling her meeting with Fortesque, she added with an impish grin, "He looks likes Mischa Auer."

I almost choked on my half of the napoleon. "You know Mischa Auer?" I gasped.

"Of course," she said. "He was the first to die in *And*

Then There Were None. It's the film version of Agatha Christie's *Ten Little Indians.*"

This was unbelievable. "But that film is over sixty years old."

"Most of the films I rent are over sixty years old." She spoke as if she was proud of the fact.

"Have you ever rented *What Price Hollywood*?"

"Rent it?" she cried. "I own a copy on tape and DVD."

"Would you marry me?" I begged.

"Only if you tell me why you got the boot at Yale."

We lingered over our coffee, chatting celluloid trivia like magpies, and when next I looked Connie and Binky were gone. Funny, I never noticed them leaving.

For the hopelessly romantic and the romantically curious I offer the following epilogue to my evening with Georgy O'Hara:

The red Miata makes its way up the long, winding drive, passing the manor house, where an old woman peers out from behind a beaded curtain, and comes to a stop before the gingerbread cottage.

He: "If you invite me in, I promise to behave."

She: "If you behave, what's the point of inviting you in? Good night, Archy. Thank you for a lovely evening."

The red Miata makes its way down the long, winding drive, passing the manor house, where an old woman peers out from behind a beaded curtain, and heads south.

Old Chinese proverb: *When one door closes, another soon opens.* ("But it's hell in the hallway.")

* * *

• The next morning dawned partly sunny, but dawn means nothing when you're sleeping in. I arrived downstairs just in time for either an early brunch or a late breakfast, depending on your perspective.

Father had left for the office, and mother, with Jamie at the wheel, was off in search of the perfect begonia, a seemingly endless quest. Pouring myself a glass of orange juice, I requested scrambled eggs, bacon and white toast.

"Boring," was Ursi's summation of my order.

"I know, Ursi, but I'm compensating for last night's dinner. It had a caloric content that read like a telephone number. Don't butter the toast and get that crock of marmalade out of my line of vision."

"Boring," Ursi repeated.

She was usually as chatty as her husband was taciturn, but not this morning. As she poured my coffee, I asked, "How were the éclairs?" and almost got the scalding brew in my lap.

"Had better," she snapped.

And there it was. Ursi was in a snit and it was all Archy's fault. Without thinking, I had brought her someone else's homemade pastries, which she had undoubtedly served for dessert last night to rave reviews from the mater and pater. Also, and undoubtedly, she had tasted a few of the minis and found them to be superb. Were they inferior she would be all smiles, compliments of Sam Zimmermann.

Unable to resist, I said, "He also sings."

"Who?" Ursi cried, attacking my eggs mercilessly with a wire whisk.

"The man who made the éclairs," I informed her.

"Then maybe he should go on the radio." With that, my eggs were dumped, unlovingly, into the frying pan.

I thought it best to keep my mouth shut until the preparation of my simple fare was history, at which time I would treat Ursi to a juicy bit of gossip to compensate for my faux pas and get back into her good graces before she ruined tonight's dinner.

After serving me, she filled a cup with java and took a seat at the table. Now was the time to make reparation for Sam's prizewinning minis. "Do you recall, Ursi," I began, "that we were discussing the Beaumont family at breakfast just the other day?"

"I'm not so old that I would forget," she countered. "It was three days ago. Mr. McNally complained because you were late coming down, like you were late again today."

Nothing like asking a simple question and getting one's life history in return. My, my, but those éclairs must have been purely ambrosial. "Well," I persevered, knowing I would win her over, "the Beaumont boy is coming to Palm Beach and he wants to see me."

Her eyes lit up like two distress flares in the night sky. "Which twin?" she exclaimed.

"I hope not the dead one," I answered. So much for her nimble mind. "Tyler Beaumont, I believe he's called."

She pushed aside her coffee mug, which I'm sure was poured just so she could sit opposite me and pout, and leaned forward. This was serious business, and make no mistake about that. "When's he coming? Where's he staying? Is he opening the house? Why does he want to see you?"

Before I could answer even one of her queries, she was on her feet. "You'll choke to death on that dry toast. Let me get you some butter. And spread on a dab of marmalade, it'll stick to your ribs. So, what's the poop, Archy?"

Ursi would pass the word of the Beaumont boy's arrival to every housekeeper along Ocean Boulevard, and even to a few less fortunate souls deprived of beachfront property and condemned to life in multimillion-dollar landlocked hovels. They would tell their respective madams. The madams would tell their hairdressers and their manicurists, who would tell all their clients who hadn't already got the news. By evening, Palm Beach would be alive with rumors and unfounded speculation regarding young Tyler Beaumont.

Finally, Lolly Spindrift, our resident gossip whose column "Hither and Yon" daily dishes the dirt to his horde of avid readers, would call me for an exclusive and, incidentally, fill me in with any tidbits he might know that I didn't.

This ploy of using Ursi to play the electronic Paul Revere was certainly not a new one. I had used it before to raise some dust and see where, or on whom, it would settle. If you can't afford legmen, you improvise. Having sowed the seed and imparted to Ursi what little I knew, I called Mrs. Trelawney to say that should Tyler Beaumont call, have him come to the office at two and, if possible, reserve the conference room for the meeting.

As I expected, she said, "Your father has been asking for you."

"I will try to get back to the office in time to see him before my meeting with the Beaumont boy." Making it sound urgent, I went on, "I'm on my way to the Lake Worth library to research certain facts pertaining to the Fortesque case. Father will understand."

My decision to visit the library was not a fool's errand

concocted to placate father. Since my initial meeting with Fortesque I had wanted to take a look at *Answered Prayers* to see if it could help me separate fact from fancy in his account of the sudden discovery of a heretofore unpublished version of the book. But as so often happens at the start of a case, I had been too preoccupied with gathering the facts and interviewing our cast of characters to indulge the whim. Not to mention my own brush with the law and where that led.

After the new assignment's heady rush comes the pause, similar to the eye of a storm where you sit, becalmed, watching pieces of the jigsaw puzzle whirl around your weary brain. My job for Fortesque was to find the elusive manuscript for which he had paid a goodly sum. The man who supposedly owned it is dead, the broker who was negotiating the deal says her partner ran off with it, and the partner says he's being framed. So where do I go from here? The library seemed as good a place as any.

The Lake Worth Public Library is the pride of the community, and for good reason. Located in the historic district of Lake Worth, North M Street, between the town's main thoroughfares, Lake Avenue and Lucerne Avenue, the library is housed in a building of Mediterranean design. It boasts a barrel-tile roof and is one of the few buildings in the area with a full basement.

Its history is as unique as its impressive facade. Some ninety years ago, the ladies of the new community saw the need for a public school and a library. Seeking book donations, they stacked a room donated by the town with the acquired tomes and had themselves a library a few years before the first school was built and some two years before electricity came to town.

A decade later, the town board voted to establish a library under Florida statutes and the Lake Worth Public Library was born and housed in City Hall. Of historic interest, the library was to be named after General William Jenkins Worth, who has been credited with ending the Seminole Wars in Florida. Congress passed a law to fund money for the new library building, but President Roosevelt vetoed the bill.

Undaunted, the good citizens of Lake Worth raised the money, without taxing the overburdened citizenry, to erect the current building, which was dedicated four months before Pearl Harbor. A generous benefactor added a wing to house the Art League. When the League moved to larger quarters, the wing became what is now the children's library. Rare for public libraries, it owns the only known collection of historic paintings by the noted artist R. Sherman Winton, whose works include themes of Florida's Spanish era depicting DeSoto, Ponce de Léon and Osceola.

A vital part of the community, the library offers public access to computers as well as a dynamic outreach program to the area's schools.

Stopping at the front desk, I told the young lady on duty that I was looking for *Answered Prayers.*

"Aren't we all," she replied. "But try the fiction section."

The fiction section is most impressive, owing to the huge Winton mural portraying the Spanish Armada that dominates the space.

Shelved alphabetically by author, I found what I had come for under the C's and took it to a comfortable reading area. The first thing I learned was that the title came from a quote by Saint Theresa, *"More tears are shed over answered prayers than unanswered ones."* The novel is prefaced with a detailed editor's note, from which came Fortesque's account of the novel's history—as far as it went.

Capote got a hefty advance for the book he said would recount in detail the fortunes and foibles of the rich and famous on both sides of the Atlantic. Hence Fortesque's interest in the work. Some four years later, Capote had completed four chapters of the book and announced that he would publish them in *Esquire.* As noted, he did publish the first chapter in the popular magazine. It caused some talk, but little else. But when he published the second chapter, "La Côte Basque," he was immediately shunned by the beautiful people he so viciously exposed, the very same people who had taken the author into their homes and their confidences.

Mortally wounded, Capote published two more chapters before stopping work on the book. The editor mentions Capote's house in Sagaponack (there is no mention of a houseboy), and he also states that Capote did write, some years later, *"I returned to* Answered Prayers," as Fortesque had asserted and upon which was based the collector's belief that the author had indeed completed the work. We are told that a very exhaustive search was made of Capote's papers after his death and not so much as a line was found to show that he had done so.

Then, the editor writes, *"There are three theories about the missing chapters. . . . The first is that the manuscript was completed and is either stashed in a safe-deposit box somewhere, was seized by an ex-lover for malice or for profit, or even . . . Truman kept it in a locker in the Los Angeles Greyhound Bus Depot."*

The ex-lover theory is the crux of my case and the basis of Swensen's claim, which sent Whitehead scurrying off to Key West and Claudia Lester scurrying off to Decimus Fortesque. Swensen had fulfilled the equivalent of a biblical prophecy and the believers had beaten a path to his door. Now the prophet was dead, the sacred scrolls missing and Bob's your uncle.

Having rinsed out enough of the rich folk's dirty laundry to satisfy the appetite of a Decimus Fortesque, I did not check out *Answered Prayers.* Bidding the Spanish Armada and the lovely lady at the front desk a good afternoon, I exited into the partly sunny day in search of a lunch counter and a much-needed digestive English Oval.

The man standing in front of my Miata said, "Mr. McNally?"

When approached by a stranger who calls me by name, my first thought is that I am going to be presented with a subpoena. "I could be," I parried, "it depends on who's asking."

"I'm Rodney Whitehead."

It wasn't a voice from the grave, but from the looks of the guy it wasn't far from it either. Rodney Whitehead had the countenance of an unhappy tourist in our sun-drenched (well, not today) paradise. Rimless specs dominated a face one could call pudgy, if one wanted to be kind, atop a body to match, and what was left of his hair was gray. He wore a dark business suit and a woeful grimace. Sad Sack would say it all in two words. Rodney Whitehead resembled a guy who would stake his job and reputation for one final chance at the brass ring—which he had done, and lost.

When people turn up in my back pocket I like to know how they got there without my noticing. Instead of a how-do-you-do, I asked, not too politely, "How did you know where to find me?"

"I called your office," he said. "Your secretary told me you were working at the Lake Worth library and would be in when you had finished. I took the liberty of coming here, saw your car and decided to wait."

"You know my car, Mr. Whitehead?"

"The night of the murder," he explained, "I was there when the witness told the police he had seen a red Miata enter and leave the Crescent. Knowing that Claudia had hired you to make the exchange, I figured it was your car—and apparently I was right."

"And what can I do for you, Mr. Whitehead?"

"I'd like a word with you," he said.

"I believe the police would like a word with you," I informed him.

"I know. I have an appointment to see them this afternoon at three." He consulted his wristwatch as if time were of the essence. "I have two hours. Perhaps you can spare me one of them."

"What do you want to tell me, Mr. Whitehead?"

He bowed his head to look at me over the rimless specs and uttered, "The truth, of course."

"The police take a dim view of me working their side of the street, Mr. Whitehead."

Going on the offensive, he argued, "You've heard what Claudia and Harrigan had to say. I think it only fair that you hear my side of this charade."

"You've talked to Claudia Lester and Matthew Harrigan?" I asked him.

"To Claudia only. She had a call from Harrigan, who, she says, refuses to see her. Naturally, I don't believe her."

Not believing Claudia Lester seemed to be an accepted fact by those who knew her. "Why tell me and not the police?"

"Oh, I'll tell the police, too. I have nothing to hide. I might have acted a little unethical, but that's not their concern. I came to you because you're working for Decimus Fortesque and I want to clear my name with him and be what help I can in getting him the merchandise he paid for at the price agreed upon."

"You know where the manuscript is, Mr. Whitehead?"

"I can lead you to the church, Mr. McNally, but not the pew."

I didn't need a partner, especially one I wouldn't trust out of my sight, but in the lull of a case you go with the flow, and right now the tide had dragged in Rodney Whitehead. Besides, a church might be just the place to find answered prayers.

I agreed to sit down with Whitehead and invited him to join me for a sandwich. It's a short stroll from the library to the Gourmet Deli House on Lake Worth Road, a favorite of mine for a quick lunch that did not smack of fast food. One comes to the Gourmet Deli House for two reasons: lox and bagels and pastrami on rye. The pastrami sandwich is enough for two, and after my late breakfast all I could sensibly handle was half. Whitehead said he would take the other half off my hands, so we sat down to share in more ways than one. Mustard, a fat dill, quartered, and two Dr. Brown's Cel-Ray tonics accompanied the main course.

After a bite of the sandwich Whitehead asked, "What did they tell you?" He wiped a dab of mustard from the corner of his mouth.

"I'm not saying. It was you who wanted to talk."

He didn't look happy, but I doubt if he knew how. Resigned, he told his story. Act One didn't vary one iota from the version given me by Lester and Harrigan. Lawrence Swensen called the auction house in New York and told them what he had. They sent their man, Rodney Whitehead, to Key West to investigate the claim.

"Was it the completed Capote manuscript?" I asked him.

"It was. Believe me, Mr. McNally, it was. And Tru

didn't miss a beat, from who murdered Marilyn Monroe to Cary Grant's long affair with Randolph Scott, and even who shot the producer Thomas Ince aboard the Hearst yacht back in the roaring twenties. Oh, yes, it was all there."

Without apology, Whitehead told me how he had seen a chance to make himself a quick profit by bypassing the auction house and brokering the manuscript himself. "I'm tired of making other people rich with the books and papers thoughtful relatives leave in the attic for their heirs to cash in on," he told me with disdain. "I want out of the rat race, and after a too-short vacation in Costa Rica I learned how one could live like a prince for a long time in that country on the annual income of most Americans. The Capote manuscript was the answer to my prayers, Mr. McNally—pun intended."

He knew Claudia Lester, as do most who make their living in the world of valuable collectibles, and told her what he had. She contacted Decimus Fortesque on the advice of her friend and neighbor, Vera Fortesque. Here, as with Lester and Harrigan, the story leaves the familiar and becomes singular to the teller.

According to Whitehead, he talked Swensen into a private deal, dangling Fortesque's name, and arranged for Swensen to come north with the manuscript and check into the Crescent Motel. He told Swensen to park in the visitors' area to facilitate parking for the people who would be calling on him—namely, the person delivering the money and picking up the manuscript and, second, Whitehead, who would call after the exchange to collect his share of the cash.

I didn't believe him. I was surer than ever that Swensen was told not to park in the space provided for tenants in order to keep the visitors from being seen driving the length of the courtyard to the guest area. Harrigan had taken Swensen's space, leaving me a sitting duck for anyone looking out their window. Fact: I was set up. As for who did the setting up, I had no idea—yet.

We had finished eating. Filling my glass with what was left of my soda, I took out my English Ovals and offered one to Whitehead. He refused, but that didn't stop me from lighting up. Oh, what bliss.

I held up a hand to stop Whitehead and asked, "What was your share?"

"Half," he said, "not that it's any of your business."

"Rather steep, don't you think?"

"No, I don't," he shot back. "It was my find. My chance to score. Swensen was a pothead, a wino, and a junkie. That's why he needed cash quick. He was up to his chin in debt with his suppliers. Whatever he got would have gone to them sooner or later. The way I see it, I was doing the guy a favor."

I guess one could rationalize anything if one tried hard enough. It seemed Rodney Whitehead didn't have to try at all.

"Second. Why didn't you deliver the cash and take the manuscript?"

That got me a sardonic laugh from the old manuscript expert. "In the world of collecting, Mr. McNally, you are a babe in the woods. Claudia Lester would not trust me to get my hands on the money and the manuscript at the same time, and rightly so. Had she, I would be in Costa Rica right now sipping a piña colada with the girl who makes my bed—pun intended. Get it?"

I got it, all right. "You needed a third party, with no interest in the deal, to make the transaction so neither you nor Lester was ever in possession of the cash and the manuscript at the same time. Are you saying that's why I was hired?"

"Of course," he said as if he were talking to an idiot.

I was getting to like Rodney Whitehead less and less. "Claudia Lester said I was hired at your suggestion because you thought Swensen might want to play rough."

Whitehead rolled his eyes in disgust. "Those bastards conspired to deal me out and walk off with the candy store. I got to the motel and found Swensen dead, which makes me a suspect. Claudia is saying Harrigan went to the motel, did in Swensen, made the exchange with you and then beat it with the money and the manuscript he took back from you in the parking lot."

"And Harrigan," I quickly rebutted, "is saying Lester crossed him and has the candy store, as you call it. That's why Harrigan is here and not in Costa Rica."

"Don't you see?" he cried. "It's a sham. They're shouting at each other while pointing the finger at me. Claudia will keep the money and try to sell the manuscript again. Knowing her, she already has a customer or will try to wheedle more out of Fortesque."

"Do you know anything about a sting operation, Mr. Whitehead?" I questioned.

"A what?"

"A Grand Sting Operation, as Harrigan labeled it. The three of you plotted to drug Swensen, take the manuscript, keep the money for yourselves and give Fortesque what he paid for."

Whitehead's face was flushed with anger. "That is the most ridiculous thing I ever heard. Why would I go for a three-way split when I had already negotiated for half?"

That had crossed my mind. "When you got to the motel you found the door to Swensen's room off the lock?"

"Yes. How else would I have gotten in?"

How else, indeed.

"Tell Mr. Fortesque," he pleaded, "they have his money and the manuscript. I'm out of a job, and given the facts there isn't an auction house in the country that will take me on. If I go into business for myself I will need customers like Fortesque, and I want him to know I play fair.

"Now I have to tell the police my story and hope they will believe me. Why would I kill a man who was drugged and had nothing to steal but the clothes on his back—and then notify the cops?"

Why, indeed.

15

• My lunch with Rodney Whitehead was not unproductive. After listening to what he had to say I was certain of one thing: either everyone was lying or no one was telling the truth.

Rub-a-dub-dub, two guys and a gal in a tub—each trying to drown the other in the dirty bathwater. To be sure, only Rodney was crying conspiracy, accusing Lester and Harrigan of stinging him, while the other two were stabbing each other in the back. But, as Whitehead had noted, it was he who was set up to discover the body and get himself listed as a suspect. But then, so is Harrigan a suspect, as is the bag man, Archy.

It would seem logical that it would take two of them to pull off the caper and walk away with the whole enchilada. However, in spite of the safeguards instituted by the partners in crime, it was only Harrigan who had his hands on the money and the manuscript at the same time. Yes, it was a short time, but when the manuscript left the room he had only to follow it out and get it back—which he, or somebody, did. This results in the same weary question: if Harrigan had it all, why did he return to Palm Beach?

Nor did I miss the more salacious tidbits Whitehead quoted from the Capote book to verify his find. He must have passed most of them on to Claudia Lester, and she, in turn, used them to bait poor Decimus Fortesque. After Lester's sales pitch poor Deci must have had his tongue, as well as his checkbook, hanging out.

As I drove to Royal Palm Way I put together what few pieces of the puzzle I could call fact. There was no question that the events leading up to Whitehead's discovery of the manuscript and Claudia's striking a deal with Fortesque as narrated by the trio was true. Because Lawrence Swensen had rented the room at the Crescent Motel, where he met the grim reaper, I would say that Whitehead had told Swensen to book in there with the manuscript and wait there that night for the arrival of the money. Swensen may have been a junkie, but he was not about to let the manuscript out of his hands before he had his mitts on the cash. So, that rainy night, the doomed man sat in unit number nine with a bottle of hooch, rolling funny cigarettes and dreaming of solvency. Then he went where no bill collector would care to follow. Swensen was drugged, then murdered.

I got to the motel about nine, made the exchange with Harrigan and saw no sign of anyone else in the room. I left ten or fifteen minutes after nine with the manuscript, was mugged in the parking lot, and when I awoke, about ten, I went back to the room and tried the door. It was locked. Some fifteen minutes later, Whitehead arrives on the scene and says he found the door open. The latter, by the by, is not a fact.

Swensen's car was in the visitors' parking area and Harrigan's car was in Swensen's space when I arrived, and gone when I returned.

As good old Al Rogoff would say, *"And them is the facts."*

Lester says I was hired at Whitehead's suggestion, in case Swensen proved difficult. Whitehead says I was hired to keep all parties from never being in possession of the book and the money at the same time. Harrigan says I was hired so I could tell Fortesque the exchange was made should the duped Swensen run to Fortesque or the police crying foul when he woke up with nothing to show for his trip north but a hangover.

I say Harrigan comes closest to the truth. As I had long believed, I was hired to bear witness that the exchange was made as agreed by all parties concerned. Why? Because someone knew that once I had done my job, everything would go haywire and everyone could claim their innocence.

Harrigan admits to drugging Swensen as part of the sting operation. But why murder him, too?

If Harrigan's G.S.O. story is true, there would be no reason for Whitehead to go to the motel after the exchange, as they now had the book and the money—nor would Whitehead agree to a three-way split when he was going to get fifty percent from Swensen. So it isn't true.

If Claudia Lester's story is true, Harrigan would have kept running with the book and the money. So it isn't true.

If Whitehead's story is true, that Lester and Harrigan have the book and the money, we are back to square one. Harrigan would have disappeared with the cache, rendezvoused with Lester when things cooled off, and tried to sell the book to another buyer or bilk more out of Fortesque. So it isn't true.

Fact. Everyone is lying and no one is telling the truth.

I arrived at the McNally Building just in time to put the pieces back in the box upon which a picture of the completed jigsaw puzzle did not appear.

• Tyler Beaumont was standing at the window, looking down on Royal Palm Way. When he heard the door open he turned to face me.

"I hope I haven't kept you waiting too long, Mr. Beaumont, but I was unavoidably delayed."

"Not at all," he said with a congenial smile. "I'm grateful that you were able to see me on such short notice."

We both maneuvered our way around the long table that separated us and shook hands when we met. "If you haven't had lunch, I could send out for something," I offered.

"Thank you, no. I'm at the Colony and had a bite there before coming here. I also had tea with your father when I arrived. He remembered doing some work for my father when I was a wee boy. How kind of him to remember us."

I almost said father does not forget millionaires but invited Tyler Beaumont to sit instead. He was a handsome young man in his early twenties with brown eyes and reddish-blond hair that appeared to fall haphazardly across his forehead, but, as life among the very rich taught me, it had been expensively cut to do just that. By dint of either nature or his trust fund, his smile displayed a row of perfect white teeth. He wore jeans, a nondescript white shirt with open collar and a gray linen jacket. In short, he looked like a native, but I'm sure Tyler Beaumont would look like one of the regulars in any of the rich watering holes here and abroad. It's what he was brought up to do.

As we settled in, I couldn't help but remember that just three days ago I had confronted Claudia Lester as I now sat vis-à-vis with Tyler Beaumont. That earlier meeting had kicked off a case I had dubbed, as you know, "A Voice from the Grave." After hearing what the Beaumont boy had to say, I would find that title spine-tinglingly suitable for this new assignment.

"It's been some time since your family has been here," I said when we were seated. "Forgive the gossipy prattle, but after all, this is Palm Beach." His smile told me that I was on safe ground. "I know the house is closed, but do any of you visit the area and stay elsewhere?"

He shook his head. "We left twenty years ago, when I was four, and never returned. We still have the house on Gin Lane in Southampton, which is only slightly less antediluvian than the one in Bar Harbor. The locals call it Disneyland, because it really does look like the dreadful castle you see on the TV adverts. Twenty-six bedrooms and ocean view, in case you're interested in renting."

I imagine the spiel was supposed to be humorous, but it somehow came off as an apology on behalf of the landed gentry, who must be forgiven because they were born that way. Sad to say, but I got the impression that Tyler Beaumont didn't know how to laugh. Even that congenial smile lacked warmth. He was not condescending. Far from it, in fact. He was polite to a fault and—I searched for the word and finally found it—preoccupied. Tyler Beaumont was preoccupied. His expressive eyes seemed to look right through me, but what they saw I hadn't a clue.

"We are not known for quaint Cape Cods and raised

ranches in Palm Beach," I said. "Are you planning on opening your house here?"

This got a reaction that was more engaging than blasé. He actually started. "How do you know I'm here because of the house?" he asked as if my ESP was showing. Was this guy weird or had that celery soda gotten to my noggin?

"Well, Mr. Beaumont," I told him, "there was a story about your family house in our local press just the other day, and almost immediately you blow into town wanting the help of a discreet inquirer. Being distrustful of coincidences, you could say I took an educated guess."

He looked either hurt or disappointed. "You think I'm strange?"

Now he was a little boy who didn't know why he was being punished—and I was losing patience. "What I think is strange is that you flew all the way down here from New York, made an appointment to see me, and now that we're both in the same room at the same time you want to play word games. What do you want from me, Mr. Beaumont?"

Without missing a beat he answered, "For one thing, I would like you to stop calling me Mr. Beaumont. My name is Tyler. Friends call me Ty."

"Okay, Ty. Now what do you want?"

He leaned forward in his chair and began to speak, carefully articulating every word, like one who had rehearsed for a long time and was now ready for his audience. "I had a twin brother," he said.

Seeing no reason to feign surprise, I responded with a nod.

"What do you know about him?" he asked.

Now, that was weird. This attractive, personable young man seemed to vacillate between the sublime and the ridiculous, with no stops between. "I know that he's dead. An accident, I believe, and soon after your parents closed the house and left Palm Beach."

"He fell down the marble staircase that led from the entrance hall to the second floor," Tyler said.

This, I recalled, was our Jamie's version of the accident.

"My mother loved that staircase," he went on in a sort of reverie, as if he were describing something to a blind man. "She used it to make her grand entrances at the balls she and father were forever giving. Maddy, that's my brother, Madison Jr., and I used to sneak out of the nursery and watch from upstairs till nurse found us and ordered us back to bed. Father said mother missed her calling and should have joined the follies. I think he meant the ones orchestrated by Mr. Ziegfeld."

Then, quite suddenly, he picked up speed and the reverie became a nightmare. "Maddy tripped and fell down the marble steps. He tumbled over. His head bounced off each step till it split open and you could see the blood everyplace. . . ."

He was near hyperventilating, and I reached out a hand to stop him. "Tyler, I get the picture. There's no need to go on." I poured out a glass of ice water from the carafe Mrs. Trelawney had thoughtfully placed on a tray beside two glasses. "Would you like some water?" He waved me off, and short of calling for help I could do nothing but listen and stare. It was not a pretty sight.

"I was in the hall. At the bottom of the staircase. I watched him fall. Saw the blood spout like it was coming from a fountain—"

This was too much. I shouted, not caring who heard, "Tyler! Please stop! Right now, just stop! I don't understand why you're telling me this or why you're doing this to yourself. Are you in Palm Beach alone? Where are your parents?"

That did the trick. He stopped talking, his eyes glossed over, and looked contrite. The little boy again. The four-year-old who had witnessed his twin brother's bloody fall to his death.

"I'm here alone, Mr. McNally, and I'm perfectly capable of being on my own. Sometimes, when I talk about Maddy, I get carried away. And my parents are in London visiting with the nobility, where they are all no doubt reading racing forms and losing money."

He was himself again, but I wasn't sure who that self was. I pushed the glass of water toward him, and this time he accepted it with a nod of thanks and drank.

As much as I wanted to avoid the subject, there was no getting away from it. "You read or heard about the incident that took place in front of the house several days ago. Is that why you're here? Why you wanted to see me?"

"We still have friends down here," he said. "The crowd that summers in the Hamptons. One of them called to tell us about the article in the paper. Yes, that's why I'm here." He took another sip of water. I wondered if I should offer him a cigarette—and have one myself. "The light," he stated. "The policeman saw a light in an upstairs window. The nursery window."

"How do you know it came from the nursery?" I got in.

"This wasn't the first time someone reported seeing a light coming from an upstairs window. Friends from here told us what they had heard when they arrived in Southampton. Their description was very clear, and it was the nursery window. My parents had the house checked and everything was secure. No one had broken in and nothing was disturbed."

"Sometimes people see things that just aren't there," I said. "Especially at night. The moon, a passing plane winging too low, anything like that could have caused a reflection bouncing off the shutters. But once the rumor started, the more impressionable kooks and meddlers joined the chorus. The same crowd that spotted flying saucers nightly. Of course, your parents did the right thing and happily found nothing. Why are you so disturbed by it, Ty?"

"This time," he asserted with a great deal of feeling, "it wasn't a kook or a busybody. It was a policeman. A trained observer. If he saw a light, there must have been a light."

Al Rogoff was a trained observer and a very good one, but, I said aloud, "Even the police officer said he thought he saw a light, and this led to the discovery of some perpetrators on the property and nothing more. The light, or what he thought was a light, was gone when he got out of his car for a closer look. I assume the electricity has been turned off all these years. Correct?"

He was silent. Probably debating with himself whether or not to go on or leave. We were both skirting the issue and we both knew it, but I wasn't about to break the ice. Not with this one. If he didn't look so pathetically forlorn I would have stood up and ended the meeting. Tyler Beaumont was hard to walk away from, and he played it for all it was worth.

Then he started to say what I knew was coming and, as feared, it came. "Maddy is in the nursery, Mr. McNally."

Give unto me a break!

"That, young man, is too preposterous to deserve an answer. And, if you'll excuse my presumption, maybe you should be seeing someone more qualified to deal with fantasy."

"Like a shrink or a seer?" he posed with a knowing

smile that told me he had been down this path before. "I've been to both. One discourages me and the other encourages me, both at an hourly rate that many families could live on for a week."

"Good. Then you won't faint when you get my bill."

"Will you please listen to me, Mr. McNally?"

"I thought that's what I was doing."

"With an open mind," he added.

"My mind is so open you can see through it. Okay, kid, have your say, but remember, my time is money."

The sparring seemed to put him at ease. When he spoke, it was with a great deal of sincerity and much less fervor. He might be a fruitcake, but he sure was a likable one. I imagine women doted on this guy, and not just because of his bank account. Not being of the opposite sex, I will own up to listening to his nonsense only because of his money. Is that crass of me? Well, I beg your pardon, but could you honestly resist being taken into the confidence of Tyler Beaumont, descendant of presidents, scion of wealth on par with the Mellons and Du Ponts, whose folks, as we spoke, were perusing scratch sheets with England's royals? Really!

Besides which, the man in the executive office next door would give me the boot without misgivings should I show young Ty the door before I heard him out. And where would I go? Back to Yale?

All things considered, I heard him out and will say this audience of one was moved by his story. As he watched his brother take that fatal and harrowing fall, Tyler was literally struck dumb. He couldn't scream or cry or utter a word, and remained silent for almost a week after the accident. Doctors advised his parents to remove him from the scene as quickly as possible. The Beaumonts, themselves eager to escape from the scene of the tragedy, were quick to return to New York, leaving staff to close the house.

It also struck me as uncanny that the setting of Mrs. Beaumont's theatrical entrances was to become the horrendous cause of her beloved son's demise. The gods are not to be upstaged.

"The blood soaked into the marble," Tyler said. "I remember the servants scrubbing the stairs, but, like Lady Macbeth's bloody hands, they couldn't scrub out the dark stains. They may still be there."

What a fanciful simile and, as would be borne out in time, a very apt one.

The family left Palm Beach two days after the accident. What Tyler did not know was that young Maddy's body was flown to New York, where a service was held before interment in the family plot.

"You see, I thought we had left him there, on the hall floor, and ran away. I imagined him alone, crying, unable to get up."

For a moment I thought he was going to go off the deep end once more, but he rallied and continued.

"As you can see, I regained my voice and went into therapy with a much-acclaimed child psychiatrist. I didn't like him very much, because all he wanted from me was to forget Maddy, which I refused to do. In fact, I think the daily session with the shrink only served to keep my brother's memory alive. Alone, in bed, I used to talk to Maddy the way we did before he left us.

"That was my parent's expression, *'Maddy left us.'* I believed we left him. One night I told Maddy how much I hated the doctor and how nice it would be if I didn't have to see him ever again. The next day the doctor was killed. Run over by a taxi while crossing Madison Avenue."

Tyler was very lucid, very matter-of-fact, which made the macabre tale remarkably believable. There were other incidents where he beseeched his brother's help and the request was granted. Answered prayers? Now who was being capricious?

"Coincidences," I said. "They do happen, Ty." No sooner were the words out of my mouth than I realized I had put my foot in it, and judging from the coy expression on Tyler's face, he too recalled my censorious opinion of coincidences not ten minutes ago.

Relenting, I said, "Okay, I goofed."

He leaped on that like the proverbial drowning man and the straw. "No, you didn't," he pointed out. "You said what you believed, and now you're ready to disbelieve it. So why can't you give me the benefit of now believing what you were ready to disbelieve when I started talking?"

I did get the point, however obtusely stated. The very rich are different from you and me. They can spare the time for idle chatter. Alas, I cannot. "Ty," I said, trying not to show my exasperation, "what do you want from me?"

"Friends told me you were the best investigator in Palm Beach and you know how to keep your mouth shut."

I took that as a compliment, although I was a little dubious about his being so keen on my ability to keep a secret. Who didn't he want to know about his visit here? His parents?

"Do you want me to go into the house and search for . . ." I really didn't have the heart, or the nerve, to finish the thought. Nor did I care to think about the stains on those marble steps.

"No, they've done that. It proves nothing. I mean, such things don't hang around waiting for company. Why and when they manifest is a mystery."

Such things? I really liked that. "So, once again, what do you want?"

"I want you to set up some sort of surveillance. Watch and wait till it happens again. The light, I mean. Then determine if it's a fact or an optical illusion. I have to know, Mr. McNally."

He was pleading, and I didn't have the heart to bid him farewell. I wish he wasn't such a charismatic young man. Also, I didn't have the time or the staff for such an operation. I was up to my chin with "A Voice from the Grave" and had no inclination to go looking for a body to match.

"Mr. McNally," he expounded, "people have seen something coming from that window, and now even a policeman admits to seeing it. No matter what you think of my theory, you have to grant me that it's worthy of investigating."

Put that way, he was right. People had surely seen something emanating from an upstairs window of the Beaumont mansion. I would like to know what it was only to prove this young man wrong and perhaps lay the tragedy of twenty years ago, along with his brother, to rest. I knew I would hate myself in the morning, but I said it anyway. "I'll think about it."

His charming smile now had the warmth it lacked earlier. "I'm at the Colony. You can get me there. And maybe you'd like to have dinner with me one evening, or a drink in the lounge. With your wife if you like."

"I don't have a wife."

He came right back with, "Do you have a girl?"

"That, Ty, is more profound than the enigma of the light in the nursery window."

16

My respite in the eye of the storm was short-lived. After Tyler Beaumont left, dazzling Mrs. Trelawney with his megawatt smile, I was plunged into the tumult.

"What a lovely boy," she commented when the elevator door closed on his radiance.

What old women don't know about pretty boys could fill volumes better left unwritten. "I have several things to impart, Mrs. Trelawney, if you can get your mind off thoughts unseemly for a business office."

As intended, she smarted at that one. "And I have several dozen items for you, Mr. Celebrity. You've had umpteen calls this morning from the local press, the wire services, an auction house, a New York publisher, Officer O'Hara twice, Decimus Fortesque three times and Lolly Spindrift ad nauseam. I've taken the liberty of ordering an answering machine installed in your office."

"If it's bigger than a safety pin, it won't fit," I answered, thinking that had she truly ordered such a nefarious gadget I would pull its plug. After my session with Tyler Beaumont, the last thing I contemplated doing was listening to disembodied voices.

My sudden popularity was no doubt a result of the police having finally made a statement regarding the murder at the Crescent Motel, naming people, places and things. Given the Capote angle, the statement was surely taken up by all the wire services and radio and TV yack shows, and perhaps even given the stature of a breaking story on CNN.

I took the list she had compiled, thanking her for her assistance, then asked if father had seen the afternoon papers.

"He has, as has everyone in the building, and he isn't exactly overjoyed. It's not the kind of thing he likes to see associated with the firm's name."

Now I smarted. "I don't pick my cases. I take them as they come, and sometimes they come with a lot of baggage. Is he free at the moment?"

The question was pure rhetoric, for if the boss were free he would have buzzed Mrs. Trelawney the moment he heard me outside his door. Besides the current hoopla, he would want to know what Tyler Beaumont wanted with me. And wait till he heard that story.

Unable to resist, she asked, "Did you read the manuscript, Archy?"

I assured her I did not and felt the back of my head. The bump was gone but not my ire. "I will take care of the calls," I said, "but I did want to mention a rather large dinner item that will soon appear on my expense report. Circumstances necessitated my picking up two rather large tabs at the club last night. Circumstances in the line of duty, of course."

"Has it got anything to do with the Capote book?"

"In a way, yes," I said.

"Has it got more to do with the green-eyed blonde you wined and dined last night?"

"I suppose Binky has told you all," I charged.

Unperturbed, she said he had.

"Then why do you ask?"

"To watch you squirm," she said with great satisfaction. "And please include an itemized account of the dubious expenditure."

"I will, along with a dubious good day to you, Mrs. Trelawney."

• The phone was jangling as I entered my warren, and from the urgency of the ring I would guess our resident snoop was once again trying his luck. I picked up, because now seemed as good a time as any to deal with the inevitable and because Mrs. Trelawney would kill me if I didn't.

"Finally." Lolly Spindrift exhaled. "I've been trying to get you all day. I'm on my cell phone outside Bunny Weaver's place, so if I cut off suddenly you'll know why."

No, I wouldn't know why, and foolishly asked what he was doing staking out Bunny Weaver's place.

"I'm on duty," he confided. "The telephone repairman went in an hour ago and he's still there."

"Maybe he's having a hard time making a connection," I said, thinking it rather clever.

"Oh, he's made his connection, all right. He's been there more than once this week, and there's nothing wrong with Bunny's phone. If you saw the repairman, you'd know what I mean. I've put in a service call a dozen times and haven't hit the jackpot. I don't know how Bunny does."

"Her sex might have something to do with it," I reminded him.

"Don't be such a smart-ass, Archy, and if you insist on talking about sex, what were you doing drinking negronis with that policewoman last night at your odious club? Were you surprised to see Connie there? I hear you couldn't care less."

Lolly had a spy at the Pelican and, it seemed, at every restaurant, bar and dinner table in PB. Like all gossip columnists, he was also fed by those who hoped for a mention in return for ratting on their best friends. *Sic transit gloria brotherhood.*

"How do you know she's a policewoman, Lolly?"

His rag's crime hack went to the briefing in Juno this morning that was given by Officer O'Hara. He told Lolly about my role in the case as reported by the curvaceous blonde trooper. "When I heard about your date last night, I put two and two together and came up with Archy McNally. I have more questions for you than a Senate investigating committee looking into reports of copulation in the cloakroom. That naughty Capote book, Deci Fortesque, a classy auction house in New York, a murder . . ." He paused either to inhale or because the repairman cometh. Then he was back, good as new. "And who should alight on your crowded doorstep but Tyler Beaumont. Archy, you are a fountain of trash gab—so come fill my cup."

"I don't have time right now, Lol, but when I do you'll be the first to know what little I know." I didn't want to offend Lolly, as he was a valuable source for me, our working relationship being one of give-and-take. Lolly gave and I took him to expensive dinners. He was a little guy with the appetite of a horse and the tastes of a gourmet, but he had his ear to our sandy ground and a foot in all the right doors. To be sure, he could be a bitch, as poor Bunny Weaver would soon learn. You see, Bunny was on all the A lists and had forgotten to include Lolly in several major social events last season, and, if she was indulging in banal liaisons, she would soon pay for her transgressions.

When Lolly called to ask if her telephones were now in working order, Bunny would giggle and invite Lol to lunch at the Club Colette, which, in PB, is on par with being knighted by Her Majesty. All would be forgiven and *sic transit gloria scruples.*

"Oh," Lolly moaned, "just give me a crumb for the late editions to upset the news editor. Did you read the manuscript?"

The police briefing had told the press all they needed to know, but did they really want the scoop on this mess or did they just want to know what other carnal secrets Capote had revealed? Decimus Fortesque's alter egos were legion. And did anyone give a hoot who killed Lawrence Swensen and why? I did. And so did Georgy girl, whom I had resolved not to think about until time and distance had cooled my fevered brow. "Just give me a quote," Lolly urged. "I can jazz it up."

Lolly was very good at jazzing up quotes. His expertise bordered on libel. "Lawrence Swensen hoped to make a fortune from his former employer's labors and learned, too late, that more tears are shed over answered prayers than unanswered ones."

"I love that," Lol squealed, already plotting to change "former employer" to "ex-lover."

"It's not exactly original," I warned him.

"Dear heart, there is nothing original on this earth except the sin of the same name. Now tell me quick, are you and Connie history? I mean, first she is seen all over town with that dreamy toreador and then you are seen at your lowlife hangout in the company of a gun-toting blonde with Connie practically at the next table. *Mon Dieu,* there's not been so much talk since Binnie and Barry Rabinowitz discovered they were both committing adultery with the same woman. So what's the story, morning glory?"

"Connie and I have always had an open relationship, unquote," I told him.

"The only thing that was constantly open was your . . ." A pause pregnant with innuendo. "No, I won't say it. I write for a family newspaper. All the news that's fit for the dustbin. And if Connie is trading you in for Alejandro Gomez y Zapata, who could blame her? I'd dump you for the toreador in a trice."

"Sorry to hear that, Lol. I was near succumbing to your tiresome advances."

"Really?" he cried. "I could change my mind."

"Too late, Lol, your loss is the world's gain."

"The world?" he said. "Or the lovely state trooper's?"

"No comment," I commented.

"May I quote you?"

"Be my guest. Now I have to run."

"Not so fast, Archy. What's with the Beaumont boy? Is it true he came here explicitly to see you?"

"It's true, but I can't tell you any more at this time. We spoke in confidence."

"Has it anything to do with the item that appeared in our local the other morning? You know, Sergeant Rogoff and those vulgar youths?"

Never sell a snoop short. Lolly had picked up the connection, as I'm sure others had. Ursi had spread the word, and now I was a tad sorry I had started the ball rolling. There's nothing like a haunted house story to attract the crackpots, and Ty Beaumont needed them like Deci Fortesque needed a murder investigation. Now it appeared my poor clients had only Archy to defend them from both. I didn't need a break, I needed passage on the next liner to Zanzibar.

"What do you hear about the Beaumont family?" I asked the man who was sure to know.

"Not fair, dear heart. Give and take. Give me a nibble and take back a reliable answer."

"Okay." I sighed. "He's here in connection with that news item. He's worried about trespassers. The house wasn't emptied of all its furnishings." The latter was pure hoke, but it made sense.

"I'll buy that, but with reservations," Lolly said. "Is the boy here alone?"

"Why do you ask?"

"Because I hear he has a constant companion—or valet, or secretary, or bodyguard, or a nanny by any other name is still a nanny. Tyler Beaumont is rumored to be a teensy unstable. Among the common folks it's called off one's rocker."

This wasn't totally unexpected, but still I didn't like hearing it. And hadn't I, perhaps instinctively, asked Tyler if he was here alone? Both cases seemed to be going down the tube in leaps and bounds, dragging me with them.

Before letting Lolly go I insisted on asking him a question.

"Fire away," he agreed.

"What are you going to do when the repairman leaves Bunny's house?"

"Take him home to inspect my instrument."

Ask a foolish question . . .

I rang off and stared at the list Mrs. Trelawney had

given me. Procrastinating, I put a check mark next to Lolly's name. I didn't want to talk to Fortesque just now, as I could neither assure him that the police were finished with him nor be optimistic regarding the return of his cash or the manuscript.

I didn't want to talk to the wire services or the Miami papers, because I had nothing to add to what they learned at the police briefing. If I gave them the quote I had just given Lolly, they would crucify me in print. Too, I thought it best to heed Mrs. Trelawney's warning and keep my name, and thus the firm's name, out of the tabloids.

I wouldn't talk to Capote's ex-publisher or the New York auction house without a lawyer present.

Last, but far from least, I did want to talk to Georgy girl but didn't know what I would say when I got her on the line. Had she enjoyed our supposed business meeting? I would be happy if she did and happy if she didn't. My love life was sitting atop a net and I didn't know whose court it would fall on. Nor did I know who would rush to claim it. Could I play on both courts, hopping the net at will? There was a time when I could, but that time has been and gone. It was now decision time, and given my current emotional state, I doubted I could make the right one.

R. Chandler said, *"When in doubt have a man walk in the room holding a gun."* What I got was Binky Watrous, pushing his cart.

"Well, well, well," I greeted, "if it isn't Diamond Jim Watrous, the man with champagne tastes and a beer wallet. I'm surprised you weren't drinking it out of Connie's slipper. It's a darn sight bigger than those flutes."

"Can it, Archy. The fuzzy wine gave me a sour stomach and a headache."

His complexion did look sallower than usual, which is

saying a lot, but nothing more than what he deserved. Without mercy, I told him as much. "And your head will ache even more when you get the bill," I warned.

"You said you weren't lying," he sniveled.

"Well, I lied about not lying. It's my nature."

He paled even more. "All my credit cards are maxed out," he told me as if I cared. Binky may look like Bambi, but he whines like a stuck porky. Since attaining gainful employment he had applied for, and was given, every piece of plastic available to those who live beyond their means. Intent on reaping a zillion air miles, he went on a spending spree for the necessities of life. Binky now owns everything preceded by the word "digital" and dozens of cashmere sweaters. If he resided in the North Pole, I'm sure he would have stocked up on Bermuda shorts and bathing trunks.

"You told Connie I was paying for the dinner," I stated rather than asked.

"It might have slipped out."

"Slipped out?" I cried. "And did the events of last night you passed on to Mrs. Trelawney also just happen to slip out? Like England, we have our own BBC. The Binky Broadcasting Company. How many times must I tell you that your job is to deliver the incoming mail, take away the outgoing mail and mind your own business?"

With that, he began to back himself and his cart out my door. "I have no mail for you, Archy," he announced.

"Then what are you doing here?"

"I came for a social visit, not to be attacked after I got myself sick and hungover doing your bidding. Next time you take a state trooper to dinner, you can do it without Connie and me in attendance."

Did I hear right? Was nothing sacred? "Just a moment,

young man. Halt or I'll shoot. How did you know my lady friend was a state trooper?"

A white-on-white complexion is a ghastly sight. Without looking directly at me, he mumbled, "I think Al Rogoff told me."

"And when did you chance to speak with Sergeant Rogoff?"

"I stopped by his trailer this morning to borrow a teaspoon of sugar for my coffee."

This was truly too much. I expect the only reason Binky is alive to tell about it is that Al wasn't wearing his gun belt when Binky came begging with an empty teaspoon. "And you thought it necessary to give him a blow-by-blow of your intemperance at the Pelican?"

"It may have slipped out," he admitted.

"Really? With the way things slip out of your mouth, I think you should apply a gag to stop the flow."

Binky described my date to Al, and Al immediately recognized the policewoman I had described to him earlier. If I weren't a gentleman, I would describe my two best friends as trailer trash.

"She's a beauty, Archy," he said.

Angling for a return on my hefty investment, I casually said, "Well, now that you mention it, may I ask what Connie thought of my date?"

"You told me not to gossip," came his maddening answer.

Binky was being intentionally obtuse, no doubt on orders from Connie. She knew what I was up to the minute Binky told her how eager I was to have her dine at the club last night. Her response was to rack up a huge tab and, enlisting Binky's help, pretend not to notice me and my date. One could say my ally, Binky Watrous, was now a double agent.

I counted to ten, backwards, then bellowed, "Tell me what Connie said or I'll throttle you."

"She said it was a cheap trick."

"Cheap? I don't call champagne and tournedos of beef cheap. It was an expensive, if tawdry, trick. Does that suit you?" Getting no reply, I asked, "Was the champagne her idea?"

Without a missing a beat, he said, "No, it was my idea."

The lie brought a little color to his cheeks. I must say you had to admire the guy for the way he had just taken the blame for that bit of extravagant tomfoolery. Chivalry was not dead, and Binky was here to prove it. But that didn't excuse him from telling me what I wanted to hear. "What did Connie think of my date?"

"She said you were robbing the cradle."

"Moi?" I was as close to a seizure as one could be and remain standing. Separated from Binky by his cart, I rattled it instead of his head. "She's five years younger than Alejandro."

"You're ten years older than the blonde," he responded, pulling the cart out of my reach. "Stop spinning your wheels, Archy. If you don't want to make a move, maybe Connie does and all you're doing is blocking her way."

When one gets rational advice from Binky, one's number is up. I was not only spinning my wheels, I was also spinning the mail cart's wheels. "Did Connie say anything last night that makes you think she's made a decision?"

"She said nothing, but the way she avoided the subject of you and Alejandro made it clear she was thinking of nothing else."

Out of the mouths of babes. I must remember never to denigrate Binky's sagacity. Or was my problem so obvious that it took less than a whiz kid to sum it up and spit out the answer?

Binky then counseled, "You both need a push."

But in which direction? To or fro? "You're right, Binky, and I'm sorry I got you involved in this. I will bite the bullet, pay for your dinners and apologize to Connie. My only excuse is that I'm involved in a couple of cases that defy resolving and they seem to have exhausted my common sense."

"I read about one of them, Archy," Binky commiserated.

It was so easy to sway him that even my somewhat exaggerated excuse had me feeling guilty.

"Is Claudia Lester the blonde who came to see you a few days ago?" I gave him a nod. "That's what I thought. I passed her on the Esplanade the other day and recognized her. She was with her girlfriend."

That was interesting. I didn't know Claudia Lester knew anyone in Palm Beach except the two male members of her sting team. However, I was presently too flummoxed to give it much thought, and more's the pity for that.

"Were you and the policewoman discussing the case last night, Archy? I mean, it's kind of unusual to compare notes with the police over dinner."

This was just what Georgy had feared. If it got around that she was playing footsie with a PI her boss would not be happy, and it was me who had put her on display at the Pelican Club. Let's face it, I was a heel. Avoiding the question, I told Binky, "Her name is Georgia O'Hara, and she's called Georgy."

Being loyal to Connie, I could see that even this introduction by proxy embarrassed him—think what it was doing to me. He scooted around that one by asking, "Do you know who did in the Swensen guy?"

"Not a clue, Binky."

Next came the inevitable. "Did you read the manuscript, Archy?"

"No, Binky, I did not. I had it in my hands but was forced to let go."

He began his retreat, saying, "If you need any help with your cases, just yell."

"Thank you, Binky, but I don't need . . ." And the little bulb in my head went *POP* and lit up the sky. "Perhaps there is something you can do, if you have the time."

He pounced, as I knew he would. "To work on a case I'll make the time. What is it, Archy?"

"Do you remember the article in the paper the other day? The one that began where Al Rogoff thought he saw a light . . ."

"Succotash," she announced with the élan of Georges Escoffier presenting his boeuf Wellington to a panel of hungry epicures.

As I entered these words in my journal I smiled at the recollection of the amusing dish and the chef who was a namesake of the renowned Frenchman. I am alone in my garret a few hours before dawn, and, in case no one has noticed, in a poetic frame of mind.

After rendezvousing once again with Officer O'Hara to discuss further developments in the ongoing investigation of "A Voice from the Grave," I am transported back in time to when we children would pick a daisy from the earth and pluck its petals while chanting, "She loves me; she loves me not." The line that coincided with the last petal would seal our fate with the pigtailed enchantress of our daydreams.

Stuffed with succotash, tipsy on a pretentious wine and not yet recovered from a good-night kiss that gave new meaning to the word *lingering,* I am the embodiment of a charming lyric from my favorite Broadway show, "... *full of foolish song.*" And, mayhaps my fate is sealed, but before the cement sets let me digress to the events that led to this rapture before it cools in the warmth of the rising sun.

• I engaged Binky as a ghost breaker, and, I'm afraid, he showed little enthusiasm for the role.

"It's creepy," he complained when I explained his assignment.

"All you have to do is check out the old Beaumont mansion a few times every evening between ten and midnight." These hours were as arbitrary as everything else about this bit of nonsense, but before I sent Tyler packing I could honestly say we set up surveillance and found nothing.

"Do I have to get out of my car?"

"It wouldn't hurt. A quick turn around the lawn and back to the safety of your armored tank."

Binky was not convinced. "Suppose I trip over people bonking?" he posed.

"Excuse yourself, move on and keep your eyes on those upstairs windows. Really, Binky, this is a very simple commission."

Looking pensive, he challenged, "What if I see a light in one of those windows?"

Now, that was something I'd not thought of because I didn't believe such a light existed, and I told Binky so.

"Then my assignment is to look for something that doesn't exist," he concluded.

"Exactly."

"That's nuts, Archy, and you know it."

"It's not nuts," I informed him, "it's integrity. I will not tell my client I looked and found nothing unless I look and find nothing. He might be a disturbed young man, but he's sincere and I intend to act in good faith."

"He's also a rich young man," Binky commented. "Ten to midnight is time and a half, and after midnight it's double time."

What was this? Did he expect payment for his services? It was those damn credit cards that made him so mercenary as to forget his apprentice status. "Keep your eyes on those windows," I ordered, "and off my billing sheet. After the champagne and tournedos, you'll be indebted to me for the rest of your life."

Remembering his hangover, he began his retreat in search of ice water. "If I see a light," he mumbled, "I'll run."

"If you see a light, get on your cell phone and dial nine-one-one. They'll relay the call to the nearest patrol car and in minutes you'll have company. If Sergeant Rogoff is still pulling the graveyard shift, it may be your neighbor who comes to the rescue."

Relieved, Binky managed a sad smile, saying, "Thanks, Archy. That's just what I'll do."

Insisting on the last word, I reminded him, "You will then owe Al your life as well as a teaspoon of sugar."

Alone once more, I looked at my list of calls, all marked urgent. I put a tick next to the tick next to Lolly Spindrift's name. That made it look as if I had called him twice. I put a line through the second tick and told myself that if I did not light a cigarette I was cured of the habit. Then I told myself that if I had one now and skipped the one after dinner I would still be true to my regimen. Here, I was saved by the bell. The telephone bell, that is.

It was Mrs. Trelawney. My father was free and would

like a word, if you please. Before I could oblige, the phone rang yet again, causing me to reconsider the installation of an answering machine. A ringing telephone is anathema to my nervous system, but I was immediately appeased when I heard the caller's voice. It was Georgy girl. I opened my desk drawer, found the hidden pack of English Ovals and lit one.

"My first call was a bread and butter," she said, "and the second was to let you know that Rodney Whitehead was coming in to be questioned. This call is to tell you he's been and had his say."

I remembered her cautioning me to lay off her suspects so kept quiet about the pastrami on rye I had shared with the man. Was it Euripides who wrote, *"The gods wear many faces/And many fates fulfill, to work their will."* Loosely translated, God works in mysterious ways. My decision not to disclose my meeting with Whitehead got me a second date with my clandestine collaborator.

"Would you like to know what he had to say?" she teased.

"I'm all ears, officer."

"Not on the phone," she said. "Are you free this evening?"

Having nothing on my agenda that couldn't be broken, I said I was free without consulting my calendar. "Do you want to meet in the dark corner of a disreputable pub? I'll wear a beard and shades."

"And I'll put on a black wig like Dietrich in *Witness for the Prosecution,"* she joined in. I must say she knew her flicks. "But it would be more comfortable at my place. If you promise to behave, I'll cook."

"I'll be there at eight, but I make no promises."

"Then I'll have to take my chances."

"Is this a business meeting, officer?"

"It is," she said, sounding as if she meant it. "This case is dragging on too long for comfort, and my boss wants to give the papers something to shout about, like 'Murder Solved' in bold type, and I need your input. He's close to reading Harrigan or Whitehead their rights."

"Does that mean I'm out of the running?"

"It means you're on a back burner. If we get desperate, we'll turn up the heat."

"Georgy, would you cook dinner for a suspected murderer?" I asked her.

"If I thought I could nail him, I'd even let him stick around for dessert."

That pert answer was rife with innuendo, and I felt myself flush. Why do I always fall for women lacking in timidity? Freud would say it's because opposites attract, reducing me to a Milquetoast. I say it's because such women have humor, street smarts, are independent, exciting and a challenge. They might also know how to cook, but that remained to be seen.

"Tell me," I said, "why not Harrigan *and* Whitehead?"

"Let's toss that around over dinner. See you about eight."

I would rather toss it around over dessert.

• Father was in neutral, meaning he was neither stroking nor tugging at his whiskers. I hoped to keep him idling for the duration of my visit. As always, he was immaculately attired in a vested business suit, white shirt and a rep silk tie. Father abhorred anything garish in his apparel, and therefore the Old Glory lapel pin he now wore with pride was a conspicuous sign of the times.

His desk was cluttered with briefs, perhaps a result of his last client meeting, but two newspapers took center stage. Even reading upside down, the names Capote and Fortesque stood out in both headlines.

"This business has certainly taken on a life of its own," he said when I was seated.

"It's the names involved, sir," I responded, nodding at the newspapers. "The murder of a relatively unknown man in a shoddy motel would be relegated to page five, if nothing juicier turned up to knock it off the editor's desk. The author and the playboy have always been gist for the tabloids' mills." Calling Decimus Fortesque a playboy had me suppressing a smile.

"It's just unfortunate that you had to get involved in this one," father said.

"As you know, sir, I wasn't aware of what I was getting into when I agreed to help Claudia Lester." This implied that had I known I would have refused the assignment, which was not true. There was nothing I liked better than a case that garnered public notice, especially when it extended beyond the borders of my county and state. It boosted my image as well as my fees. Contrary to father's more conservative opinion, I think it helped rather than hindered the cause of McNally & Son. However, this was neither the time nor the place to argue the point.

"What's your position now?" he asked. "I assume the murder investigation is being conducted by the police and that you are cooperating."

The last time I had discussed the case with father I had met with O'Hara and spoken to Claudia Lester at Bradley House. Now I brought him up to date with an account of my interviews with Harrigan and Whitehead. Being a lawyer, father is a good listener. Being a good lawyer, he jotted down a few notes along the way.

When I was done, he leaned back in his chair and began, "It seems to me that the sole object of this escapade is to get more than fifty thousand for that manuscript by either selling it again to another buyer or forcing Fortesque to come up with more money if he wanted to hang on to what he almost had. Were they content with the original sum agreed upon, we would not be having this conversation. It seems someone is running a private auction with Fortesque and an unknown or unknowns vying for the prize."

I agreed, saying, "I think Fortesque made them an offer and wouldn't go a penny more. If they canvassed the manuscript to other collectors and received a better offer, Fortesque would not now be minus fifty thousand and I would have been spared a bump on the head."

Unspoken was the fact that I would also not have met Georgy girl.

I went on to say, "Fortesque was their target because they had inside information regarding his taste for the esoteric. I speak of his third wife, Vera Fortesque, a friend of Claudia Lester."

Gadzooks! The lightbulb did not merely pop—it exploded. That's always the way with a case. The break comes when you least expect it. I wanted to jump up and clap my hands, but that would be uncouth. It would also be foolish. My epiphany could not be taken on faith alone. It needed proving, and stealth, not exposé, was the means to that end. I would have to play my hand close to the vest or it could cost me the game.

Distracted, I heard but did not perceive all father said,

but did manage to snap out of my silent musing in time to hear him ask, "Of the three, who do you think might be telling the truth?"

"Harrigan," I said, without a moment's hesitation. "He's the novice of the team and the easiest to be duped by the other two. Also, I don't think he has the smarts or the nerve to lie to the police and keep his cool. The other two could walk away from a third-degree grilling with dry foreheads. Harrigan contacted me because he wanted information. I think he was genuinely surprised to learn I never delivered the money to Lester and even more shocked to hear about Swensen's death.

"I say this knowing his story is flawed. Why would Whitehead agree to a three-way split when he was getting half from Swensen?"

Father shook his head. "It seems to me, Archy, all three are malefactors and congenital liars, yet you credit or discredit each of their statements based on the testimony of the other two libelers. Because Whitehead told you he was getting half from Swensen is not proof that he had struck such an agreement with the murdered man. The only fact I conclude from your evidence is that all three are intent upon making the other two look like rotters."

Everyone is familiar with Murphy's law, which, incidentally, Mr. Murphy borrowed from the mathematics genius, Pythagoras, who observed a few thousand years ago that *"anything which can happen can happen to you."* But a lesser-known, and perhaps original, Murphy edict is the Law of Forgiveness, which asserts that one can be forgiven if wrong, but *never* if right—and Prescott McNally was right. 'Nuff said?

"I take it," my learned colleague was saying, "that you

have severed your ties with Claudia Lester and have now been engaged by Decimus Fortesque to retrieve that confounded manuscript or his money. Correct?"

"That is correct, sir."

"And just how do you intend to do that, Archy?"

"I have no idea, sir."

"Nonsense," father insisted, slipping out of idle and going into high gear. "The only way you can learn what became of the manuscript or Fortesque's money is by solving the murder of Lawrence Swensen, a job better left to the police."

I jumped on that like a cowboy mounting a bucking bronco. "As you hoped, sir, I am cooperating with the police."

"Over cocktails and dinner?"

From the mail boy to the secretary to the CEO. So much for my stint at the rodeo. "I will admit to mixing business with pleasure. We did discuss the case."

Father sighed as if he were much put upon. "You know, Archy, I never interfere in your personal life, and I have no intention of starting now."

That declaration is always followed by the word *however,* and it came right on cue.

"However, I think it was imprudent for you and this policewoman to be seen carrying on in public while you are both involved in a murder investigation."

"In all fairness to Officer O'Hara, sir, the dinner meeting was at my suggestion. Remember, I was a possible suspect. I wanted to sit down with her to clear myself as well as offer my help."

"Granted," he said, "but I wish you would have chosen a more appropriate venue for the conference. When and if this goes to trial, a defense attorney could make much of such a meeting to the detriment of the prosecution. Officer O'Hara should be aware of that."

This was true, if rather far-fetched and not like father. I had collaborated with the police before this, especially with Al Rogoff, and father had never opposed the stratagem. Based on this and my refusal to act covertly with my boss and kin, I told father that I was meeting yet again with Officer O'Hara this evening, and this time in her home.

My candor was rewarded with an appreciative nod. "I assume the relationship has taken on a more personal aspect."

Not retreating, I answered, "I hope that is the case."

He gave that some thought before changing the subject or, better put, taking a different route to where this was leading. He told me mother, too, had read the newspaper account of the murder and my attack in the parking lot. "She's worried, Archy, which aggravates her condition."

I would forsake everything dear to keep mother healthy and happy, which was not a secret in the McNally household. Not having to defend my position, I simply sidestepped the issue. "I will talk to her, sir. I have before, and it helps."

"I'm sure it will," he said, "but what would please her most, and myself, is to see you settle down. We have long thought that you and Connie—"

"We were never formally engaged, sir," I cut in, none too gently, "and at the present, as we all know, Connie is seeing another man."

"Then perhaps you should be more demonstrative," he advised.

Father had never sat me down to discuss the birds and the bees, and I hoped he wasn't going to now. In truth, I found this conversation rather embarrassing and was certain that he was doing it only because mother had asked him to. It was surely as disconcerting to him as it was to me. Perhaps even more so.

The thought only made me feel worse. Would I ever know a love even approaching my father's for my mother? Did I want to know such a love? As if in answer to my thoughts, I heard myself say, "Right now, sir, I don't know that I want to be more demonstrative."

"I don't mean to meddle, Archy."

"I'm sure you don't, sir." Not being a C. B. DeMille, I couldn't shout "Cut" and have done with this painful scene, so I did the next-best thing and asked, "Now, would you like to hear what Tyler Beaumont had to say?"

With evident relief, he answered, "That's why I wanted to see you."

Really? You could have fooled me.

After relaying Tyler's bizarre tale, father looked as if segueing from my love life to Tyler Beaumont's fantasy life was akin to leaping from the ludicrous to the preposterous. "It's hard to believe Lolly's assertion," father said. "I chatted with the boy over a cup of tea, and he sounded perfectly normal. In fact, I thought he was rather charming."

"That he is," I acquiesced, "and perfectly lucid. What he has to say is the problematic part of the equation."

"Is Lolly a reliable source on this matter?"

"When it comes to high society, Lolly is a walking encyclopedia. Trust me on that, sir. I've engaged Binky to keep a sporadic watch. I may also mention it to Al Rogoff, as he was the catalyst of this inanity. I refuse to ignore Tyler's request with a wink and a nod."

Father liked that, as I was sure he would. "I wonder if we should contact his family?" he said.

"That would be a betrayal of his confidence and against my ethics. If they're concerned, I'm sure they'll find him. He has friends here who seem to be in touch with his people."

"Very good, Archy." Father made a display of removing the newspapers from his desk, indicating our meeting was over. "You will keep me posted."

"Of course, sir."

"On the Fortesque case, too," he quickly put in.

I stood up to leave. "I may have a breakthrough to report on that sooner than expected."

"You sound more optimistic than you did when you came in."

"If I am, it's because of our talk." I stopped at the door and turned to face him. "Nothing you said went unheeded, sir."

18

I knew I would find mother in the sitting room of the guest suite, the one she had so generously offered me should I take a bride. The room contained a chaise longue of royal proportions, upon which mother enjoyed taking a siesta in the late afternoon, before dressing for the cocktail hour with father.

She slept so lightly, her eyes opened the moment she heard the door creak. "Don't get up," I said, pulling a chair beside her. "I just wanted to visit for a few minutes before going out."

Her florid complexion and blue eyes made one think of an old-fashioned daguerrotype that had been hand-painted to produce an ersatz Technicolor print. "Out again?" she complained. "It's been so long since you've dined with us, Archy. I miss your company."

Like a halfback who sees an opening, I ran with the ball. "If I married, you would see even less of me."

Looking guilty, and more flushed than ever, she said, "But I wouldn't have to worry about you getting hit on the head in parking lots late at night."

This, of course, intimated that when married I would sit by the fire evenings with my pipe and slippers, never venturing out after dark without the little lady to protect me from myself. For many mothers, getting a son wed is like retiring from duty and transferring her charge into the hands of a younger, more ardent caretaker.

"You've been reading the newspapers and listening to Ursi's account of the incident. You know how both tend to exaggerate. It was hardly a life-threatening blow, and it could happen to anyone, anyplace, anytime. In fact, Mrs. McNally, it's a proven fact that more married men are hit on the head with rolling pins than single men."

This got more of a laugh than it deserved, but that's one of the perks of having a fan club. "What an exciting case," she whispered as if it were a family secret. "Decimus Fortesque, Truman Capote and all those people chasing after the lost manuscript. It's a pity about the man who owned it, but then, he didn't act very honorably himself."

I said I enjoyed a case that got a lot of fanfare but one of the drawbacks of notoriety was that people tended to ask questions and offer advice. More of a problem in our home was that mother would learn the more sordid aspects of my occupation and fret over them. Father and I tended to avoid the topic in toto or, when cornered, make light of it, which I now did.

"I'm a little forgetful, Archy, and even a little dotty at times, but I don't have to be protected, like a maiden aunt, from the facts of life," she said, quickly adding, "however I do appreciate the gesture."

I took her hand. It was warm and slightly moist. "Humor the men in your life and stick to your begonias. Now I have to go."

She refused to relinquish my grip. "Ursi told me you're seeing the Beaumont boy. Is the family coming back to Palm Beach?"

Here I drew the line on discussing cases with mother. Ghosts on top of murder could prove a noxious mix, and when her mind wandered, as it sometimes did, there's no telling what demons might pop out of the wainscoting. "He's here to see friends and check on the house. Nothing more."

"Then why does he want to see you?"

Madelaine McNally, even in her golden years, was no fool. The thought was heartening. "A personal matter not meant for the ears of a spinster aunt," I replied.

The only subject in our abode more taboo than murder is sex. With a flutter of her free hand she withdrew the question, but I imagined she would press father on the subject. The poor squire—this was not his day for inquisitions.

Proving thoughts have wings, mother then asked, "Are you seeing Connie tonight?"

"No, ma'am. In fact, I am seeing a police officer, so I will be in protective custody all evening."

"Sergeant Rogoff?" she asked.

"No, mother. Lieutenant O'Hara. Georgia O'Hara, in fact. She's a policewoman."

"Is this in regards to your case?" she questioned hopefully.

"Ask father. He will tell you all about it."

This led to "You had a talk with father?"

"Yes, ma'am. I'm sure he will tell you all about that, too."

"You're mad at me for butting in."

Playing for sympathy, she could draw tears from the dress circle to the last row of the balcony. I raised the hand I was holding and kissed it. "I'm flattered that you care enough to pry, but right now I need some elbow room. You see, mother, I don't know what I want or, for that matter, who wants me."

She squeezed my hand and, spoken like a troth, affirmed, "We want you, Archy. We always have and we always will."

• I went into the kitchen to grab a cold drink and discovered a pitcher of fresh-brewed iced tea in the fridge. Ursi knows I'm partial to lemon lift, and I was not disappointed. Ursi clicked off the small telly that keeps her company most of the day and turned to me for a live update. "Have you seen the Beaumont boy?" was first on the agenda. "What does he want? It's about that item in the paper, isn't it, Archy? They say he's staying at the Colony. Everyone wants him for dinner."

That last item was disquietingly cannibalistic, but I ignored it as I filled a glass with ice and poured tea atop the cubes, then added a chubby wedge of fresh lemon. Tyler Beaumont's visit was the talk of the town because of my big mouth and Ursi's chronic telephonitis. I know I asked for it, but now I regretted it. More tears over answered prayers? I felt a chill that had nothing to do with the ice-cold glass in my hand.

I told Ursi the same thing I had told Lolly Spindrift, giving her a chance to air it before Lolly could print it.

"Did you read the manuscript?" was next on Ursi's agenda.

I told her I had not and remembered to say I would be dining out this evening.

Acknowledging this with a nod, Ursi continued her newscast. "Mrs. Marsden tells me that Lady Cynthia is beside herself with worry. She is sure the Capote book contains an entire chapter on her life before she became a Lady."

Not seeing the capital L, a listener could make much of that statement. Mrs. Marsden was Lady Cynthia Horowitz's housekeeper and Ursi's dearest pal. Lady Cynthia had had many husbands in her long life, all of them parting with millions to get rid of her, except the last one, who fell out of a tree and died, leaving her only a title.

I'm sure that her life was rife with scandal; however, her belief that Capote would honor her with even a footnote was wishful thinking. There are far too many more important people who have made fools of themselves for our Lady Cynthia to be noticed, but the rumor, self-started, would go a long way in giving the agile septuagenarian and hostess a certain cachet.

I escaped from the kitchen and ran upstairs to change into my swimming togs. I would just have time for my aquatic ritual before eventide. In late September the days grow noticeably shorter, but as a wise old owl has noted, the shorter the day, the longer the night.

After a bracing swim followed by a quick shower, I wrapped myself in a towel and debated whether or not to have a cigarette. I had already given up my after-dinner smoke for the one I enjoyed when Georgy girl called. If I had one now, I would have to surrender the one I could have before I lay me down to sleep. Not knowing what shape I would be in when I returned to my aerie, I thought it best to keep the option of having a late-night smoke wide open. The ability to procrastinate encouraged me to believe that I may still lick the habit in my lifetime.

Kings, presidents and generals are often called upon to make decisions, but none could be as daunting as what to wear when invited to dine in a gingerbread cottage with a policewoman. It was truly unprecedented. Flannel seemed too formal, denim too casual, seersucker too summery and sharkskin too mafioso, given the nature of my date's line of work.

After much soul-searching, I went for a pair of linen trousers in a gray I believe is called mouse and a fuchsia pima cotton polo, and topped it all off with a lightweight wool blazer in an inky black. Rather natty, I thought, as I slipped my size-eleven hoofs into a pair of Belgian loafers.

Not wishing to raid father's wine cellar, I stopped to purchase my obligatory offerings on the drive north. A red Rhônes, a White Burgundy and, feeling patriotic, I tossed in a bottle of New York state rosé. Going up the drive, I got the fish eye from the landlady and gave a friendly beep, which rattled her beaded curtain. I parked next to Georgy's Subaru and made my way up the path leading to her front door.

She was in a pair of black slacks, a white sweatshirt and an apron. Shod in sandals, I learned she painted her toenails a bright red. Her hair was pulled back and tied with a shiny blue ribbon. In a word, she looked adorable.

"I never know if I should serve the wine I bought for dinner or the one the guest brings," she said, taking the package from me.

"I'll answer that when I see what you're pouring. Good evening, Georgy. You look ravishing."

"Thanks. You look like an ad for pipe tobacco. English briar, actually." Vanishing behind a paneled folding screen that had been set up to hide the galley kitchen, she went on, "Take off the jacket and relax. I hope that shirt isn't fuchsia."

"It is," I called back.

"Then take it off, too," she pleaded.

"That comes later, dear, in the bedroom."

"Fat chance, buster." She emerged from the kitchen. "What would you like to drink?"

"What do you have?"

"What you see is what you get," she said, pointing to a small sideboard in the breakfast nook where a bar had been set up.

What I saw was vodka, scotch and rye. All unopened. She had gone out and bought them especially for tonight's dinner. Georgy girl was being very accommodating and Archy was in a dither. I have always approached a new romantic liaison with the confidence of a traveler holding a round-trip ticket, but as I boarded this one I didn't know if I wanted to return to from whence I came.

For mixers there was tonic, club soda, ginger ale and ice water. No Coke, so Cuba Libres, and all they implied, were impossible. In such predicaments one is thankful for small favors. "What can I get you?" I politely asked.

"Whatever you're having."

"You are a trusting soul," I said, deciding on vodka and tonic. No need to ask if she preferred lemon or lime, because neither was in the offering. As I poured, I noticed the table had been set with care. The silver was stainless steel, the plates delftware with a blue print glaze and the wineglasses perfect for a small apéritif. Lest I seem unkind, I must add that the napkins were in bone rings and a posy of flowers in a crystal vase stood in the center of the table. It was frightfully like the newlyweds' first night home after the honeymoon—but I get ahead of myself.

She popped out from behind the screen saying, "When Joey traded all this for a gilded cage with an ocean view he took our one bottle of booze and I never bothered replacing it. I like beer."

"Certainly not with dinner," I gasped.

"Especially with dinner."

"So his name was Joey," I stated.

"And still is, unless he changed it to something more catchy, like Guy or Brad or, Lord forbid, Jeb. Joseph Gallo. No relation to the Napa Valley Gallos. Joey's father was a mason."

"Serves you right for falling for an Italian," I said, drinks in hand. Turning, I almost ran into the screen. I put down the glasses, folded the screen and propped it against the nearest wall.

"What are you doing?" she cried.

"I can't have you popping in and out from behind that screen all evening. As Gertrude Stein so cleverly put it, a kitchen is a kitchen is a kitchen. Also, I can see you don't put arsenic in the saltcellar. Hmmm, something smells good."

"Thanks. It's Liz Arden. Very expensive."

"I am talking about the aroma emanating from the oven."

"Oh, that. Cut up chicken, cut up potatoes and cut up onions. Sprinkle with olive oil and bake till tender. Garnish with basil and oregano. The potatoes go in first, because they take the longest."

"Sounds Italian. One of Joey's recipes?"

"No, Archy. My mother's. She's Italian."

"Like I just said, a lovely people, the Italians. *Salute, bella.*"

"Cheers," she toasted, then proudly proclaimed, "I uncorked my wine to let it breathe."

I looked at the label and told her it had breathed its last hours ago. "We'll have the wine I brought."

"Archy McNally, you are opinionated—and pompous."

"I am an invitee. Be nice."

"An invitee who's taken over my dinner party."

"Dinner party? I thought this was yet another business meeting," I said, and was rewarded with that lovely neck-to-forehead blush.

"It is," she barked. "We can sit for a while. The chicken won't be ready for forty minutes. I set the timer."

The living area was furnished with a settee, club chairs, coffee table and lamps, comfortable but nondescript. Georgy said, as we took our places, that the cottage had come furnished. "I never got around to changing anything except the bedroom furniture, which you will never see."

"Then I won't show you mine," I quipped and got the blush. Oh, I could play her like a Stradivarius.

Until Georgy began giving me a summary of Whitehead's statement to the police I had almost forgotten the reason I was here. To make amends for this dereliction of duty, I listened attentively and could find no discrepancy in what the man had said to me and what he told the police.

"What do you think?" Georgy asked when she was finished.

What followed was a give-and-take very similar to the one I had had with father that afternoon. When done, we were no closer to a solution than when we started. As Binky might say, we were spinning our wheels.

"How can your boss hand over Harrigan or Whitehead to the District Attorney? Where's his proof that one of them murdered Swensen?"

"It's circumstantial," she said, "but it's all we have. They were both involved in the sale of the manuscript to Fortesque, and they were both in the motel room with the dead man. Harrigan even admits to giving Swensen the dope."

"I was also involved in the manuscript deal, even though I didn't know it at the time, and I was in the motel room," I told her. "Why isn't Delaney thinking of arresting me?"

"You're not off his list, Archy. I told you that. You three were the only ones to have been in the murder room, which makes you all prime suspects. Your saving grace, for now, is your good standing in the community and your lack of motive. But that could change. There's no witness to say you were mugged and the manuscript taken. You have no alibi on that score."

"I had a bump on my head, but it's disappeared. Good-bye alibi." Getting up to freshen my drink, I held out my hands. "Put on the cuffs, officer."

Refusing a refill, Georgy said, "Captain Delaney would have a fit if he knew I was collaborating with you. My job is on the line, Archy."

When I came back I promised, "I might yet make you the envy of the squad, Georgy girl."

"How so?"

"Listen and be enlightened. Do you see how we keep arranging and rearranging three cards, like a shark running a game of three-card monte? The three of us in the motel room. The three of them dealing with Fortesque. We're so intent on watching the cards, we forget to keep an eye on the dealer."

"But one of the cards is the dealer," Georgy said.

"A card can't be a dealer. A card is nothing more than a device. A means to an end."

"But all we have are those three," Georgy insisted.

"Really? I believe, and I'm sure Delaney does, too, that

two of our three darlings are working together. One, working alone, could not have created all the mischief that took place the night I made the exchange at the Crescent Motel. But which two?

"Something I heard this afternoon made me think there might be a joker in the deck. With your help I would like to flush it out."

She seemed leery. "My help? What did you have in mind?"

"A C.S.O."

"A what?"

"A Counter Sting Operation. Are you game?"

"Will it get me fired?"

"My dear, it may just get you a medal."

She was still dubious, but curious. "I'm listening."

The oven timer told us our forty minutes was up.

"It can wait till after dinner," I said. "Time, tide and a cut-up chicken wait for no man."

• Succotash," she announced, displaying the steaming bowl with pride. "From scratch. I scraped the corn off the cobs, and the limas are fresh."

It was delicious. As was the platter of chicken surrounded by crisp potatoes and onions. It was a down-home meal, and, amazing myself, I felt very much at home. We drank enough wine to make us scintillating and clever, but not enough to dull our senses. The evening, after all, was before us. I learned that Georgy is an Aquarian. I told her I was a Pisces.

"We go together like fish and water," she exclaimed.

Like I said—scintillating and clever.

19

The only thing Binky had seen on his evening vigil was Tommy Ambrose and friends.

"What were they doing on Dunbar Road at that hour of the night?"

"Coming from a party and on their way to the next one," Binky said, now without a hint of envy in the delivery. "You know that crowd."

I knew that crowd very well and cared for them not at all. Locals referred to the clique as Tommy Ambrose and Co. I called them the Nighthawks, a name borrowed from the famous Edward Hopper painting. For those not familiar with the term, Nighthawks are a strain of our breed who emerge after the last bar closes to gather in all-night diners, sipping coffee and puffing on unfiltered Camels. Where they emerge from and where they flee to at the first sign of dawn is questionable, but theories abound.

In Hopper's work we see them through the glass facade of the diner; a study in quiet desperation, forlorn and forsaken, they seem to be focusing their attention on the clerk behind the counter, his hands engaged in a task hidden by the counter's top.

An artistic entrepreneur with a flair for the macabre redid the work, substituting the faces of dead film stars for Hopper's threesome, adding the figure of the late James Dean peering futilely in the window as if wondering, as he did in life, if this was where he belonged. The poster enjoyed a vogue far exceeding Hopper's original, proving that we get what we deserve.

No, I don't care for Tommy Ambrose, and since he began taking book on my love life I find him even more insufferable. Knowing it was hopeless, I said to Binky, "I hope you didn't tell him what you were doing there."

"I had to say something," came the expected reply.

"And . . ."

"I said I had read about the light in the window of the Beaumont house and was curious. I didn't say I was on a case or mention any names."

Except the name of the house, which said it all. Well, what difference did it make? All of Palm Beach knew that Tyler Beaumont was in our midst, and those who hadn't seen the article in the newspaper had certainly heard about it by now. I would bet my personally autographed photo of King Kong that Binky would have company on tonight's watch.

"Did Tommy give you the latest odds on my bout with Alejandro?"

"He said there was a lot of action after you showed up with the blonde. When the odds began dropping in your favor, Tommy put out the word that you got the blonde from an escort service."

I was sorry I had asked. The best way to handle Tommy Ambrose and his ilk was to ignore them. Anything more only encourages them.

I told Binky that after tonight we would call it quits on Dunbar Road, as it was an exercise in futility. Binky readily agreed. He deposited a pathetically small packet of mail on the desk and, backing out of my space, told me, "Al Rogoff is back."

Now, that was news. "Back from where?"

"A quick hop to New York. Just one night. You think he has a girl up there?"

He sure does. She's a ticket broker who gets him choice seats to the opera, ballet or the kind of concerts that get sold out the minute the performing artist is announced. Not knowing what Al had told his cohorts in blue, I suggested to Binky that he direct the query to Al.

"I did," Binky said. "He told me to mind my own business."

Minding my own business was just what I was not going to do this sunny Palm Beach day. I put in a call to Decimus Fortesque and the first step in my C.S.O. was put in motion. The butler, Zimmermann, informed me that the master was at his club and was expected home directly after lunch. I said it was imperative that I see him this afternoon and would come to the house at three.

"I'll wait if he's not home yet, and should he get there before me, keep him there," I commanded Zimmermann.

"Very good, sir."

I then put in a call to Al at home and got him there.

"They ain't arrested you yet?" Al said, sounding disappointed.

"They have not, and I'm going to make sure they never do. Are you working tonight?"

"The graveyard shift," he said.

"Can I buy you lunch at the Pelican?"

"Are you still a suspect, pal?"

"Like the thirteenth juror, I get called if someone falls out. The odds are a zillion to one they'll put me in the pokey."

"Sounds like your chances of routing Alejandro from your harem."

"Binky Watrous has a big mouth."

"You're telling me. I'll meet you at the Pelican, because I want to see you on another matter. I'll be there at noon but can't stay more than an hour. I have to get a haircut, pick up my laundry and stock the pantry."

"If you had a wife, Al, you wouldn't have to do anything but get a haircut."

"If I had a wife, pal, I wouldn't need a haircut. I'd have pulled them all out."

I chuckled, told him we would indulge in a hamburger at the bar and signed off, having no idea why he wanted to see me. Having enough on my plate to keep me noshing all morning, Al's tidbit could wait till lunch.

Now for step two of the C.S.O. A bit premature, I'm afraid, as I had not completed step one, which was to get Fortesque's permission to proceed. That would have to come after the fact, as time was of the essence. If he refused to go along, which I doubted, we would be back to square one and, perhaps more damaging, alert our trio to what was afoot. But the gist of a sting operation being *cojones,* I called my ex-client, Claudia Lester.

"Oh, it's you," she said when I identified myself. "Have you found the money and the manuscript?"

"That's what I was going to ask you, Ms. Lester."

"You've come to the wrong place. Try Mr. Harrigan."

"You know he's back and has been to the police?"

"I can read, Mr. McNally. Are they buying his story?"

"Right now they're not buying any of your stories, but my client, Decimus Fortesque, is once again in a buying mood. Interested?"

There came, as the hacks say, an audible silence, and I defy anyone to say it better. "Are you there, Ms. Lester?" I prompted.

"What do you mean?" she asked, wanting not information but confirmation.

"I mean he's a foolish old man with more money than sense, but he is my client and I am doing his bidding. He's willing to make another offer for the manuscript."

"To repeat, Mr. McNally, why call me? I don't have it."

You had to hand it to her. A pro right down to the wire. Not even the promise of more loot was going to catch the lady off guard. She wouldn't give an inch until she knew exactly what Fortesque's offer entailed, which, alas, poor Decimus didn't know himself at this juncture.

"You say Harrigan has it. He says you have it. And Whitehead says you both have it. Deci Fortesque figures that one of you must have it, and he wants it."

"He's in for fifty thousand," she replied. "Isn't he concerned where it went to?"

"Sure he is," I told her, "but in for a penny, in for a pound, as those who have *beaucoup* pounds like to say. He's an avid collector, Ms. Lester, and in your trade I'm sure you know how tenacious they can be when it comes to getting what they want. Haven't some been known to do murder as the means to that end?"

"Are you saying Deci murdered Swensen, Mr. McNally?"

"Who murdered Lawrence Swensen is the concern of the police and of no interest to me or my client." The lie rolled off my lips with genuine conviction. "And we both know Mr. Fortesque didn't murder anyone."

I could hear the match strike on the other end, followed by the delicious intake of the first puff. "So what's the deal?" she said, exhaling.

"He would like to meet with the three of you this evening at nine and make his offer. Will you come?"

"Have Matthew and Rodney agreed to be there?" she wanted to know.

"This is my first call, but I imagine they will."

"I'll think about it," she said.

I had her. She couldn't stand being left out if there was a chance her partners would attend. "Do you have Fortesque's address?"

"I have it." And she rang off.

Thanks to Georgy girl, I now had the numbers of the motels where Harrigan and Whitehead were stopping. I called both and gave them the same story I had given to Claudia Lester. They wanted to know if the other two would be there, and I assured them they would. Harrigan told me Claudia Lester hung up on him every time he called. "The bitch is made of ice," he whined. "Do the police believe her or me?"

"Not my business, Matt. I want that manuscript for my client, and when I get it you can all go to the devil."

"I didn't kill Swensen," he protested.

"That, too, is not my business. See you at nine. Dress is informal."

Whitehead was the only one who betrayed his greed. "Well, we're finally getting down to business," he gloated. "If Fortesque is going to make an offer, I want not only my cut but my share of the fifty those conniving pirates stole."

This implied that there was no question of the manuscript's surfacing should an offer be made. Encouraged, I said, "After you hear what Fortesque has to say, you can make your own arrangements with the pirates. See you at nine."

"Are they going to arrest Harrigan for the murder?" he quickly got in.

"What do you think?" I asked.

"After what I told the police, they should arrest both of them. One for murder and the other for conspiracy."

"You are not without blame, Mr. Whitehead."

"I was only trying to make a dishonest buck. Arrest everyone in this country who does that and we'd need to build a wall around Texas to imprison them."

Not wishing to honor the inanity with a reply, I hung up on Rodney Whitehead and placed a call to Tyler Beaumont at the Colony. I told him I was just checking in, had nothing of note to report, and asked how he was getting along.

"Just fine, Mr. McNally. I see the press knows I'm here."

I told him that was inevitable in a town like Palm Beach, especially after the incident at his parents' home. "Are you seeing friends?"

"Afraid not," he said. "I'm being a recluse. Would you like to rescue me from boredom and have a drink with me this evening?"

"I have an appointment at nine, but am free before. What about seven?"

"Seven it is, Mr. McNally. The Colony on Hammon Avenue."

"I know where the Colony is, Ty. Till later."

• We were Simon Pettibone's first customers, taking him away from Wall Street via cable TV and to drawing a couple of lagers for Sergeant Rogoff and me. In uniform, Al Rogoff looks like Attila the Hun in uniform. In civvies, Al Rogoff looks like Attila the Hun in civvies. But don't judge the man by the facade. Al is kind, gentle and cultivated.

"So what did you see in New York?" I asked after tasting the beer, which was choice.

"Voina y Mir," he answered, as if recalling a particularly pleasant dream.

I had to think about that one. *"War and Peace?* The one by Tolstoy?"

"You're pretty good, Archy. The book is by the count. The opera is by Sergei Prokofiev."

I was impressed, but when Al drops names I always am. "It's a grand and very long tome," I said.

"So is the opera. Over three hundred supers and four and a half hours long with intermission. Magnificent from start to finish."

I assume he meant from the war to the peace. "A man named Ernest Newman," I told Al, "said he didn't know which would be better—an opera without an interval, or an interval without an opera. I might go for the latter."

"Your taste is in your mouth, Archy."

"I wouldn't want it anyplace else," I admitted. And speaking of which, I beckoned to Priscilla as she drifted by in a pair of white jeans that looked as if they had been painted on and a cotton T-shirt that looked on the verge of erupting.

"Well, well, well," she remarked, "if it isn't the PI and the flatfoot. You still looking for the guy who clobbered you, Mr. Spade?"

"Would you marry me?" Al asked as if he meant it.

"Depends," Priscilla told him.

"On what?"

"Your bank balance."

Al shook his head. "Right now I'm overdrawn, but I get paid tomorrow."

"Stop it, both of you," I cut in. "Sergeant Rogoff is bemused by Russian music and not responsible for what he says. I know for a fact that he does not get paid tomorrow."

"Then I'll have to decline, Sergeant Rogoff. Would you like to see a menu instead?"

"No need," I answered for Al, "we're eating at the bar. Leroy's burgers, more rare than medium, a side order of fries, very crisp, and a few kosher dills, sliced."

"Two death-wish specials coming up," Priscilla proclaimed, and marched off.

"She's probably right," Al lamented over our lunch order.

"Would you rather have Jell-O over a mound of cottage cheese?"

He winced. "God forbid."

"Then shut up." If one goes, one may as well go all the way.

I asked Al what he knew about the murder at the Crescent Motel. Not being in his jurisdiction, and having been away for two days, he didn't know much, but thanks to his neighbor, Binky, he was up to snuff on all the vital statistics concerning Georgia O'Hara. "Some dish, quote and unquote, Binky Watrous," Al said.

"That she is, Al." Being in need of a confidant, I told him what was happening with Georgy and me socially, not professionally.

Al grimaced, which, on his mug, was frightening. "I told you I didn't want to discuss the case with you because you were a suspect, and now you're telling me you're dating the officer in charge of the investigation.

Cripes, I don't know who's being more loco, you or the dame."

"What's the big deal? You and I have worked cases together."

"Never when you were a suspect, pal, and we never dated."

"Are you bragging or complaining, Al?"

"Come off it, Archy. You know what I'm talking about. What does her boss have to say about it?"

"He doesn't know."

"That's what I thought. If I was you, I would can it or at least wait till the case was closed."

Hoping to have closure in a few days, I nodded as if in agreement. Of course, Al was right and I was wrong to make him privy to my indiscretion. Coming from a discreet inquirer only compounded the issue. Sensing this was as far as he wanted to go with the subject, I dropped it and reminded him that he had something he wanted to discuss with me. "What is it, Al?"

"The Beaumont house. Binky tells me you have him on a midnight watch but he won't tell me why. Will you?"

"Why do you want to know, Al?"

"Because the more I think about it, the more I'm certain I saw a light in that upstairs window. Now I read in Spindrift's column that the Beaumont boy is here in Palm Beach. What gives, Archy?"

Here I was up against that old dilemma. How far could I go without breaking my client's trust, however bizaare the confidence. I owed Al something, and if he now believed there was a light in that window, I owed my client Al's professional opinion. Avoiding telling Al who Tyler thought was playing with the light switches in the house, I settled on telling him what I had told Ursi and Lolly, which wasn't exactly a fabrication but a slight distortion of the truth. Tyler Beaumont had heard about Al's sighting and asked me to investigate the possibility that someone was prowling around the place.

"How come his parents didn't come, too?" Al commented.

"His parents are in England, playing the ponies with princes and earls."

"You serious?"

"Cross my heart and hope to die. The Beaumonts do things like that, and some people sit through *War and Peace* set to music." I told Al that the family had had the house looked at this past summer when they heard similar reports, but nothing was found. "I'm doing this as a favor to the boy," I said. "The only thing Binky saw last night was Tommy Ambrose."

"Tommy Ambrose? Now, ain't that interesting," Al reflected.

Priscilla arrived with the death-wish specials just as Mr. Pettibone positioned our place mats. Al was as reluctant to discuss the light in the Beaumont window as he was to hear about my relationship with Georgia O'Hara. In the game of give-and-take, we had both given a little but took nothing in return—except a scrumptious lunch. This evened the score, and, hey, you can't have everything.

20

"Do you have the manuscript?" Fortesque pounced as soon I entered the library where he was seated.

"Good day to you, too, sir," I said. "I don't come bearing the manuscript but a plan to get it."

"A plan? When Sam told me you had urgent business, I thought you found my property. Since the press and the TV got onto this thing I've been hounded by everyone, including the police and a New York publisher who seems to think that if the manuscript turns up it belongs to them. Wishful thinking, I told 'em."

Once again, father knew best. Thanks to the murder of Lawrence Swensen, the once clandestine discovery of the Capote papers was now in the public domain. If the manuscript ever did reappear and it was what Whitehead claimed it to be, Decimus Fortesque might just need a lawyer to hang on to his treasure. And there was nothing father liked better than a challenge attached to a hefty fee.

In spite of Fortesque's vexation with the publisher, one could see that he was very pleased to have, or almost have, a collectible that was causing a minor sensation. This might yet prove more famous than his collection of wives.

On that subject, he ranted, "Whenever my name appears in print it's followed by the names of all my brides. One rag even wrote that my monthly alimony bill equaled the average American's yearly income."

I was impressed. "Is that true, sir?"

"If it is, the average American is doing okay for himself. Now, what's this plan? Is it guaranteed to get me the manuscript, or my money back?"

"Nothing in this world is guaranteed, Mr. Fortesque, except death and taxes."

"And alimony," he added.

"Of course, sir. And alimony. May I sit?"

With a protuberant gaze, he indicated a chair and waved me into it. "Sorry, but when I get worked up I forget the niceties. Can I offer you something? I'll ring for Sam."

Knowing what Sam would bring, I declined, saying I had enjoyed a larger than usual lunch.

"I ate at my club," he reported. "Salad and a sip of white wine. Tiresome, but healthy. So what's the plan? Does it involve the police? If it does, the answer is no. Don't like the police, man. Nosy bastards. But I must say the one who came about the bloody manuscript was an eyeful. Nothing like that on the force in my day. If I hadn't given up marrying for collecting, I would have signed her up for the alimony brigade."

I couldn't wait to tell Georgy this. "What makes you think she would accept, sir?"

"Why wouldn't she, unless she's a Communist and opposed to money and a life of luxury? One of my wives was a stewardess for a big airline. 'Marry me and fly free,' she said, and I took the bait. She quit her job and lost her privileges with the line. To keep her promise she bought a jet, hired a pilot and fell in love with him. I got custody of the plane, and she got custody of the pilot. You wouldn't be in the market for a used jet, would you?"

If Fortesque's marriages had lasted as long as his diatribes, he might still be married to number one. "I'm not in the market for a jet, but if I hear of anyone who is, I'll send them around. Now, about the plan . . ."

"Yes. The plan. What about it?"

"I invited the three principals in this affair to meet with you at nine this evening."

"Don't know as I want to, man. One of them is a murderer."

"There's a possibility we may find out which one," I said.

"That's a matter for the police. Why not tell them?"

"Because you just said you don't want anything to do with the police."

"So I did. Go on. What's the deal?"

I told him what I wanted, which was to offer the three another fifty thousand for the manuscript.

"Funny," he said. "A hundred thousand was the original asking price. I offered half and they accepted it."

Or pretended to accept it, I was thinking. It was now clear that the scheme to get another fifty out of Fortesque was hatched the day he held firm on his offer.

"This is a tough crowd and not easily fooled. You're going to have to convince them that you are desperate to get your mitts on that book. You're willing to forgive, forget and pay. Let's keep Swensen's murder out of it. It's police business and might make them suspect that finding the murderer, not the manuscript, is our goal."

"And it's all a sham," he said.

"Of course," I assured him.

"Good," he replied, "because I won't give them another cent, but they're not going to admit they have it and hand it over just like that. If that's your plan, forget it."

His acumen was right on target. Just when you thought you were dealing with a man who's always out to lunch, he lets you know he's playing with a full deck. I was now confident that he'd rise to the challenge and play the game according to my rules. After all, he was a zillionaire looking to get his money's worth and woe be unto the interlopers.

"There's more to my plan than just the offer, sir. Trust me."

"Let's hear it."

"After you make your offer, I will tell them how the exchange is to be made." Here, I delineated just what I would say and do. He listened, eyes bulging with glee, and nodded his assent.

"So the police are in on it," he said when I had finished.

"Strictly speaking, sir, they are not. I mean, should it work, they'll make an arrest. Should it not, they'll claim ignorance of our intentions."

"Who's the murderer, Archy? And why kill if they had the money and the manuscript?"

"Who? I don't know. Why? Because they wanted more money, and now we're going to give it to them, in spades."

"Answered prayers," he said.

"I hope so, sir."

When I took my leave, Fortesque asked me what I knew about Tyler Beaumont's visit to Palm Beach. "It's all the talk at the club today. Is it true he came down especially to see you?"

Now so used to the story I had concocted, I dished it out to Fortesque with the ease of a politician on the campaign trail.

"That house is cursed," Fortesque said. "I suppose you know what happened there. The steps should have been carpeted, but I heard they never were because Sarah Beaumont didn't want anything clashing with her fancy ball gowns when she made her grand entrances. I met Dmitri and Audrey at one of the Beaumont parties. He was a Romanov and she was an Emery. Not the first title-and-money combo to settle in Palm Beach."

I left Fortesque nodding in his chair, perhaps envisioning the night Sarah Beaumont came down those steps to have her hand kissed by the Grand Duke Dmitri Pavlovitch.

As Sam led me to the door, I recalled his comment when last he ushered me out. "You once told me to beware of answered prayers," I reminded him.

"So I did, sir."

"Will you tell me what you meant?"

With the air of a sage counseling a monk in training, he lectured, "When Mr. Fortesque gave up marrying for collecting, I turned to baking and Prince Siddhartha, both very calming after having to adjust to eight mistresses in as many years. The Prince believes that everything is nothing, and therefore nothing is everything. So one should pray for nothing. I believe he had the edge on the Carmelite mystic by a few millennia. Mr. Fortesque's quest for *Answered Prayers* has led to nothing but grief. Should he find the book, I imagine it will prove even more grievous. And tell me, sir, did the éclairs you wished for and got bring you joy?"

"As a matter of fact, Sam, they didn't. My housekeeper was very put out at having to serve someone else's pastry for dessert, and I got the blame."

"Just as I thought, sir. Good day."

Before I got the door closed on me, I said, "Prince Siddhartha?"

"Buddha, sir."

"Carmelite mystic?"

"Saint Teresa of Avila, sir."

Seeing he was in an answering mood, I fed him, "Ethel Merman?"

"A third cousin, once removed, sir."

• As they say up the road a piece, all systems were go and the countdown had begun. When a case reaches this point it starts an eddy of adrenaline bubbling in my veins, and I was hard-pressed to keep my foot from gunning the Miata's gas pedal to the floor. I went back to the office to give father a wrap-up but was too late. He had left for a business meeting and wasn't expected to return. I put in a call to Georgy and told her that we were poised on the launching pad.

"Tomorrow night?" she asked.

"That's what I'm hoping. I don't see any reason to prolong it."

"In fact," she said, "it's not a moment too soon. We're state troopers and not equipped or mandated for long-term investigative work. The case is about to be turned over to those who are. Also, Archy, we have to cover three sites.

I'll take one, but who can I assign the other two when I'm not supposed to be in on this?"

"Can't you assign it to a couple of subordinates? What's a lieutenant for?"

"For taking the blame, that's what for. I'll try to come up with something. How is Fortesque taking it?"

"With all the aplomb of an actor on opening night. By the by, Georgy, he was quite taken by your charms. He said he thought of making you number nine."

"Really? The last time Swathmoore and I sat down to chop suey my fortune cookie said, *'The best times of your life have yet to be lived,'* and gave my lucky number as nine. If this all pans out, I'll have it all."

"Everything is nothing, Georgy."

"Really? Says who?"

"A very wise man, that's who. What are you doing tonight?" I asked.

"I'm going to watch *Hotel Berlin.* I'm in love with Helmut Dantine—posthumously, I'm afraid."

"That's on tape?" I cried.

"It is for me. A friend of mine has it on sixteen-millimeter and pulled a tape for me. You know it's the campiest war film ever made."

What an extraordinary woman—and she could cook, if one liked succotash. "Would you marry me?" I proposed.

"Only if Decimus Fortesque changes his mind."

Then I got an idea that I would later regret but, at the time, seemed inconsequential. "How would you like to meet a millionaire who's younger and richer than Fortesque and handsomer and more alive than Helmut Dantine?"

"Twist my arm," she begged.

"I can't pick you up, drive you home and be back in

time to be at Fortesque's at nine, so meet me at the Colony at seven and say hello to Tyler Beaumont."

She squealed like a teenager. "*The* Tyler Beaumont?"

"Is there any other?"

"What should I wear?" she moaned.

"As little as possible."

"You're a dirty old man, Archy McNally."

After dealing with Georgy, I got ready to pack it in on Royal Palm Way and head for a swim before meeting with both clients this evening. Halfway out the door my phone rang. I vacillated in the doorway, stepped out, came back, shrugged and returned to answer it. On such trifling decisions are our fates decided? I fear they are. It was Connie.

"Did I get you at a bad time, Archy?"

"No, not at all. I was just getting ready to call it quits."

"Same here," she said, "but it's been on my mind all day and I wanted to do it before I left."

"Do what, Connie?" I must say it was good to hear her voice.

"Apologize for the champagne dinner. Binky said you might have to sell the Miata."

"I'd sell Binky first," I told her. "Look, Connie, let's say we both acted a little foolish and forget it happened."

"Okay. But some of us acted more foolishly than others."

She had to turn the screw one more time, but I was so happy she was still speaking to me I acquiesced by keeping my mouth shut.

"If you're free tonight," she said, "I'll take you to dinner at Café L'Europe and you can order champagne."

I was truly touched. "Connie," I pleaded, "I would like nothing better and would even go dutch, but I have two client meetings this evening. Seven and nine. Can we do it some other time?"

"Sure," she said, and went on, "I've been reading about the Capote case. Lady C is telling everyone who'll listen that she's in the book. I hope you're keeping out of dark alleys, Archy. We would hate to lose you. When you told me about the murder, I didn't realize you were in so deep. Sorry if I sounded crass."

I was even more touched. It seemed I was being offered an olive branch. I think Connie was as undecided about our future as I and not burning any bridges. We parted with a promise of talking the next day.

• Georgy wore what I believe was once called a sack dress, and perhaps still is, in gray. This is a shapeless garment that hangs straight from the shoulder to the hemline, which, in Georgy's rendering, was mid-knee. That print silk scarf, last seen around her neck, was now wrapped around her waist, shaping the dress to her lithe figure. She was shod in black low-heeled espadrilles.

For my two, and diverse, engagements I had gotten into a pair of baggy flannels favored by rich gentlemen and British royalty, topping them with a navy hopsacking jacket with toggle fasteners. I must say we made a fetching couple.

Tyler was already seated in the lounge and waved us over as we entered. "He is adorable," Georgy whispered.

"And alive," I reiterated.

The young man stood when we arrived and I introduced him to Georgy, leaving out her profession and rank. Given Tyler's rather precarious emotional state, I didn't want him to think I had come to arrest him. "You told me you didn't have a girl, Mr. McNally, and you turn up with Miss America."

"Girl? Oh, Georgy. I picked her up on my way here. She was hitchhiking on Ocean Boulevard. Shall we sit?"

"I'm delighted he gave you a ride, Ms. O'Hara."

Georgy seemed to enjoy being the centerpiece of conversation and, with a toothy grin, told Tyler how thrilled she was to meet him. Georgy girl is a bit ingenuous when it comes to the social graces. One can be "thrilled" to meet a person of note. A celebrity, as it were. Tyler's only claim to fame was his wealth, which was now clearly the reason for Georgy's elation. The rich don't like to be reminded of the fact. They want to be loved for themselves.

But what could one expect from a little girl from Little Rock? Come to think of it, Georgy wasn't such a little girl. With her in heels, we could walk shoulder to shoulder. However, like a diamond in the rough, her charm lay in the expectation of things to come. To pipe poetically, *"Heard melodies are sweet, but those unheard are sweeter . . ."*

Tyler had a beer before him, in a fine pilsner glass, and, summoning a waiter, asked us what our pleasure would be. Eschewing negronis, Georgy went for a white wine, saying a Pinot would be fine, and I joined Tyler in a beer. After ordering, we lapsed into one of those embarrassed silences that descend upon strangers in social situations. With smiling faces we were all thinking, Where do we go from here? In the universal language of resort communities, we spoke of the weather.

After giving Tyler a blow-by-blow of our Palm Beach summer, he favored us with the droughts, rains and sun-filled days experienced on the east end of Long Island. We refrained from telling him what we expected this winter, as it was very much like what we experienced this past summer. Besides, Tyler would have no comeback, as he never stepped foot in the Hamptons between the days Labor and Memorial.

When our drinks came, Georgy announced her acquisition of *Hotel Berlin* on tape. Explaining her find, Tyler was immediately interested and made her promise to send him a copy. The ice broken, there followed a lively and interesting conversation on topics ranging from the classics to the comics and a few stops between. Thanks to Georgy, our impromptu cocktail party was a roaring success. Tyler Beaumont was bright, witty, interesting and, yes, even adorable.

We ordered another round and were so engrossed in our repartee that we didn't notice the man standing over our table until Tyler looked up, spotted him and blanched. All conversation ceased.

"I didn't know you were in Palm Beach," Tyler said.

"I didn't know you were till this morning. Aren't you going to introduce me to your friends?"

The party broke up shortly thereafter. "Who do you suppose that was?" Georgy asked of the uninvited one.

"I would guess he's Tyler's caretaker."

"What?"

"Can't explain right now, Georgy, but I will when next we meet. I'll call you at home after my next meeting. Did you secure extra help?"

"I'm working on it. Why didn't you say hello to your friend in there?"

"What friend?"

"The lovely Latina lady you spoke to at the Pelican Club the other night."

It was my turn to blanch. "Connie? Are you telling me Connie was in the Colony Lounge tonight?"

Georgy shrugged. "If that's her name. She was sitting a few tables from us, having a drink with a girlfriend."

"Did she see me?"

"I know she saw me," Georgy answered. "She looked right at me."

O death, where is thy sting?

21

Deci Fortesque gave a performance worthy of a Barrymore. The set was the great room of his Lake Worth home. Bigger than life—as drama should be—and reeking of money, it put the audience in a position of supplicants come to hear their fate. Mother Nature, in charge of the lighting and special effects, had turned off the stars and caused a mist to rise from the lake, dappling the party lights of the occasional craft navigating the waterway to give it the eerie appearance of a Flying Dutchman.

But even with this support, it was the leading man who stole the show. Dressed in a green velvet smoking jacket, with black lapels, over a tuxedo shirt and hand-knotted black bow tie, Deci was every inch Mr. Noblesse Oblige, ready to suffer the poor, sink his hands into his deep pockets and come up with pardons and compensation for his wayward serfs.

Now, no thinking gentleman would receive guests in a

smoking jacket, but Deci was playing to the stalls and, by gum, getting away with it. His audience, awed and expectant, stared and listened in rapt attention as he made his offer.

However, lest we forget, this audience was also playing a part. Three swindlers posing as victims, all eager to get what they had come for—more money—without libeling themselves. One of them had what Fortesque was willing to trade for another fifty thousand, but how to get their hands on the cash without soiling them was the question. Oh, what a fine fiddle they were in.

Arriving separately, they chose to sit as far from each other as availability allowed, which was very far indeed. Claudia Lester, looking very smart in black, sat with her shapely legs crossed at the knee, chain-smoking. When she wasn't looking at Fortesque her eyes darted about the room, appraising its worth and regretting that she had never had the old geezer to comfort on a nonstop from L.A. to Sydney. Had she, she would now be sitting beside him, not before him or, at the very least, on his monthly payroll.

Rodney Whitehead had thought to get his suit pressed for the occasion, but it didn't help the sad sack look any happier. Twice he removed his rimless glasses to give them, and his forehead, a wipe with his handkerchief. Each time he replaced the glasses, his ample frame heaved with an audible sigh. Surely he was envisioning what Fortesque's house and its contents would buy him in Costa Rica.

Poor Matthew Harrigan looked the worst of the lot. Tired, drawn and unable to sit still for two consecutive minutes, he kept watching the door as if expecting the police to raid the joint with weapons drawn, ready to cart him off to Death Row. When Sam wheeled in the tea trolley, now serving as a portable bar, Harrigan actually rose from his seat, hovered in the air, then fell back into it. I thought he had fainted.

Lester took a scotch and soda; Harrigan a neat scotch; Whitehead a bourbon and branch water. I stood behind Fortesque, who faced his audience with Lester on his right, Harrigan to his left and Whitehead between the two.

Fortesque made his offer with all the pathos of a rich collector determined to get his spoils and damn the cost. I think he did it so well because he was typecast for the part and the surroundings spoke for his ability to deliver the cash if they, or one of them, would deliver the goods.

Naturally, it was Claudia Lester who broke the silence after Fortesque made his offer. "Mr. Fortesque," she opened, "as a professional with her reputation at stake, I want you to know that I carried out, to the letter, the bargain we struck. Mr. McNally can vouch for the fact that I had him count the money in my presence and gave it to him to be used for the purchase of the manuscript from Lawrence Swensen at the agreed-upon price."

Harrigan was out of his seat, spilling scotch down the front of his shirt as he pointed a threatening finger at his former partner. "She's a liar," he shouted. "A damn liar. She had me go to the motel and drug Swensen. That's why she had to tell McNally he was buying her diary from a young guy. McNally gave me the cash and I gave him the manuscript—"

"Mr. Harrigan," I broke in, "please don't shout and be seated. We're not here to—"

"No way," he bellowed. "She had her say, now let me have mine. These bastards are setting me up to take the murder rap, too. I drugged Swensen, that's all. I gave her the money," here he pointed at Claudia Lester as if there were another "her" in the room, soiling his shirt with more scotch, "and she told me Mr. McNally brought her the manuscript. I didn't even know Whitehead was in Palm Beach. She told me he was back in New York."

Looking bored with Harrigan's oft-told tale, Lester blew smoke rings at the high ceiling, secure in the fact that he who shouts the loudest loses.

"Please be seated, Mr. Harrigan," I tried again. "Sam, perhaps you can freshen Mr. Harrigan's drink." Sam nodded woefully, no doubt enjoying all the misery *Answered Prayers* had visited upon those who lusted after it. "I did not deliver the manuscript to Ms. Lester," I told Harrigan, and the room in general. "Someone took it from me in the Crescent's parking lot."

Now seated and swilling the scotch Sam had just poured for him, Harrigan cried, "Not me. I got in my car and drove back to the Ambassador to deliver the cash to Claudia. Whitehead showed up after I took off, or maybe he was there all the time."

Hearing his name prompted Whitehead to take the floor. "Mr. Fortesque, I must protest Matthew's insinuation. I went to the Crescent to get my finder's fee from Swensen and found him dead. I did not clobber Mr. McNally or remove the manuscript from his car. I don't have it or your money. Furthermore, Mr. Fortesque, I am out of a job and have no hope of getting another in my chosen field.

"Unlike others I could name, I am a true professional, an expert on old manuscripts who could be very helpful to you in acquiring texts from private collections. Texts one has heard of but never hoped to—"

"Mr. Whitehead," I said, cutting him off in his bid to become Deci's personal purveyor of purple prose, "I must again remind you and the others that we are here for one reason only—to initiate an exchange of fifty thousand dollars, in cash, for the completed and unpublished manuscript of Truman Capote's *Answered Prayers.*"

"I don't have it, Mr. McNally," Whitehead stated.

"Nor do I," Claudia Lester joined in.

Harrigan laughed, the sound more hysterical than joyous. "One of them has it," he said, and giggled. "Give them a lie-detector test. Would you be willing to take one, Claudia? You, Whitehead? I would." He offered his arm. "Go on, hook me up." This, of course, unhooked more scotch from his glass, this time anointing a most embarrassing portion of his trousers.

At the start of our little theatrical I was ready to give Decimus Fortesque the Tony for his performance. Now, I wanted to call it a three-way split and hand one to Claudia Lester, one to Matthew Harrigan and one to Rodney Whitehead for the most convincing portrayals of our young century. They were making it perfectly clear that they had nothing to lose by sticking to their squalid tales. At worst, they could walk away with the money and the manuscript. I had to show them how they could double the ante without risk of exposure.

Their refusal to cave under pressure had me toying with the idea of aborting my C.S.O. Why risk making a fool of myself—yet again—on this evening of ignominy? There was no stopping now, as one of them had latched onto the line we tossed out and turned it into a noose—not with a lie, but with the truth.

"It seems to me, Mr. Fortesque, and Mr. McNally, that this meeting has served no purpose in getting any of us what we want," Claudia Lester wisely announced. "I don't have the manuscript or the money, so I thank you for your hospitality and now I really have to run."

She began to rise, and Whitehead followed her lead. "I don't have what you want either, Mr. Fortesque."

"They're both lying," Harrigan ranted, not wanting the party to break up until he had been absolved of all sin.

Fortesque, who had not spoken a word since making his offer, now tugged on my sleeve. "Get on with it, man," he ordered.

Arms raised as if I were about to conduct the Boston Pops, I began my pitch. "Please, keep your seats for just another few minutes and listen to our proposition." That got their attention. "Mr. Fortesque and I don't believe any of you." There was some grumbling and a shuffling of feet. "If we did, we wouldn't have called this conclave. One of you has what Mr. Fortesque wants, and we aim to get it without putting any of you in an awkward position."

"I don't have it," Harrigan shouted.

Again, I raised my arms. "Please hear me out. Mr. Fortesque, as he has just told you, is willing to double the price for the manuscript, which, I believe, was the original asking price. He doesn't care who's doing what to whom, or why. Least of all does he want to get involved with a murder investigation. He just wants what's owed him, albeit at a premium, after which you can all go on your merry ways, or as far as the police are willing to let you go.

"None of you have the manuscript? Fine. If you happen to be in contact with the person who does have it, tell said person that I will deliver fifty thousand dollars, in cash, to him or her in return for the manuscript. To show Mr. Fortesque's good faith, the exchange will be made as follows.

"I will be in front of my club, the Pelican Club, at eight tomorrow evening. Said person can hire a car and driver to pick me up and take me to wherever said person awaits with the manuscript. The driver will make sure he is not being followed. No tricks, no traps. After the exchange, said person can ride off into the sunset, but not before arranging transportation for me back to the club. Any questions?"

There were no questions, only blank stares. Then a foghorn wailed across the lake and, as if it were a furtive signal, the three of them were on their feet, all suddenly eager to be off and running. But to where? Or to whom?

They thanked Fortesque for his hospitality, except Harrigan, who was hot on Claudia Lester's tail, babbling at the back of her head. Whitehead, mumbling inaudibly, brought up the rear. Curtain.

"How did I do?" Fortesque erupted like a neophyte after an audition.

"Splendid," I complimented. "And me?"

"I don't think they believed you."

• I called Georgy from my garret and told her that we were on for eight tomorrow night.

"How did it go?" she asked.

"I think they took the bait. Did you get more help?"

"Swathmoore and another rookie. Neither will be officially on duty, Archy. All they can do is observe. And I told Delaney what we were up to."

That was a shock. "Why, Georgy?"

"He was going to bring in Harrigan tomorrow for another interrogation and maybe even hold him overnight. You wanted them all on the loose, didn't you?"

"It's essential," I said. "How did Delaney take it?"

"He wasn't overjoyed, but he has to turn the case over to

the big boys on Monday and this is his last hope of handing them something more than an empty plate. There's a lot of competition on the force, Archy."

So Al Rogoff had often told me. "Let's hope we don't disappoint, Georgy."

"Do you have a cell phone?"

"No. But I can borrow Binky's."

"You really should get one, Archy."

There were a lot of things I really should do, and getting a cell phone was the least of them. I told Georgy what position I wanted her to take.

"Why that particular one?" she questioned.

"An educated guess. How was *Hotel Berlin*?"

"Divine," she gushed. "When this is over, we'll watch it together."

When what is over? I pondered, as I bid her good night.

I washed, brushed, undressed and wrapped myself in a comfy robe. I poured a generous mark and lit an English Oval. I sat at my desk, opened my journal and stared at the blank page. I was miserable.

In all the years I had lied to Connie about my extracurricular activities, and got away with them, I never dreamed that the truth would trip me up. *But it was a client meeting,* I heard myself insisting.

In answer, all I heard was Georgy saying, *I know she saw me. She looked right at me.*

And the truth shall set you free. From what? From having to make the decision I had been putting off all week because it had now been thrust upon me? I didn't even have a daisy to tell me I love her; I love her not. Right now I was certain only that Consuela Garcia loved me not.

The other certainty was that I would have another cigarette before bed. When one goes, one should go all the way.

William Riley Burnett, the distinguished writer of gangster novels and screenplays, summed up life in this vale of tears in eight words: *"You're born, you get in trouble, you die."*

22

I was late for breakfast by design, not torpor. I just didn't want to face the mater and pater, who might ask if I had plans to see Connie this weekend. Alas, I was not late enough. Father had delayed his departure to await my arrival. Mother had delayed her morning visit to the greenhouse for the same reason. Ursi was standing before her stove, and Jamie stood guard at the back door. Conversation ceased when I entered and eight eyeballs focused on me.

Blessed mother of Maude Adams, had they heard about last night's faux pas? It's my attire that usually gets the gawks, but this Saturday morning I couldn't be more pedestrian in jeans and T-shirt emblazoned with a silk screen print of Batman and Robin on the hoof, capes billowing in the breeze.

Father cleared his throat and announced, "The Beaumont house was raided last night," thus opening the floodgate.

Mother: "Were you there, Archy?"

Ursi: "Binky was on the TV."

Father: "Perhaps 'raided' is too strong a word. They apprehended the drug ring as they prepared to vacate."

Ursi: "Binky said you had him casing the place because you knew something was going on."

Jamie: "Not in the papers yet. Too early. We got it on the morning news."

Mother: "I was so worried, Archy, I sneaked up to your room to make sure you were home and safe. I hope you don't mind."

Ursi: "I told her the Miata was here so you must be here, but she had to make sure."

Father: "Sergeant Rogoff refused to comment, but his commanding officer said it was a joint effort. Did he mean the police and you, Archy?"

Ursi: "Did the Beaumont boy put you wise, Archy? I've had a dozen calls since the news broke on the TV. The local network sent a camera crew there when Binky alerted them as to what was happening. It looked so exciting. The images were all dark and shaky because it was real life."

Father: "I don't think the police appreciated the presence of the TV crew."

Jamie: "Tommy Ambrose is being held until bail is set. Do you know him, Archy?"

Ursi: "What can I get you, Archy?"

"A black coffee and three extra-strength aspirins, please."

• If Al had pulled the graveyard shift and indulged in the drug bust, as Ursi—or was it mother?—had labeled it, he should now be at home. I knew from experience that Al did not go directly to bed after patrolling our fair island all night, but had a bit of breakfast before nodding off, Al's breakfast being a Bud and two franks with mustard and kraut. Covering Batman and Robin with a rugby shirt in blue and white, I drove to the Palm Court.

"I was expecting you," Al said, opening the door to his trailer. The background music was loud and tumultuous. In a robe and barefoot, Al went to the stereo and toned it down. "Boito's *Mefistofele,*" he told me. "The peasants are cuttin' up. . . . *'Tutti vanno alla rinfusa/Sulla musica confusa.'* It translates, 'All is going to dire confusion/With the music in collusion.' "

Great. The guy's English is atrocious, but he can spout Italian librettos. In a tartan robe Al looks like Smokey the Bear in a tartan robe. "Dire confusion is what I'm here about, Al. What the hell happened last night?"

"You wanna beer, pal?"

"At ten in the morning? No, thanks."

"How about a foot-long dog?"

"You're turning my stomach. Is coffee even a remote possibility?"

"On the stove, help yourself. So you heard, eh?"

I poured myself a cuppa and added a drop of milk. "Heard? It was the talk of our breakfast table. Where's the sugar?"

"I'm out," he said.

"Go borrow a few lumps from Eliot Ness."

Al roared. "You shoulda seen him, Archy. He looked like he was directing World War Three and lost the script. Kept running in circles. I had to put him in the patrol car to keep him out of the way." Al lit a cigar and puffed contentedly.

I took a seat at the table. "I heard he alerted the TV station."

"The captain wanted to kill him."

"Why didn't you let him?"

"Don't be unkind, Archy. Binky is your biggest supporter. He told the TV guy that you was onto the scam before us."

A drug bust at the Beaumont house and now Al defending Binky. I had heard two impossible things before lunch. What next?

"I had shoved him into the patrol car, so he had to give his statement looking out the window. Then he spots the Ambrose kid being led off in handcuffs and he shouts, 'Hey, Tommy, whatta you doing here?' "

Al's grin broke into a raucous laugh. A moment later, I joined him. It was the Keystone Kops, with Binky leading the chase. When our giggles subsided, I asked Al to sock it to me from the beginning.

"I told you I kept thinking about the light in that upstairs window. What I didn't tell you was that I talked to the captain about it."

Knowing that Al Rogoff was the PBPD's biggest asset, the captain let Al in on the fact that the odd couple Al had arrested at the Beaumont site had not gone onto the grounds to engage in sex, but to purchase drugs from the back door of the Beaumont mansion.

"The Bennett dude, on the advice of his lawyer, fessed up in return for pleading guilty to unlawful trespassing. Mitand, who had the dope in his purse, also copped a plea." From that point on, the house was being watched by the vice boys from Miami.

When Al read that Tyler Beaumont was in town, he came to me to find out what Tyler might know about the operation. When I told him my version of Tyler's quest and added that I had set Binky the task of keeping his eye on that window, Al got the picture. I also told Al that Binky had run into Tommy Ambrose while on duty. Knowing his neighbor, Al suspected that Binky had told Ambrose that he was snooping, thus alerting Ambrose to the fact that his safe house maybe wasn't so safe anymore.

"We had been watching Ambrose and his crowd, giving them enough space to incriminate themselves. They was comin' and goin' like they owned the joint."

It seems the gang had been using the former nursery, on the second floor, to store their wares, even bringing in portable battery-operated lamps. A few times during the summer, and since, it got so hot up there they foolishly opened a window and loosened the shutter to let in some air. Hence the mysterious and occasional light in the upstairs window. And, wouldn't you know it, the nursery window.

Al was puffing away, occasionally tapping his ashes into an ashtray that looked suspiciously like a huge terracotta flowerpot coaster because that's what it was. Judging from the mound of cigar ash it contained, I would guess it hadn't been emptied in weeks. Al was in need of a domestic engineer.

"With Binky hanging around and yakking it up with Ambrose, we knew we had to strike last night or lose the game. And we was right. We caught 'em moving out like their lease was up and they was going to greener pastures."

Amazing. Just amazing. "I never did like the Ambrose boy," I admitted.

Al chuckled. "He was takin' book on your chances of zapping Alejandro, and now the bank's gone bust. How is Connie, anyhow?"

"Don't ask, Al."

"Bad as all that, eh?"

"Worse," I told him.

"So there ain't gonna be no wedding."

Did Al realize that a double negative made a positive? "There might yet be a wedding," I said, "but the face under the veil is still a question mark."

"Careful, it might turn out to be Binky's mug. Now, get outta here, I gotta get some shut-eye."

"Thanks for the java," I said. "And for the record, I didn't know a damn thing about what was going on in that house."

"I know that, Archy."

"Your boss told the TV people it was a joint effort."

"He was talking about us and the vice boys from down south."

"Have a good snooze, Al."

Before the door closed behind me, I heard the *musica confusa* swell and wondered if Dr. Faustus was dancing with the devil.

• Binky pushed his mail cart into my office all bright-eyed and bushy-tailed. "The Unmasked Avenger," I said in awe. "May I have an autograph?"

"What a night, Archy. Did you see me on the TV?"

"No, Binky, I missed the first performance. Perhaps I'll catch you on the late show. Now tell me why you told the reporter I had you watching the house because I suspected what was going on there?"

"Well, didn't you?"

"No, I did not. I told you why I had you snooping around there."

"I didn't believe you," Binky said.

"I never lie to you."

"You always lie to me," he contested. "And you don't believe in ghosts, do you?"

"No. But my client obviously does, and the client always gets the benefit of the doubt." Here I remembered that it was my duty to call Tyler and give him the bad news, which, I was sure, he had already heard. I really liked that boy, and so did Georgy.

"After last night," Binky informed me, "I think I've served my apprenticeship and graduated. I'm a shamus, Archy."

"A shameful shamus, you mean. I heard you had to be locked in a patrol car."

"I wasn't wearing a bulletproof vest, that's why."

"I don't believe any shots were fired," I said.

"How do you know?" he accused. "You weren't there. You were smooching with the blond trooper at the Colony."

Did I hear him correctly? Of course I did, and I wanted to retreat into denial. But how do you deny the truth when it's being decreed by a guy with the face of Bambi, the movie star fawn? That would be un-American. "How do you know where I was and with whom?"

"Connie told me. She called me this morning to make sure I was okay. Some people care, Archy."

"After your face appeared framed by the window of a patrol car, I think you will have a legion of caring fans. Yes, I was at the Colony with my client Tyler Beaumont. I met the officer in the lobby and invited her to sit with us. Also, it was hours before the assault on Dunbar Road and it was a business meeting."

Were I Pinocchio my nose would be longer than Palm Beach Island. "I will call Connie and explain. I trust she's at home today."

"You trust wrong, Archy. By this time she's halfway to Miami."

"She's gone to Miami for the weekend?"

"That's what she told me. She's going to a political rally with Alejandro. He wants to run for mayor."

With Connie at his side, I thought. "I think I'll kill myself," I said to our mail person.

"Well, don't let me keep you," he encouraged, backing out with his cart. "You have no mail, Archy."

"Thanks—and I would like to borrow your cell phone before I leave today."

"Okay. But be careful with it. It's not fully paid for. Why do you need it?"

"Business," I said.

"The Capote case?"

It had now become the Capote case, and the poor man had been gone all these years. "If you must know, yes," I said.

"Will you need me, or just my phone?"

"Just your phone will do, Binky."

"Good, because the girls are taking me to dinner tonight."

"What girls?"

"The girls in the typing pool are treating the hero to *vitèllo alla Milanese* at Bice on Worth Avenue."

Now Binky was spouting Italian menus. Seated at my desk, I buried my face in my arms and wept.

The ringing phone interrupted my crying jag, which I was really enjoying. It was the reception desk in the lobby. A Mr. Milo Wentworth wanted to see me.

"I don't know a Milo Wentworth," I told her, anxious to get back to my crying.

"He says you met him last night at the Colony, sir," she responded.

Caramba. It was the man who had horned in on our little cocktail party. The man I thought might be Tyler's sentry. With Tyler on the loose and the house all over the morning news, Mr. Wentworth must be tearing his hair out. "Send him up," I said, hoping my eyes weren't puffy.

When Tyler introduced him to us, I vaguely remembered hearing the name before in connection with the Beaumont family. In fact, I think the Wentworths are the Beaumonts' poor cousins; however, with this crowd, poor is relative, especially when applied to relatives.

He knocked before entering, and when he did I was able to appraise him more carefully than I had last night. There was nothing poor about his designer jeans and lightweight blazer that bespoke tailor-made at Chipp's. Milo Wentworth was near six feet tall, possessed a full head of layered brown hair, I believe lightly hennaed by the barber who layered it. He also had clear blue eyes and an affable smile.

I would guess his age to be about thirty. His handshake was manly, an approach most likely learned at the fraternity house of some Ivy League school when greeting hopeful candidates for admission into the brotherhood. That same hand could drop a black ball with all the aplomb it had offered friendship.

"I hope you forgave my intruding on your little party last night," he said, "but we all have to do our jobs."

"And your job is to be intrusive in the life and times of Tyler Beaumont." It was blunt, but I wanted to get back to my crying. "Please have a seat, Mr. Wentworth, and excuse the cramped quarters, but my office is being refurbished."

His smile told me he didn't believe me. So, you win some and you lose some, and I was on a losing roll. "You know what my job is, Mr. McNally?"

"I've heard rumors, and I've talked with Tyler, and I agreed to help him," I said.

"Why did you agree to help him, Mr. McNally?"

"As you said, we all have to do our job. Also, I rather like the lad."

"Most people who know him like him," Wentworth said. "He's perfectly normal, you know, in every way except for his obsession with the death of his twin brother. The family has spared no expense in getting him help, believe me, but all to no avail. He insists on keeping Maddy, his late brother, alive. They talk, you know."

"So he told me. Does he have to be watched constantly?"

Wentworth shook his head, causing the layers to ripple. "*Constantly* is a very exacting word. Let's say he has to be monitored so he doesn't run off to Palm Beach and hire detectives to find out if his brother is roaming the halls of the family house. All the doctors, and there have been many, agree on one thing: keep Tyler away from the scene of the accident. So you can understand my apprehension when he disappeared from New York and came here. His arrival was noted in your local newspaper and friends called me."

"Now the mystery of the light in the window has been solved," I said. "Will that help Tyler cope?"

"For a while, but not for very long. I talked with Sarah and Madison, who are currently in London. They've given me permission to deal with the police and again secure the house. I'll do what has to be done and then get Ty out of here as quickly as is possible. If you give me your bill . . ."

"There is no bill, Mr. Wentworth."

"How generous. Did Tyler tell you what happened in that house some twenty years ago?"

"He did." I briefly related what the boy had reported.

Wentworth thought a moment before answering. "Tyler was not at the bottom of the staircase, Mr. McNally. He was at the top of the staircase."

The hair on my neck bristled. "You mean . . ."

"Maddy was in the new fire truck the boys received for Christmas. Ty was pushing him across the upstairs hall. The truck's bells clanging—the boys shouting—children seldom look where they're going . . ."

I could see the scene as clearly as if I were watching it on a movie screen.

"The truck toppled on the first step, tossing Maddy out, headfirst—"

"Please. That's enough."

"I didn't mean to upset you, Mr. McNally. I just wanted you to know why Ty is so desperate to bring his brother back to life. Like Lady Macbeth, the damn spot won't go away. Even under hypnosis Ty swears he was at the bottom of the staircase, looking up."

Poor Ty. Poor, adorable Tyler Beaumont.

"Well, it's been a pleasure, Mr. McNally," Wentworth said, extending his hand. "I must be going, as we all have our jobs to do, don't we?"

Yeah, we all have our jobs to do.

23

I stood in front of the Pelican Club in a slouch hat, a raincoat with a bulging left-hand pocket that contained Binky's cell phone, not a .38, and toting a briefcase. The only thing missing from the scene was a foggy mist and a cigarette dangling from between my lips, but times change and we must change with them or get left behind. As I saw the approaching headlights, I wished I were getting left behind.

It was a black mini-limo the car service people refer to as a Town Car. It stopped where I stood on the curb. I opened the passenger door, and before I entered another car pulled up behind us. The glass partition between the driver and his fare was raised. The driver wore a black jacket and cap. He didn't turn when I got in but pulled away as soon as I had closed the door. The car behind us followed.

I didn't like this one iota. I felt as if I were being led up the garden path with an escort to see that I got there. I tapped on the partition, and it lowered a fraction. "Do you know we're being followed?" I said.

"It's the people who hired me." The partition went back up.

The response was barely audible, and the faux basso made me believe my driver was a woman. I am aware that woman chauffeurs are no longer an oddity, but if my conjectures were correct this particular one was our odd man out. If not, why the closed partition and bogus voice? My C.S.O. was off to a good start. Now all I had to do was stay alive to see it to completion.

When I had asked Whitehead why he hadn't made the trade with Swensen, he told me: "*. . . you are a babe in the woods. Claudia Lester would never trust me to get my hands on the money and the manuscript at the same time. . . .*"

The money and the manuscript were once again poised to be in the same place at the same time; ergo, in the car behind us were all or two of the following: Claudia Lester. Matthew Harrigan. Rodney Whitehead. I ticked off my candidates as we drove through the dark streets of Palm Beach and West Palm Beach, crossing the Flagler Memorial Bridge and returning on the Royal Palm Way Bridge.

We did the South American circuit—Brazilian Avenue, Chilian Avenue, Peruvian Avenue—and traversed Seminole Avenue, Atlantic Avenue and even Dunbar Road, where a patrol car stood guard at the gates of the Beaumont house. Sergeant Rogoff? Up Worth Avenue, where all the storefronts were ablaze with lights to display their costly wares, we passed Bice, where the hero was eating veal.

It was all very boring, and just as I was about to tap

once more on the glass partition a glance out the window told me we were now heading back to where we had started. We pulled up to the club's entrance and stopped. Our tail car stopped at a distance that made it impossible for me to see who was in it. The partition came down and, without turning, the driver passed over the familiar package. It was still wrapped in brown paper and tied with string. I took it and put the handle of the briefcase in the driver's now empty hand, which hovered over the padded black shoulder.

Very clever. First the almost one-hour car ride to be sure we were not being followed, and now the exchange in the car so I would never see the face of the person I was dealing with. But I had seen the hand of that person with its perfect manicure and tinted nails. Flamingo pink, if I wasn't mistaken.

The car drove off immediately. The second car lingered until I had turned my back, heading for the lot and my Miata. I heard it rev past before I reached my car. Taking *Answered Prayers,* which I had checked out of the library this afternoon, from the car, I headed back to the club with it and the package wrapped in brown paper. The moment of truth.

Nine o'clock on a Saturday night and the Pelican was jumping. I did manage to find an empty stool in a far corner of the bar and commandeered it, resting my cargo and Binky's cell phone on the counter. Priscilla was too busy to verbally accost me, and I noticed that Todd, the young man who assisted Priscilla on busy nights, was also working the floor. Todd, who was born Edward, wanted to be an actor and I believe he had taken his stage name from his idol, the producer Michael Todd, who once announced that he believed in giving his customers a meat-and-potato show, which our Todd was now doing. However, M. Todd defined meat and potatoes as *"Dames and comedy."*

"You heard about Tommy Ambrose?" Mr. Pettibone said when he had a chance to come my way.

"Ad nauseam," I replied.

"They say Binky made the bust."

"Who's they, Mr. Pettibone?"

"Binky," he said with a wink. "You look like you could use a martini."

"A gin martini," I ordered, "with a few of those tiny onions."

"That's a gibson, Archy."

"What's in a name, Mr. Pettibone?"

"A lot if it's Rockefeller, Du Pont or Astor."

You know, he had something there.

I untied the string and opened the package that had caused so much trouble and a death. A typed cover page said *Answered Prayers* without benefit of authorship. I began the task of going through the pages, most in type, some handwritten with annotation in the margins, diligently comparing it to the published text.

When Simon Pettibone brought me the gibson, he asked, "Is that the manuscript, Archy?"

"It's *a* manuscript," I answered. Happily, he was far too busy to hang around and snoop. I suspect Mr. Pettibone can read upside down.

A half hour later, I started when an unfamiliar buzz began to emanate from Binky's cellular. I picked it up, pressed what I hoped was the right button and said hello, never expecting anyone to answer.

"Bingo!" It was Georgy. "A car just came into the space outside Whitehead's room and three of them went in. Two of them are wearing pants."

"Never judge a book by its cover," I said, "or a manuscript either, for that matter. Do nothing till I get there, and alert your cohorts to join you."

• Georgy had given me the address of Whitehead's motel in West Palm and, should it be necessary, Harrigan's digs in Juno. I knew where to find Claudia Lester. I drove into the parking lot, which, I must say, was larger and better lit than the Crescent's. Rodney Whitehead had gone upscale for his stay, perhaps thinking he could now afford to do so.

Georgy, in uniform, was waiting for me. "They're all in the room. I called my assists and gave them the room number. I told them to wait outside till they were needed. Is that the manuscript?"

"It is," I said. "Let's go."

Georgy had her hand on her holster. "I don't think that will be necessary," I told her.

"The first thing we learn on the force, Archy, is to assume nothing and treat every speeder as a potential assassin."

"You sound like your old landlady."

"I've been standing out here so long, I feel like my old landlady."

Florida motels come in all shapes, sizes and colors, mostly pastels. The Lakevue, which did not have a view, or even a vue, of the lake, was a long, narrow rectangle, two stories high with a balcony running across the second story and a wood deck fronting the first-floor row of units. Its stucco facade was painted yellow and its doors, perfectly aligned above and below, were painted a glossy black, each sporting an overhead light.

Whitehead's room was on the lower level. The shade

was drawn on the unit's only window. "You wait here," I told Georgy. "I'll go in and call you if I need you."

"Why?"

"Because if they see a uniform they'll clam up and demand to call a lawyer. And if it's a washout, you won't be involved and your boss can't say he told you so."

She agreed but wasn't happy with the idea. "I'm tired of waiting for something to happen," she said.

"All things come to he who waits," I preached.

"Well, make it snappy or I'll leave you to the wolves."

I knocked on the door, which a brass plate told me was number twenty.

"Who's that?" I recognized Whitehead's voice.

"Archy McNally."

There was a hush, followed by a great deal of activity behind the shade. Shadowy figures running in circles, as if tidying up before receiving guests. Could they be flushing the money down the toilet? Never. This crowd had too much respect for America's legal tender.

I knocked again, louder, the noise attracting the attention of the Lakevue dwellers in numbers nineteen and twenty-one. I saw someone hanging over the balcony above our heads.

The door opened a crack and I pushed my way in, shoving Whitehead aside. Claudia Lester was seated, smoking. I addressed the woman standing behind Lester: "Mrs. Vera Fortesque, I presume."

"You have no right to break in here like this," Whitehead said.

"I didn't break in," I answered, "you opened the door."

"What is this?" Whitehead shouted, removing his glasses as if they interfered with his ability to grasp the situation. All it did was make him squint.

"A sting," I said. "Like the one Matthew Harrigan told me you were going to pull to get an extra fifty out of Fortesque—and almost succeeded."

"Harrigan is a liar," Whitehead ranted.

"No, Mr. Whitehead," I said, "Matthew Harrigan is the only one who was telling the truth. The fact that he's not here proves it. Trouble was, he didn't know the whole truth. He thought he was part of a trio, not the expendable patsy of a quartet. Which, incidentally, I believed until my associate told me he saw Claudia Lester strolling on the Esplanade with a girlfriend. I didn't think Ms. Lester had a lady friend in Palm Beach, unless it was one who had joined her here from New York. Correct, Mrs. Fortesque?"

The two women, one seated, one standing, had said nothing till now. Smart cookies, they knew the value of silence.

"How did you find us?" Vera Fortesque asked. She was a woman approaching fifty, looked a good ten years younger and must have been a knockout twenty years ago. Dark hair with streaks of gray she smartly didn't try to conceal, dark eyes, good skin and a full figure that was a welcome relief from the current craze among fashionable women to emulate Olive Oyl. She had discarded her chauffeur's cap and jacket but was still in black trousers and white shirt.

Good question, and one the hysterical Rodney Whitehead had not thought to ask, relegating him a drone to the Queen Bee. Not wanting to give away Georgy's position, I gave Vera the old standby: "I'm not at liberty to reveal my source."

"How clever," she said with a snide glance at Whitehead. "And what are you accusing us of, Mr. McNally?"

"Extortion, times two," I stated. "The bills I gave you a few hours ago were marked, and this," I wielded the manuscript, "is pure poppycock. It may, or may not, have belonged to Truman Capote, but it contains nothing more than the stories that appear in the published text of *Answered Prayers.* By the way, Mrs. Fortesque, you sure do know your way around Palm Beach."

"I used to live here," she said.

Of course, could this be Deci's ex-stewardess who had encumbered him with a jet and took off with the pilot? If so, she hadn't married the guy. None of Deci's ex-wives had remarried. That foolish move would cost them their alimony.

"If it is a fraud," Claudia Lester spoke up, "I was unaware of the fact. I am an agent, and was given the provenance of the manuscript by a supposed expert before contacting Mr. Fortesque."

"Ditto," Vera Fortesque announced.

Whitehead almost jumped out of his skin. "Liars. They're both damn liars. I told them it was just one of Capote's working drafts and it was her idea to sting Fortesque for a hundred grand." Whitehead was pointing at Vera, who, like Claudia, appeared unperturbed by the accusation. Poor Whitehead was as far out of his league as was Matthew Harrigan.

I hoped Georgy had her ear glued to the door, although she had no interest in who stung Decimus Fortesque. The extortion case would be played out in court, if, in fact, it ever got that far. If Fortesque got his money back, he might not want to bring charges against an ex-wife and a disreputable agent of collectibles who might serve him well in the future. A court case would only prove salacious fodder for the tabloids and expose Deci's voyeuristic tendencies. In short, it would be all the talk of Deci's club, and among the Palm Beach elite, the only crime is to get caught.

Georgy was here on a far more serious matter, and she was giving me space to wrap up my case with the expectation that I do the same for her. Pray I didn't disappoint.

From Whitehead's sometimes disjointed invective I mentally put together the jigsaw puzzle, and the picture it formed was much what I envisioned since suspecting that Vera Fortesque was in town. Whitehead got back from Key West and his visit to Lawrence Swensen. At one of those New York cocktail parties where those who have, those who have not, and those who want, gather, he told Claudia and Vera about his unproductive tip and the manuscript he had rejected.

Vera was aware of the mystery and conjecture surrounding the Capote book, and of her ex-husband's penchant for collecting such esoterica. She got Claudia to contact Fortesque and the plot was hatched.

"She was a third wife," Whitehead blasted. "It was almost twenty years ago, and alimony doesn't keep up with inflation."

Vera Fortesque nodded her head as if in agreement. Claudia lit another cigarette. Watching someone chain-smoke is the best inducement for quitting.

When Deci would only go fifty it was, as Harrigan had said, Claudia's idea to pull the sting, keep the fifty, retrieve the manuscript and hit Deci for another fifty. Vera and Whitehead were delighted. The plan needed two fall guys. One to swear to Fortesque that Lester had made a fair exchange—label him Archy McNally. And one to drug Swensen and get the money back to Lester without implicating the other three in the swindle—label him Matthew Harrigan.

"What no one expected," I said, "was a murder."

"That crazy Harrigan." Whitehead was once again off and running. "He lost his head."

"Why did you go back to the Crescent that night, Mr. Whitehead?" I asked him.

Suddenly he had nothing to say. Neither did the two ladies, who had assumed the air of curious but disinterested observers. What a pair!

"Come on," I urged. "You just admitted to the sting operation. Harrigan took the money to Claudia and you went to the Crescent to get back the manuscript. Someone had to take it from me. If I had delivered it to Claudia, she might give it to Fortesque, as agreed, and keep the money."

Whitehead removed his glasses before mopping his forehead with a handkerchief that was seeing a lot of duty tonight. "Harrigan attacked you in the parking lot and took back the manuscript," he charged.

"He did not, sir," I rebutted. "Harrigan was told I was going to bring Claudia Lester the manuscript and believed I had. You were assigned to get back the manuscript." Vera Fortesque gave an almost imperceptible nod. She would see Whitehead fry to save her own skin. She might be charged with extortion, and probably get away with it, but not for a murder she had nothing to do with.

"You were in that parking lot the whole time I was making the exchange with Harrigan," I continued. "Last night you said you didn't take the manuscript from my car. Only the person who clobbered me and took it would know I had tossed it in the car before getting in. I am charging you with assault with a deadly weapon and murder, Mr. Whitehead."

"This is outrageous," he cried.

"You slugged me, took the manuscript from the seat of

my car and went back to Swensen's room. The door was open because Harrigan had not hit the lock switch when he left. You locked the door behind you, strangled Swensen and waited until you heard me try the door and leave before unlocking it and calling the police."

"Why would I kill Swensen?" he insisted.

"Because you were the only one Swensen knew by name and place of employment. The only one he could trace. When he awoke with the manuscript gone and not a cent for his trouble, he wouldn't have gone to the police. He would have known better. He would have come after you, not these lovely ladies or Harrigan, whom he probably wouldn't remember.

"If Swensen was into drugs, those connections would help him get what was coming to him, and them, even if they had to travel to Costa Rica to get it. You would have to sleep with one eye open the rest of your life, while your cohorts never missed a minute of their beauty rest.

"Also," I went on, "it was the Fortesque name that had Swensen agree to a private swap. Both you and Harrigan told me that. If Swensen went to Fortesque with his tale of woe, it would have alerted Fortesque and jeopardized the scam and the second fifty thousand. He might have even described the contents of the missing manuscript to Fortesque, and that would have been the kiss of death for all of you. Lawrence Swensen was more of a danger alive than dead, and you went for the better odds."

"Prove it," Whitehead said, eyeing the door.

"That ain't my job, sir."

Turning nasty, he ordered, "Then get out of my face." To make sure I did, he pulled a gun from his jacket pocket and aimed it at me. "You see, I prepared myself for a possible visit from Swensen's goons, and how fortunate. I killed once, Mr. McNally, and I'll do it again if I must. Beware a desperate man holding a loaded pistol."

"Don't be a fool, Whitehead. How far do you think you can get?"

"As far as a hundred thousand dollars and the Palm Beach international airport can take me." Without taking his eyes off me, he ordered the women to remove the briefcase and the attaché case from the closet. "For the record, Mr. McNally, a more urgent need to do away with Swensen was the fact that when I returned to his room he had come out of his stupor. He was an addict, remember, and the few pills Harrigan had given him wouldn't keep him unconscious for long. That's how pill addicts die, you know. They keep waking up and popping more to put them back down until they ingest the fatal dosage.

"Swensen was muddled, but awake. And guess what? He told me that stupid Harrigan, who pretended to be Fortesque's man, told him that the fifty thousand dollars was on its way. Can you believe it? I should have killed Harrigan. As you said, I was the only one in contact with Swensen, and, looking to make a little extra for my trouble, I had told him that Fortesque was willing to pay ten thousand for it, not fifty. Swensen had no idea what such a thing might be worth, and to him ten thousand was a fortune and fifty was a king's ransom. He wasn't very happy, but, lucky for me, he was very groggy."

The women, who seemed to have lost their cool at the sight of Whitehead's gun, stood holding the briefcase and the attaché case.

"Take the money and go," I said to Whitehead. "Leave me and the women alone."

He laughed. "I'm taking the money, and all of you. My car is outside. Vera, as we now know, is a very good driver.

She takes the wheel. Claudia, my love, you sit next to our driver, and Mr. McNally and I will head up the rear. We will drive some fifty miles to a desolate area, where you will all get out and we will part company. Sorry I can't offer you a ride back. The gun will be on Mr. McNally. Any nonsense and he gets it first. Mr. McNally, please remove the cell phone from your coat pocket and leave it on the dresser."

"How do you know it's a cell phone?"

"If it were a gun, you would have shown it to us long before now."

"You won't get away with this," Claudia Lester said. "You don't have the brains."

"Do you want to come with me, Claudia dear?"

She hesitated. For a woman like Claudia Lester, a hundred thousand bucks was hard to part with, especially when you had half of it in your hand. "No, thanks. Are you taking the manuscript with you?"

"No," he said. "You and Vera can fight over it."

Vera told him what he could do with the manuscript, which was a physical impossibility.

"Open the door, Mr. McNally."

"With pleasure, Mr. Whitehead."

24

"And he walked right into the three waiting cops?" Fortesque said the next day when I reported to him the results of our Counter Sting Operation.

"He did, sir."

"Capital, man. Capital." He applauded, eyes bulging with delight.

I also brought him the attaché case containing the first fifty thousand, explaining that the briefcase with the marked bills and the manuscript were in police custody pending his decision to press charges against Vera and Claudia.

"How naughty of Vera." He sighed. "She called to apologize, you know. How does she look, man?"

"Lovely, Mr. Fortesque. She's put on a few pounds, but on her it looks good."

"She always was a bit zaftig, if you know what I mean.

Between us, Archy, I'm taking them to dinner at the club tonight."

"Them, sir?"

"Vera and Claudia. They want a chance to explain their transgression while under the influence of the dissolute Rodney Whitehead."

I almost laughed in his face. Poor, bug-eyed Deci. He would be like a hunk of clay in their hands, begging to be kneaded and molded to suit their fancy. Either Vera would get an increase in her monthly stipend or Claudia would become the ninth Mrs. Fortesque. But one thing was certain. The ladies from Sutton Place would be forgiven their transgressions.

"Why don't you join us," Fortesque invited.

"Sorry, but I have a date to watch *Hotel Berlin* with a woman who is in love with the late actor Helmut Dantine."

Fortesque's eyes bulged. "Dantine? I've met him, man. He was married to Charlie Wrightsman's girl. You remember Charlie, the oil baron. They had a house down here. Maybe still do. Friends of the Kennedys. In fact, the Wrightsmans' place was called the winter White House when Camelot was in full bloom.

"Charlene, that was her name. Charlie's girl. She divorced the actor and married one of the Cassini brothers. Not the dress designer. The one who wrote a gossip column. Then she took her own life, man. Charlene, that is. Sleeping pills it was. Very tragic. Do you know why she did it, Archy?"

"No, sir, I don't." And I hoped he wasn't going to tell me.

"Neither do I. Thought the Capote book would have something to say about it. Which reminds me, Archy. I got a call from a dealer in California. He says a porter at the Greyhound Bus Depot in Los Angeles, who was in charge of breaking open the lockers of people who rent them and never return to claim what they stored, contacted him. It seems the man found a manuscript in one of those lockers years ago. The man was a closet collector, and he took the manuscript home to add to his cache of other items he had found in unclaimed lockers. The man is now retired. Well, he was watching a biography of Truman Capote on the television and . . ."

This is where I came in—so I left.

On the way out, Sam Zimmermann gave me a neatly packaged box of his mini-pastries.

"Why, thank you," I said. "I wasn't expecting this."

"That's why you got them, sir."

• I charred burgers on Georgy's little outdoor grill. She was making fries from a package of frozen shoestring potatoes and an iceberg and romaine salad mix that came cut and washed in a plastic bag. The Thousand Island dressing came in a squeezable plastic bottle. When it comes to convenience shopping, Georgy girl has no peer.

"I work odd hours, Archy," she defended herself. "I don't have the time to fuss."

Strangely enough, I rather enjoyed the meal. In fact, it was hard not to enjoy yourself in Georgy's company.

"We make a good team," she said while passing the ketchup. It, too, came in a squeezable plastic bottle. "I wish you could have seen Whitehead's face when you opened the door." Her green eyes sparkled like emeralds.

Needless to say, Georgy's boss was overjoyed with the results of our little operation and was putting her in for a commendation along with Swathmoore and the other rookie, Anita Doolittle.

"It was all thanks to me, and what do I get for my sweat, blood and tears? Not to mention my remarkable noodle."

"You're a genius, Archy."

"I'm not," I said. "But knowing I'm not makes me smarter than most."

"And what you get is a hefty fee from Fortesque," she pointed out. "How much do you make, Archy?"

"That's a most indelicate question for a young lady to ask."

"I'm not a very delicate lady," she confessed. "I do okay, but Uncle Sam zaps me. I would do better filing a joint return."

"For that you need a husband."

"How odd you should bring up that word. Is it on your mind, Archy?"

"What's on my mind would make you blush."

"Really? Try me."

We watched *Hotel Berlin,* and it was as campy and enjoyable as I remembered it from previous screenings in New York and New Haven at cinemas that specialize in showing movies that were made before they became something called "films."

I didn't tell Georgy about Dantine's marriage to the oil baron's daughter, leaving ancient gossip and scandals to the master, Decimus Fortesque.

Instead, I showed off and said, "Did you know that Helmut Dantine was in *Casablanca*?"

"No."

"He was." I nodded sagely. "Might have been his first film. He plays Jan Brandel, the Bulgarian who tries to win at Rick's roulette table to save his wife's virtue. A bit part for which he didn't get a credit."

Georgy was impressed. "I'll rent *Casablanca* for our next night at the movies."

• It was almost midnight when I left the gingerbread cottage. I beeped the landlady on the way down the drive, and I think she waved. I still hadn't seen Georgy's bedroom, but who knows? After watching Bergman leave Bogart in the lurch, would Georgy have the heart to part with me in a similar manner?

Driving through the cool night under a sky full of scudding dark clouds and a half moon, I listened to an instrumental version of "Sentimental Journey" coming from the Miata's radio and asked myself, *"Quo vadis,* Archy McNally? *Quo vadis?"*

Was Connie, at this very moment, driving north? Or had she decided to spend yet another night in Miami and come home in the morning? Or not at all? I don't think Connie would enjoy being Mrs. Mayor, but then I never thought I would enjoy dinner garnished with the contents from squeezable plastic bottles.

I drove past Dunbar Road to see if Al Rogoff might still be hanging around. I needed a shoulder. But no, the patrol car was gone and all was quiet. The house had been secured once again, and Tyler Beaumont was back in New York.

I stopped for a moment to look at the old mansion that had played host to grand dukes and ex-kings. A cloud obscured the moon for a moment, and I swear I saw a light come on in the upstairs nursery window, where it glowed brilliantly for a few seconds, dimmed and disappeared. In the distance the *clang, clang, clang* of a fire truck bell pierced the still night.

About the Author

Lawrence Sanders, one of America's most popular novelists, was the author of more than twenty-two bestsellers. **Vincent Lardo** is the author of *The Hampton Affair* and *The Hampton Connection,* as well as three previous McNally novels. He lives on the East End of Long Island.